Death On The Coast

A West Country Crime Mystery (Book 3)

By Bernie Steadman

Also By Bernie Steadman

West Country Crime Mystery Series

Death In The Woods (Book 1)

Death On Dartmoor (Book 2)

Chapter One

Kegan waited outside the rough circle of stones until the moment was right. Faces, made hideous by red and black paint, stared at him through the swirling flames of the fire. He found Tana's eyes, so black in her white face. It was time. The rock, cold in his hands, scraped at his palms as he lifted it high and smashed it down on the back of the man's head. The crack of stone on bone was loud enough to make one of them flinch, but they held firm, watching intently as Kegan hauled the unconscious man into his arms, before rising – each taking a limb of the inert body – and throwing it messily into the heart of the fire.

PC Gareth Evans warmed his hands. Above his head, stars filled the black sky, competing with the rising smoke and the dying flames below. 'Looks like kids started it,' he said.

His partner scanned the area close to the fire with her torch. There were many footprints in the sand, crossing over each other, wandering off at a tangent, obliterating useful evidence. She tutted and rolled away an empty beer can with her toe. 'Hmm …' Six boulders had been pulled into a rough circle, and behind them lay a tideline of empty cans and discarded food wrappers. 'Looks like it was quite a party,' she murmured.

'I'm surprised anyone bothered calling it in at five in the morning. Nobody lives near this end of the beach.' PC Evans stepped closer to the fire and stared into its yellow heart. It would burn itself out soon enough once the tide came in, no need to alert the fire brigade. 'Halloween party, probably. Nothing better to do with their time, eh?' It would only get busier as bonfire night approached. There were just too many students in Exmouth to keep an eye on them all. 'I hate students,' he said.

PC Tracy Mulligan stood at the far side of the fire, boots lapped by the sea, peering into the flames. One of the larger branches shifted and dropped as it was consumed in a quick, orange flare. 'What the ...' Tracy grabbed a long piece of driftwood in both hands and rammed it into the centre of the fire, poking and pushing one burning log, then another, out onto the sand. 'Gareth,' she said, 'you better come round here and look at this.'

The body fell forward out of the inferno: its mouth a gaping hole, hands clawed against its chest. Tracy turned horrified eyes up to meet Gareth's. 'Oh my good God,' she said.

'Right,' said Evans, his florid face paling. 'Stand back, Trace. You start to secure the scene and I'll call the station. This is more than just a fire.'

DCI Dan Hellier perched on a rock and glared at the waves lapping the shore. How the hell were they supposed to maintain a crime scene when the tide came in twice a day? He sipped from a takeaway coffee and watched the gentle wash of the tide. Of course, it could be a clever ploy to avoid detection, or just a party that got out of hand. And if the body turned out to be a drunk who'd fallen into the fire in the middle of a Halloween party, he'd be even more annoyed.

The forensics team stood listlessly on the promenade, chatting to Sergeants Bill Larcombe and Ben Bennett. They were waiting to process the scene but there wasn't a lot they could do until the tide had gone out again. They'd lifted the body, but that was all.

Hellier almost felt guilty about being there, as there was a mountain of stuff he could have been doing, but sod it, they could manage without him in the office for an hour or two. He took another swig of coffee and gasped as it burnt its way down his oesophagus. At least they'd had time to retrieve the body before the tide took it; what was left of it. He hated fires.

'DCI Hellier?' Campbell Fox, the pathologist, yelled, and waved a beefy hand in his direction. Dan heaved himself up, every muscle complaining from the forty-mile bike ride he'd completed the day before. He'd allowed himself to get out of shape over the summer, and that had to stop. No way was he going to become some desk-bound wally, old before his time and shuffling paper, DCI or not. He jogged across sand and flat rocks towards the promenade, where a make-shift crime scene separated the police from the general public behind crime scene tape and a tent.

Fox beckoned him again, impatience in every gesture. Dan put a spurt on. He couldn't quite get used to being DCI Hellier. It felt like someone else. The interview process had nearly seen him off, too. But, there it was, and here he was, jumping over boulders on Exmouth beach.

'Enjoying the view, are we?' asked Fox as Dan stepped up beside him. 'You won't be in a minute.' The body was lying in a bag on a stretcher, ready for transporting to the hospital path lab. 'I thought you might like a wee peek, before I take him away.' He unzipped the bag and exposed a body, half-consumed by fire, settled in a stance like a boxer about to fight, arms curled into fists.

Dan took a shallow breath, covered the lower half of his face with his jacket sleeve, and put his cup down on the concrete. 'Oh, that is horrible. Burns victims are the worst.'

'Aye, they are. Luckily this one was rescued before the fire completed its work, so there should be identifying marks that we can use. Unlike on our Bog Bodies case, eh?' He scratched his beard through his mask. 'On first look, he's clearly male. There is a small amount of head and facial hair on the skull. The skull has a massive fracture at the rear, on the occipital bone, which may indicate that he was dead, or at least unconscious, before he went into the fire. I've alerted the coroner.'

'Right, it looks like we need the murder investigation team after all. Okay, thanks. Let me know when the post-mortem will be.'

Dan went back to his perch on the rock. Dead before he was burnt on the fire? At least unconscious? Could kids having a Halloween party really have burnt a man to death? He glanced at the two evidence bags full of the rubbish that had littered the site. It had been collected up by the two PCs on duty, and Dan made a note to thank them for their quick thinking in beating the tide. It certainly looked like it had been a bit of a party: beer cans, takeaway boxes, the black ends of joints. If one of the partygoers had fallen into the fire, would the others have left him to burn? Not if it was an accident they wouldn't.

He slid off the rock and walked back to the promenade and the scientists standing by. Bill Larcombe would be fine on his own as crime scene manager, and it would be another couple of hours before forensics could get in to examine the fire in more detail. 'Bill,' he said, 'we'll set up back at the station. It seems pointless having the primary site here. Come back as soon as you've cleared the scene.'

Larcombe nodded. 'Looks like murder then, boss?'

'Or manslaughter. Whichever, I don't think a bloke with a massive hole in the back of his head jumped into that fire, Bill.'

Chapter Two

Tana sat cross-legged in the middle of the bed with her eyes closed and her hands at rest in her lap. Around the room, the others rested on the floor, propped against the wall.

Jay sneaked a look at his phone. It was almost 7.30 am. Light showed through a crack in the curtains. He would have to get going or he would be late for college, and he didn't want to attract anyone's attention today. He shook Scarlett's hand to check she was awake. She looked bombed out. Dark hollows under her eyes, mascara tracking down her face in black streaks. 'Come on,' he whispered, 'gotta go.' He nudged Amber, who looked as if she'd dropped off to sleep.

Tana's eyes flickered open. She stared at Jay, as if from a place far away.

'Err … we have to go now, Tana,' he said, pulling Scarlett and Amber to their feet.

'No problem. You were brilliant.' Tana tugged on Amber's hand. 'I'll see you all tonight and we'll talk.'

In the small bathroom near the front door, Jay scrubbed at his face and hands with soap and water to remove the dirt from the fire and the make-up Tana had made them wear. No problem? That's what she thought? The face he saw in the mirror was not the person he had looked at the night before, where the world was a shitty place, yeah, but where the charge of murder could not be added to his list of sins. Squeezed in next to him, Scarlett washed herself, digging in her shoulder bag for a clean top. They hadn't said more than a couple of words.

He grabbed his guitar from the living room, shrugged on his overcoat and opened the door. Amber was waiting outside for them, leaning against the railing. He could see that her head was far, far away. Far away from normal. Things had changed for all of them now, a step had been taken, and soon the dam they had built around them would break. It was bound to.

As soon as the front door had slammed shut on the last one, Tana rose from her bed and stretched. 'What a night. It was amazing, wasn't it?' She tore off her smoke-stained clothes and stood naked before Kegan. 'I'm starving. Do you want to make us a coffee?' Before he could answer, she jumped in. 'No. I know, a quick shower then down to Costa for brekkie.' She grinned at him and headed for the bathroom.

Kegan swallowed. Tana's body, laced as it was in the lattice of burn marks and silver scars she had gathered over the years, was both exotic and repulsive. He knew his body would soon look the same if he stayed with her. He held his right forearm up and examined the weeping burns. Weird how there was no pain when they were all in the grip of the fire, but it burned like hell the next day. He fumbled in his rucksack and found the gauze to wrap his arm, pulling on the ends of the cloth with his teeth to tighten the knots a little. 'Always be prepared' was more than just a motto since he'd been with her.

He was in it deep with Tana. Deep in the grip of the Irish witch. Again, he tasted the burning and the flesh and the flames on his tongue and shuddered deep in his groin. Deep. She had him, and she knew she had him. It was a wild ride with Tana.

He picked up her clothes from the floor and threw them into the laundry bin. Christ, it had been scary at the start: luring that disgusting old tramp to the beach, filling him with cheap cider, and then … His brain refused to conjure up the image for him. It was there in his head, but lurking under a blanket of horror. Even when he thought really hard, all he could remember was the sickening crunch of the old guy's skull cracking.

The sound of Tana's thin voice came from the shower. She was singing a song like nothing momentous had happened. Kegan shook his head and dug out fresh clothes from his rucksack. 'Hurry up, Tana,' he yelled through the door, 'I need a shower too.' He had to get to work, though how he was going to get through the next eight hours until they were able to sit down and talk it all through, he had no idea. He didn't even think he could go to work. Better to walk away.

They had done it. Taken the step. Kegan knew he would dare more with Tana – go further than he had with anyone else. He just wished he didn't feel so frightened.

He sank back down on the bed and thought about what would happen next. The laptop was charging in the corner of the room, a small white light throbbing like the pulse in a grey neck. If she posted the pictures she'd taken last night, on her site, nothing would ever be the same again.

Chapter Three

Detective Sergeant Sally Ellis stood in front of the mirror in the ladies', tugging at the hem of her shirt. It was no good, she was fat. Fat, fat, fat. She couldn't fasten the button at the side of her skirt, and she had to wear her blouse on the outside, and that made her feel scruffy. And fat. *I've no excuse,* she told herself, *too many doughnuts have caused this, and I've only myself to blame.* She sighed, and tugged a brush through her blonde curls, which bounced back into exactly the same position. She stared at her reflection. It had hurt, really hurt, when she'd heard the younger members of the team wondering if she was pregnant again. After all the effort and IVF it had taken last time, that would have been a miracle. Instead, it was just humiliating. But that throwaway comment was the spur she'd needed. 'No, madam, you are going on a diet.' She winked at herself. 'And if I'm suffering, so is every bugger else.'

Sally had arrived at work that morning to find a voicemail from Bill Larcombe, telling her to set up the major incident room and move Team Two into it ready for when the boss arrived. She had no idea what Dan was doing down at the beach, apart from sticking his nose into everyone's business. He should have been able to trust them to get on with it by now. He had too many responsibilities to go gadding about after every major incident. Perhaps she should tell him.

She opened the MI room door and found a satisfying babble as desks were allocated and people began to collate information about the new case as it was called in. Sally tacked a map of Exmouth onto the board, cleaned the rest of it, added Dan's name to the top of it, and recharged the coffee maker. She sent young Adam

Foster out for milk and refused to acknowledge the questioning looks when she didn't order doughnuts. This would be tough, but good for them, as she was sure they would all come to understand.

Dan held the first briefing just after 9am. The team gathered in their usual places and he perched on his – on the corner of the table. 'We have a male Caucasian, major trauma to the back of the head and severe burning to most of the body. Found by PCs Gareth Evans and Tracy Mulligan at approximately half past five this morning on Exmouth beach.'

'Which bit of the beach, sir?' asked DC Adam Foster, his throat injury adding a darker, rougher edge to his voice.

'Between the end of the main promenade and Orcombe Point. Just around the corner.'

'It might mean that the perpetrators are local, sir. They'd have had to know the tide times to avoid being washed away, wouldn't they?'

'Good thinking, Adam. Sam, what time was high tide last night?'

DC Sam Knowles tapped into his computer. 'Just give me a sec … High tide was at seventeen-eighteen yesterday, sir.'

'Right, if you set the fire at, say, ten pm, the tide would have gone out far enough to expose that strip of sand for the next eight or so hours.'

'Plenty of time to start a really good fire,' agreed Sam. 'And have the evidence destroyed by the returning tide the next morning.'

'A Halloween party that got out of hand?' asked DC Lizzie Singh. 'Someone had too much to drink and fell into the fire?'

'That's a possibility. But if it's one of your mates, and he's drunk and he falls in the fire, why don't you pull him out and ring for an ambulance?'

Lizzie frowned. 'Maybe because you're all too drunk to notice?'

'Or,' added Sally, 'you did try but weren't able to get him out, so you ran for it.' She made a note in her book. 'Which might make it worth checking out the local hospital for any burns sufferers. So, student party gone wrong, or murder most foul?'

'That is the question, but the answer is definitely going to be murder: he had a cracked skull.' Dan tapped the back of his head to indicate the area of the wound. 'He was at least unconscious before he went into the fire.' He gave them a few minutes to think. He'd been mulling over the event on his drive back from Exmouth.

'Sam, see if there is any CCTV in that vicinity that we could have a look at. As far as I know, Exmouth town centre is crawling with it for the Saturday night party crowd.' He stared at the incident board for a moment. 'As soon as we have the post-mortem results, we should be able to get some DNA matching on the victim. There was a bit of skin on the arms and some hair still left on the body. And PC Evans collected a couple of bags of party rubbish from the site that might yield up something useful.'

'The only trouble with DNA evidence, of course, is if the victim doesn't have a criminal record, he won't be on the database,' said Sally.

'True enough, but cheer up, we're only on day one. Okay, Sergeant Bennett, please organise a trawl of the pubs of Exmouth, there may have been a group of people getting themselves psyched up, ready for an exciting night ahead.'

Bennett made a note. 'I guess there's no point doing house-to-house,' he said, 'as no one lives close enough to see what was happening.'

'No, but there may have been other people out, early shift workers or late-night revellers, that you may catch on CCTV. Could be worth a follow-up.' He tapped his teeth with his pen. 'Not much to go on, I know, but you've all got actions to get on with. I'll see you later.'

Dan wandered down the corridor to his new office and ducked inside before anybody stopped him. He glanced at the in-tray, shrugged, and leaned on the window ledge to watch people going about their day. It made a change from staring at an old bit of Sellotape on the wall of his previous office. It was an odd case, this one. If it was deliberate, it was unheard of in Devon – as far as he knew. You did have to discount the witch trials in the past, he supposed. Of course, it could still turn out to be an accident that nobody had called in, but that just didn't seem right. The cracked skull. The rubbish in those sacks was from stuff young people ate, not old alkies keeping warm on a cold night. Was the date, Halloween, important, or just a coincidence?

Pulling his laptop closer, he sent an email asking Superintendent Oliver if she had any input for the first press statement, and prepared a new logbook for the case.

Chapter Four

Dan looked out over a sea of faces in the large public room at HQ. Four o'clock on a cold Monday afternoon but the place was steaming. He recognised many from the local press and TV. But the case was macabre enough to attract the nationals too. Not that he had much to tell them yet. He glanced down at his notebook, cleared his throat and waited until the chatter died down.

'Good afternoon, ladies and gentlemen. This will be a brief meeting as, you will understand, we have only just begun our investigations into the case.'

'Murder or accident, DCI Hellier?' came the nasal voice of reporter Lisa Middleton from three rows back. 'Shall we get to the point?'

'If you'll allow me to give my report, Miss Middleton, I'll make time for questions at the end.' Dan didn't smile at her. He was beginning to see why Sally didn't like her: pushy. 'So, Devon and Cornwall Police was alerted at just after five this morning to a fire on Exmouth beach by a member of the public, and shortly afterwards officers sent to the scene discovered a body in the embers of that fire. Currently we have no idea who the deceased may be. I will know more after the post-mortem tomorrow.'

He looked directly into the TV camera that was facing him. 'I would like to ask the person who made the phone call, or anybody else who saw anything to do with the incident, to come into Exeter Road police station, or contact us via the numbers on the bottom of your screens.'

He nodded back at Lisa Middleton. 'To answer your question, we cannot tell whether this is a suspicious death or a terrible accident until after the post-mortem. Please don't go away and speculate. You will know more tomorrow, and I'd rather you printed the facts.

'Any more questions?'

'So, was it a teenagers' Halloween party gone wrong?'

'I can only repeat myself, Miss Middleton, I will know more tomorrow. Thank you. You will be informed via the usual channels of any further information as soon as possible. Otherwise, please wait until the next press conference is called.' He got up, removed his tie-clip microphone, and stood next to Chief Superintendent Oliver as the press filed out.

'Well, you handled that a bit better than your first one,' she said with a faint smile.

'Not so scared now,' he said. 'But if Middleton runs with a "teenagers' party goes wrong" story in tonight's edition, I won't be happy.'

'It's our best guess, though, isn't it?'

'Mmm.' He stuffed his hands in his pockets and took himself back to the station and up to the MI room. His stomach growled, it had been a long time since breakfast.

Once inside, Dan made himself a fresh coffee and searched in vain for something to eat. 'Where are the doughnuts?' he complained.

Sally marched across to the drinks corner. 'There's a new regime,' she said. 'Cakes only on birthdays.' She opened a cupboard, rummaged about in a carrier bag, and said, 'Here, have a pack of these if you're hungry.' She threw him a tiny pack of nuts and raisins.

Dan caught them and stared at her. 'What's brought this on, Sal?'

She tutted and went back to her computer station, muttering, 'As if you didn't know. As if it's not blindingly obvious. As if you're not all gabbing on about me behind my back as it is. This,' she said, slapping herself on the bottom, 'and this,' poking herself in the stomach, 'have got to go. And if I'm on a diet, so are you lot. Sir,' she added.

'Right, that's me told,' said Dan, running his tongue around the inside of his mouth. 'Glad I asked. It's good we've got that all cleared up then.' He opened the little bag with his teeth and emptied the contents in one mouthful. He chewed for a minute or two, and tried not to smile at the expectant faces peering up at him from their computer screens. 'Trainee DC Foster?'

Foster leapt to his feet and grabbed his coat. 'Yes, sir. What can I get you?'

Dan looked at Foster, aged twenty-eight and thin as a whippet, and then at Sally, aged considerably more and resembling a purple duvet in her tight suit, and decided he didn't want the fight. He took a fiver from his wallet. 'Just get me a prawn sandwich, please, and some more milk for coffee corner.'

Foster couldn't hide his disappointment as he slunk through the door.

'DS Ellis is right, you lot,' he said. 'We need to be fit to do our jobs, so healthy food only from now on in the MI room.' He picked up his coffee and headed for the door. 'Of course, what I eat in *my* office, is entirely up to me …'

Sally interrupted Dan as he was engrossed in checking the evidence folder for the Team One robbery case. He felt sick to his stomach every time he found an error in the paperwork or a lack of proper supporting evidence. Jim Waite led the team well but was not good with detail. He frowned up at her. There was no way the first court case with him in charge was going to collapse from poor evidence presentation. No way.

'Sorry, boss, know you're busy. PM's at eight tomorrow morning. Fox is cramming it in before that hit and run victim. He thinks it will be straightforward.'

'Right, I'll be there, thanks.' Dan made a note of the time. 'We might have something to go on once that's done and the flowerpot men have examined the evidence properly.'

'Bill is back at the station. They've closed down the crime scene at the beach – as you suggested. He's left a PCSO there to talk to any passers-by. He and Ben have got both sacks spread out on the tables in the evidence room. Why don't you pop down and have a look?'

The evidence room was long and narrow: the whole of one long wall taken up with scrubbable Formica-topped tables. Bagged and sorted evidence was kept in a separate locked section, the key guarded by the duty sergeant. Sergeants Bill Larcombe and Ben Bennett had emptied each bag onto a different table and were sifting through the contents, separating types of waste into piles.

'Afternoon, gents,' said Dan, pulling on protective gloves as he surveyed the piles. 'Anything look interesting?'

'Boss,' acknowledged Bennett. 'It's a pain when we can't bag it all individually on site, but we've got several cigarette and joint butts, which may yield DNA.' He tweezered another butt from the inside of a reeking beer can. 'If any of the partygoers have form, we've got 'em.'

'Good. Bill?'

'Nothing's jumped out at me so far, except this,' he said, and handed Dan a sealed evidence bag with a scrap of paper inside.

Dan turned it over. It was a sheet of music paper, with scruffy handwritten notes and staves drawn in pencil. 'Hmm, could be guitar chords,' he said. 'Maybe one of them had a guitar with them, and maybe we could pick that up on CCTV. Good find.' He placed the bag back on the sealed pile. 'Anything else?'

Bill passed him another bag. 'Rolling tobacco, almost empty. I'll send it to the lab for testing as I could detect a whiff of cannabis. Other than that, cans, bottles, food wrappers, fag ends; it's not looking too promising, boss.'

'No footprints, of course,' added Bennett. 'And there didn't seem much point in dragging in the stones they sat on.' He grinned and reached across the table. 'We do, however, have one surviving boot from the victim, and,' he held the boot up, 'judging by the state of it, I'd suggest our victim might have been a member of the homeless fraternity.'

Dan grinned back as he surveyed the boot. 'Okay, I think you might be right. That is one knackered piece of footwear. That's not bad, you know. We have two leads I can get the team working on, and the PM is early tomorrow. We should be getting results back from that within a few days.'

'Any progress on our new DI, Boss?' asked Larcombe.

'Advert's out, applications are coming in, so I guess it will happen.'

'You don't want it to though, do you?'

Dan shrugged. 'I know it's too much work for me, managing the whole department and a team, but I like what we have. Someone new could really mess with the dynamics.'

'Not if you get to choose,' said Larcombe. 'There are some good sergeants out there waiting for their chance. We could help you to house-train one.' He glanced at Bennett. 'We won't be around forever, you know.'

'I'll get on to it, but not just now,' said Dan, and he escaped into the corridor. Was he struggling with his workload? He thought he was coping fine. Although he probably wasn't the best person to judge. Ideally, he wanted to hang on to Team Two as his murder and serious crime team, and let Team One do all the domestics, burglaries, et cetera. Another DI could work across both teams, he supposed.

Chapter Five

Professor Navinder Patel dipped into a paper bag of barfi and chewed the pistachio treat, wiping sugar from his chin and off the paper he was grading. It was almost eleven and he was finding it hard to concentrate. He'd caught the morning news before leaving home and now his heart was beating erratically and he couldn't stop looking at the clock.

He jumped when the tap came at his door. Tana entered, threw her bag on the floor and dropped into the single chair opposite his desk. Her grin told him all he needed to know. Wiping his mouth more carefully with a tissue, he took a calming breath. 'So … did you do it? Did you murder that poor man?'

'Not murder, Nav. A necessary sacrifice,' she said. 'It was amazing, though. I never thought it could be like this.' She spread her hands out in front of her and raised them slowly, wiggling her fingers. 'I took them with me all the way. The fire, the booze, just enough to get them going, not to send them to sleep. Kegan was magnificent at the crucial moment, and they all helped to chuck the old tramp onto the fire. And then … and then the sacrifice burned, Nav. It burned and they were in awe. We actually did it!' She clasped both hands into a tight grip to contain herself. 'You have no idea what I've got recorded on my phone.' She dug the phone out of her bag. 'D'you want to have a look?'

Patel raised his hands to ward her off, his top lip curled in revulsion. 'Please, show me nothing. I saw enough on the television this morning. How could you, Tana? I want nothing more to do with this. And …' he pulled himself up out of his chair and breathed pistachio fumes over her as his voice became a screech, 'you must not mention my name in connection to this monstrous crime ever again. I cannot have my name associated with this ... this murder. I cannot believe that you went ahead with this madness and I will have nothing more to do with you. Now, get out.' He pointed towards the door, fear making his voice shake harder. 'I am revoking your thesis and throwing you off the course; collect your belongings and leave the university.' Face a livid purple, he crossed to the window and stood, shoulders heaving, expecting her to do as she was told.

Tana sat very still. 'Are you, now? Throwing me off the course, are you? So, have you called the police, Nav?'

He shook his head. 'I am a gullible fool, but not an idiot. If I call the police, they will know I am involved. No, get out and I will keep quiet. You have my word.'

'Too right you're a fool, thinking you can throw me out and pretend I never existed. Thinking I might go away like some child you have told off. This is my life's work, Nav. It's what I've been planning for, and I'm not giving up now, oh no.' She chewed the end of a fingernail and watched his sweating figure. 'No, if the police find out, and they won't, I've been way too clever for them, but if they do, I'm going to tell everyone it was your idea. It was, anyway.'

'No, it wasn't! Don't you try to blackmail me, you little bitch.' He made a lunge for the phone on his desk. 'I'll take you with me, I swear I will,' he said, grasping the handset and waving it at her. 'Not the burning of bodies, the murdering of people; that was all your idea. And look at the other students you have pulled into your web. What will happen to them when you are caught? What will happen to me? The lives you have ruined, Tana. Think of that. What have you done?' He rested his burning face against the window, hands tight around the handset. 'I think you have gone completely mad.'

She chuckled. 'Mad? Me? I'm saner than you are, you old creep.'

He turned back to face her. 'No, you're not. I merely wanted you to test out your hypothesis regarding the growth of a cult.

A belief system based on the Manson trials. With no risk to the students. And it was not *my idea*. You wanted to do it. I thought I was supervising a PhD, not this monstrousness. This murder of an innocent man.' '

She gave a slow smile. 'One for the cleansing, one for the power, one for the purification. That's what we said.' Tana crossed the room and poked him three times in the chest to emphasise her words. 'That's what we agreed.'

Patel's voice grew shrill. 'We made that up, Tana. Together in this room. Two years ago. We made all of it up, invented this cult. It's not real. You can't have begun to believe all this ...' His eyes bulged. 'Please, no more killing. You should go to the police yourself. End this, now.' He held out the phone.

Tana backed towards the door and shouldered her bag. 'You're scared. I should have known ...' She ran her hands through her hair and spat out a short laugh. 'I never thought you would be the weak link, Nav. Ha. Well,' she said, and placed her hand against the door. 'You're in it with me right up to your pudgy little neck, Patel, so you'd better do exactly what I tell you, when I tell you, or your life really will be over.' She stared at him, hard. 'After all, I'm a weak and vulnerable student who you have totally manipulated, aren't I? Not to mention the cash sitting in your account.' She yanked the door open and left.

Patel watched Tana swing away down the corridor. Such arrogance. Such confidence. He shuddered. He called in his secretary and told her to remove the girl from all university records. He wiped her out of existence, but waited for the reckoning that would surely come.

Chapter Six

Tana's followers met in the Reed Cafe in between lectures. Jay, gaunt, with jet black hair lying over his face, arrived first and ordered coffee, a croissant, and water, counting out the change with shaking fingers. He checked that Tana was nowhere to be seen and took his breakfast to a corner table where he could keep an eye on the door.

Next in was Scarlett. She waved at him and gave her order at the counter, shifting her bag to her other shoulder. It was, as usual, full of stuff. He had no idea what she could carry around all the time that weighed so much. He watched the door. Finally, Amber came through, eyes to the floor. She didn't acknowledge him, but he knew she'd seen him.

At the counter, Scarlett put her hand on the other girl's shoulder. Together they brought their drinks and food to the table.

Jay let them get settled and eat something while he finished off his coffee and drank his water. They were all dehydrated and starving, blood sugar all over the place. It had been a life-changing night. He stared out of the window and watched leaves fall. 'Right, I guess we need to talk about what happened and what we're going to do about it, yeah?'

Scarlett used her spoon to lick out the last of the cappuccino froth and looked up at him under her freshly blackened eyelashes. '"Do about it"?'

'It was murder,' he whispered. 'Not a night out at a nice little bonfire.'

Scarlett shrugged. 'We knew what we were letting ourselves in for, Jay. There's no going back.'

Jay winced. 'I don't think I did. I never thought she'd actually do it. Did you? And what about you, Amber? Did you expect it?' He watched the younger girl closely. Her eyes had regained some focus at last.

'It was amazing. The fire consumes and cleans,' she said simply. 'We made the sacrifice. The sacrifice has gone to a pure place, cleansed of his impurities.'

Jay was aghast. Why was she spouting that rubbish? 'Amber, we just made that stuff up, for the website, remember? That poor guy had his head bashed in by that psycho Kegan. He wasn't a sacrifice!' Jay stared at the girls. Bonkers, both of them. Couldn't they see? 'Can't you see that this has got out of hand? That Tana is off her rocker? And dangerous? That we are party to a murder?'

Scarlett held on to Amber's hand and glanced around the cafe. 'You need to be careful what you say, Jay. People might hear you, and then where would we be?'

Jay shook his head. 'I don't believe you two. Get real. The police will be all over that site. They'll be coming after us. You do know that, right?'

'But they won't find anything,' said Amber. 'Tana has arranged it all so well. None of us has a criminal record, so no DNA. We were disguised by make-up. Anyway, the police are fools, and Tana's made sure they can't trace her.' She reached across the table and took Jay's cold hand. 'There's nothing to worry about. Tana has thought of everything. This was a good thing to happen to that tramp. He'll be much happier now. Surely you can see that?'

Scarlett smiled. 'It was an amazing night, wasn't it? I never thought it would be like that. So ... so ... visceral.' She tucked into her toasted sandwich.

'Visceral? Scarlett, she's going to do more. More murders, and we are implicated. How are we going to get out of this?' Jay watched the two of them catching each other's eye and saw the gulf that had opened between them all. He stared at Scarlett; was there nothing at all left between the two of them?

He needed to get away from them before he lost it. It was almost eleven and he had a lecture to attend. 'I've got to go. Need to drop my guitar off at home then I've got a lecture.' He couldn't meet their eyes. 'See you later.'

Scarlett stood close to him and placed her hand on his chest. 'Don't be mad at us, Jay. It will be all right, you'll see. Tana will make sure it's okay. You will be there tonight?'

Jay shuffled past her. 'I guess so, yeah,' he said, lifting the guitar case from the floor and turning away.

It felt good to get out of the cafe and into clean, cold air. Of course he wouldn't be there tonight. He hurried across campus, long legs pumping. I'll run. I'll go, he thought. He pounded along the pavement, swerving past students with bags and bikes.

But he couldn't run, could he? The mad cow had made it clear that they were all in it for the duration. She'd dob him in without a moment's hesitation. They'd all known what was coming, hadn't they? Been 'hand-picked' for the mission. But he hadn't known. Not really. It had been fun and exciting, and secret, and very weird, yeah, but he'd not factored in that they would actually go ahead and kill someone. And he couldn't get his head around the fact that everybody else apparently had, and were okay with it.

The flat was hot, and stank of sweat, sex, takeaway curry, and beer. Kegan sprawled against the bedhead and watched Tana through half-closed eyes. He gave a lazy smile. 'They'll start arriving soon. I should clear the place up a bit.' He didn't move from the bed, but switched on the television for the early evening news. 'Did you upload the photos?'

'I did, they're on the website. Not much reaction yet, but you wait an hour and all hell will break loose.' Tana pulled Kegan towards her and wrapped her arm around his neck. 'Now for the next one,' she said into his ear. 'Have you got the sacrifice ready?'

'Yeah, contact made.' He couldn't take his eyes off the screen. 'Wow. The cops are throwing everything at it, considering he was just an old tramp.'

'I know. And very soon, I'll be up there with the best of them, my darlin', only nobody will ever find out who I am.' She pulled her laptop onto her knees and sent messages to the rest of the group, telling them what time to arrive. Then she scrolled down to see the responses to her photos. 'Aha, it's starting. "Are these for real?" Ha, wait until you see the rest!' She started to type.

'For Christ's sake don't answer them. You don't know who's out there.' He shut up, knowing he had gone too far. 'I mean, keep a bit of mystery about yourself, build up the excitement.'

She stuck out her bottom lip, and then nodded. 'Yeah, good thinking.'

'You know, we should ditch that laptop now,' Kegan said, staring at the images. He didn't think you could tell who anyone was in the dark, and, with the flames to help disguise him, it would probably be okay, but you never knew. 'These things can be traced.'

Tana punched his arm. 'Don't be an eejit. I stole it in Dublin from an old mate three years ago. It's impossible to trace, and if they do, it will only lead back to him, and he doesn't even know my real name.'

'I don't know your real name.'

'Ah,' she whispered, 'but you have my heart, Kegan, and you need nothing more.'

Professor Navinder Patel took a sip of the Chablis and pulled a face before he could control it. It was such a waste, a good wine imperfectly chilled. He picked a canapé from the table and popped it whole into his mouth, chewing carefully and wiping his lips with a napkin. Smoked salmon and cream cheese. Very nice. He checked his watch: 5.30pm start, he should be home by 9pm.

The other professors were sucking up to the dean and the vice-chancellor, which was what he should have been doing, but he couldn't manage it. He was worried sick about Tana. What if she actually published her photos from the bonfire? What then? Chaos. The police were trained to follow the trails back until they got to the source. And she'd already threatened him. He knew she would betray him to save her own skinny little hide in an instant. He swallowed the canapé before it choked him.

Why had he taken the money? He knew why: his wife wanted to go back to India for a holiday. The money Tana had given him to take her on the Masters course had covered the cost of the trip and more. Oh, he'd been enjoying the repercussions of that generosity for the past year or so. He patted his stomach. Had he known then what he was taking on? Really?

And now his life may well be over, unless he could keep everything under control. Clearly the girl was mad. He just needed to be prepared to argue that point. After all, he was a professor at the university, with an excellent reputation, and she was a nobody. A mad nobody. Besides, the money had been given to him in a wad of Euros. Nobody would be able to trace that back, would they? He could just deny everything. And get a good lawyer.

The chatter around him ceased as the dean tapped her pen on her glass. 'Ladies and gentlemen,' she said, 'before we get to the agenda, it is with great pleasure that I can announce the appointment of our new archaeology professor, Neil Pargeter.' She left a space until everybody had clapped. 'Neil has been doing the job brilliantly since Professor Ballard retired, and we were delighted to appoint him to the post. Let's raise our glasses to Professor Pargeter!'

Patel clapped and raised his glass as instructed. Pargeter looked delighted, he thought. As well he might. He was young for a professor, and he'd only ever taught at Exeter, so he was lucky, too. And Neil didn't have 'accessory to murder' stamped all across his head, did he?

He shrugged and took another canapé. It didn't matter who was appointed to what any more. It was unlikely he'd have a future at the university if the truth about his graduate student ever got out. It was unlikely he'd be out of prison for long either. She was an insurmountable problem, was Tana.

He caught Pargeter's eye, raised his glass at him, and mouthed, 'Well done.'

Unless he came up with a feasible plan to get rid of her, of course. That should not be beyond his capabilities. He was glad he'd just wiped her off the records and got rid of her from the university completely. No record.

He dredged up a smile for Pargeter as he wandered over. 'Good result, Neil,' he said. 'I thought you were the best candidate by far.'

Pargeter grinned. 'Thanks, Nav. The interview is not an experience I want to repeat any time soon, but it feels good now, I must admit.'

'Excellent, we need new blood at senior level. But now, you must pay for all this jollity by sitting through the weekly executive group meeting. Prepare for death by utter boredom.' He grabbed several more canapés, wrapped them up in a napkin, and hid them in his pocket.

Then he refilled both their glasses and led Pargeter into the meeting room.

Chapter Seven

Dan studied the incident board in the early evening, once the office had quietened down. No reports had been received from the hospitals on anyone suffering burns. Sam had collected whatever CCTV footage could be had. Bill and Ben were all over the evidence. He couldn't think of anything else to do and he was tired after the ridiculously early start. No, an early night was called for, and a takeaway.

He drove quickly to his flat on the quayside. It felt cold and a little empty; he hadn't been back for several days. There would be a point very soon when he would have to seriously consider whether it was time to give up his place and make a proper commitment to Claire – if she'd have him. He checked the fridge, deemed the carton of milk okay for another couple of days, and rescued two bottles of white wine. He picked up a spare jumper and his heavy winter coat, and on a whim, put his guitar in its case, and lugged it all downstairs to the car.

Claire was home when he let himself in, laden with Chinese takeaway and wine, and the guitar over his back. She was kneeling in front of the wood burner, swearing under her breath. She didn't say hello. 'Bloody thing won't catch light. Light, you bloody thing,' she said, rattling the casing with a sooty hand.

'Nice to see you, too,' said Dan, as he hurried through to the kitchen with the food. Rufus the cat glared at him, and rubbed white fur on Dan's trouser leg until he took the hint and emptied a sachet of food into the cat's bowl. 'You're welcome,' he muttered to the furball.

He loaded the food containers into the oven on a low heat, took out plates, cutlery and wine glasses, and set the table before daring to go back into the living room. Placing two glasses of wine on the low coffee table, he knelt behind Claire and massaged her shoulders. 'Bad day?' he asked.

Claire stopped fiddling with the fire, at which point it worked perfectly and flames rose up from the logs. Sighing, she slammed the door shut and leaned back against him. 'Awful,' she said, close to tears. 'Not parents' evening: earlier in the day.'

He slipped round so they could both lean back against the sofa and enjoy the warmth from the fire on their toes. He handed her the wine and watched while she took a sip, waiting for the stress to seep out of her shoulders.

'I hate being acting head of department, Dan.' She wiped her eyes with her sooty hand and made a streak along her cheek.

Dan said nothing, just reached across and wiped it off with his thumb.

'If it's not the kids playing up, it's the parents, and now, now ... ooh, it makes me so mad!' She gulped down the wine.

'Right, why don't you tell me about it before we eat, then we can enjoy our evening without all this hanging over us?' he said, wondering when he had become so reasonable. It wasn't as if teaching was life and death after all. Not like his job, which was always like that these days it seemed.

'It sounds pathetic now. I was telling a kid off in the corridor, and she was mouthing off about getting her mum in. You know, just giving me lip, when Debs Wright comes swanning out of the stockroom and gets the girl apologising to me in about ten seconds flat. Like I couldn't do it myself, and the look on her face. She enjoyed showing me up.' The threatened tears became real and trickled down her face. 'Thing is, she's right – I can't do it. It should have been her job,' she wailed.

'Hey,' he said, passing her a box of tissues, 'you were chosen because of your experience and your organisational skills, and your knowledge of the kids and all the exam stuff.' He shook her arm. 'It wasn't charity, Claire. You're the right person for the job. Debs Wright's a nasty, jealous old witch in my fully-informed opinion,' he said. 'She's undermining you, so don't let her. It's called bullying. Have a bit more faith in yourself, sweetheart.' He went silent for a moment, thinking he may have to deliver the same speech to Adam Foster soon if he didn't buck up. 'Come on, scrub up, I need food and wine, and …' He scooped up Rufus from the rug and pushed him, unyielding, into Claire's arms, 'you need a cuddle from the hairy monster.'

Claire snuffled out a laugh and squeezed the cat against her chest until he squeaked and jumped off her lap. She clambered to her feet. 'Okay, sorry about all that. I just needed to let it out,' she said, dabbing at her face.

'No worries. You should have seen me when I was leading on my first case. Total bag of nerves. Let's eat, shall we? Then I'll treat you to a few toons on the geetar …'

Chapter Eight

Dan's last post-mortem, back in June, had involved two bodies that had been killed almost ten years earlier. It was a clean, clinical process that day, unlike this morning, he thought. The room seemed unnaturally bright, the corpse wet, smelly and all too recently alive. He cleared his throat and watched the clock. Shouldn't be more than an hour, he hoped. He watched the technician measure the body using string, to follow the unnatural contours where the victim's legs had contracted in the fire, and record the results.

'He was over six feet tall,' she murmured, 'and there are indications of muscular wastage where there is enough tissue to measure it.'

'Aye,' agreed Campbell Fox, 'he was a more imposing man in his heyday than after years of self-abuse, I imagine.'

Fox had another technician snip the remaining ribs and sternum to enable him to access the chest cavity. 'Many of the organs are burnt,' he said. 'The heart seems to have shrivelled, pulled back in on itself.' He placed the heart in a tray and cut out the liver. 'The liver, burnt, of course, is the black, lumpen mass of an alcoholic on the outside.' He paused and took a slice off the lump, 'and the medium rare of well-cooked steak on the inside.' He chuckled at his wit and signalled the technicians to turn the body onto its side.

Dan made a silent vow in the quiet that followed, that nobody would ever make him eat liver again. Ever. He glanced over at Ben Bennett, who was waiting patiently for evidence, and rolled his eyes. Bennett made a throwing up motion and grinned.

Fox examined the hole in the back of the dead man's head and measured it. 'A weapon at least fifteen centimetres wide, blunt, and heavy.' He asked the technician to saw open the skull and extract the brain.

'A rock, then,' said Dan. 'Not much chance of finding the weapon on a beach full of rocks that have been washed for six hours by the sea.'

The whine of the blade made him wince as it made light work of the cracked skull. 'The brain, almost untouched by fire, also shows signs of the characteristic deterioration I would expect to see in an alcoholic of middle years.'

Dan's phone buzzed in his pocket so he left the room to answer it. He wasn't interested in the guy's brain, he wanted to be able to identify him, and as far as he could tell, they would need to rely on DNA for this poor guy. It was Sally on the line.

'Thought you might want an excuse to get out of there for a minute or two,' she said. 'Is it gruesome?'

'It is,' he said. 'And not so far telling me anything I want to know. What can I do for you?'

'Just thought you would like to know that the charming Lisa Middleton has got the front page on the Western Daily. I quote: "Teen party inferno. One dead. Police baffled." unquote. There follows a load of stuff about antisocial behaviour and half-term holidays, and speculation about whether it was an accident or murder.'

'So much for "please do not speculate". She's a piece of work, isn't she?'

'Well, I suppose, if I'm feeling kind, which I'm not, much, I can say that she is trying to do her job, but I'd rather she was on our side than agin us. And,' she cleared her throat, 'I may be to blame for her somewhat hostile attitude.'

'Really? You do surprise me. What with you being so tolerant of other people's foibles.' He laughed when she blew a raspberry down the phone. 'Okay, thanks, I'll speak to her when we do the next press briefing. Any other news?'

'I've got Lizzie and Adam in Exmouth asking in the homeless hostel and around the town, just seeing if a regular has gone missing over the last day or two. We have Paula Tippett doing a check of homeless registers in the south-west. I was a bit surprised that numbers are on the rise again. I'll have a word with our liaison team, see what's happening there. Sam's on misper – you never know, someone may have reported him missing – and Bill Larcombe's got his PCSOs doing the phone box checks. We need that description asap.'

'Right, I'd better get back in there. See you later.' He slipped the phone into his pocket, took a breath of relatively fresh air, and went back inside.

A technician was taking scrapings from under the victim's fingernails. The scrapings were red, like rust, as they dropped into a bag. Fox tweezed out several undamaged hairs from the victim's head and placed them in a bag. 'The main torso is relatively undamaged. The fire would not have burned hot enough or long enough to destroy the body, if indeed that was the aim.'

'But he could have been in there for five hours,' said Dan. 'Why isn't he more burnt?'

'It's fat that burns, not bone, DCI Hellier. A skinny, under-nourished one like this would have hardly any fat on him. The burning clothes would do the initial damage, but once they've burnt off, and the skin has gone, it would take a long time to destroy the bone.' He shrugged. 'I hope he was properly unconscious before he went in, poor soul.'

'Could you make a guess at his age, Doctor?' Dan moved closer to the slab.

Fox looked at him over the rims of his glasses. He harrumphed briefly then gave in. 'The victim appears to be a male in middle-age, although it is hard to be sure as alcoholism ages the body quickly.' He waggled his fingers, making an estimate. 'Judging by his physical state and his teeth, I'd say mid-to-late forties. Is that a good enough guess for ye?'

'Great, thanks. Any other distinguishing features?'

Fox pursed his lips. 'You know how we identified that dead woman in June, through the tattoo ink on her ankle? Well, there are similar marks on this victim, but they are all over the bits of skin left on his back and arms. I'd hazard a "guess",' he made air quotes around the word, 'that our victim was in the armed forces. Possibly the navy.'

'That's useful. Thanks very much, Doctor Fox, that'll give us something to go on while we wait for the DNA results.' Dan nodded at the doctor and left. Ben would bring along any evidence they could use, and, with a bit of luck, he could get the Plymouth lab to start on the DNA analysis sooner rather than later.

He cut across the grass to the car park and took the On Police Business sign out of his car. It was always a toss-up whether or not to use it, but the car park prices were extortionate at the hospital, and, now that he was in charge of several budgets, he was economising.

Chapter Nine

DCs Lizzie Singh and Adam Foster stood outside the imposing frontage of Swallow House, the hostel for the homeless in Exmouth. Lizzie jotted down the latest intel on the victim as DCI Hellier dictated it down the phone. 'Male, about fifty, beard, thin, possible tattoos,' she said to Foster, 'PM verbal, not verified.'

'Better than nothing,' he said, and leaned on the bell. He could hear it ringing inside the building but nobody came to the door.

Lizzie turned the handle. The door opened so she went in. 'Hello? Anybody here?' She led Foster down a long corridor, towards the sound of a radio coming from the rear of the building. Lizzie stuck her head around the door; the woman at the sink gave a little yelp and held up her washing-up brush. 'Hello, no need to be alarmed, we're police,' she said. She found her warrant card and held it out.

The woman, all of five-foot-three, with dark, curly hair escaping from a flowery headband, puffed out a held breath. 'Right. Jane Poole, I'm the hostel manager, day shift. Thought the front door was locked. We usually lock it once they're all out for the day.' She put down the brush, wiped her hands on her jeans and rested against the sink. 'Who's in trouble now?' she asked.

'It's a bit difficult,' Lizzie said. 'Early yesterday morning the body of a man we believe to be homeless was discovered inside a fire on Exmouth beach.'

Jane Poole screwed up her face. 'Oh, no, that's a nasty way to go.'

'We have reason to believe that the man concerned may have been based locally; were any of your regulars missing last night or the night before?'

Poole tucked a stray curl under her headband while she thought. 'Not our regulars, I don't think. We have a dozen or more who we've successfully taken off the streets this summer, and they all came home before I left for the day, but if he was a habitual rough sleeper, we may simply not know about him.'

Foster sidled further into the kitchen. 'This is a really nice room,' he said. 'Airy.'

'Thanks. What did you expect? Fagin's den? This is home to our clients until we can move them on to somewhere more permanent. But it's a home without the chaos they usually come from.' She picked up the soapy brush and eyed the pile of cereal bowls next to the sink. 'Look, I'd like to help, but we haven't missed anyone. If that's all, could you see yourselves out?' Poole smiled at Lizzie and went back to washing up.

Outside, on the quiet, broad road, Lizzie thrust her hands into her pockets. 'Come on, Lee Marvin, let's see if there are any likely lads in town.'

'Lizzie, why is everybody calling me Lee Marvin? Sergeant Bennett started it after my little run in with the knife, and I don't know who Lee Marvin is, and, well, should I be really pissed off that this is becoming my nickname, or pleased?'

Lizzie tried to hide her grin. 'Tell you what, Adam, look him up on Google – I think you'll understand once you hear him sing. Come on.'

Exmouth town centre was quiet. The schools had gone back after half-term break and there were no skateboarders clogging up the town square. There were, however, three men sitting on a bench, sharing a bottle and smoking roll-ups. Lizzie headed straight for them across the recently paved and updated square, which would now, she thought, be more properly called a circle. Foster trailed in her wake, attempting to discover where his nickname originated by squinting at his phone.

She stopped a metre away from the bench and scanned the faces. Two of them studied the ends of their cigarettes. The cider bottle had disappeared, probably under a coat; she could smell alcohol and an undefinable sweet smell. The one on the left was hideous but at least he was watching her through his one good eye. She smiled at him. His dog, a square, squat thing with a triangular head and big shoulders, growled at her. She buried her hands in her pockets.

'What do you want, girly?' he asked, pleasantly.

Lizzie checked behind her for Foster. He was oblivious, head stuck in his phone. She wished she'd brought a local PCSO with her, but she hadn't, so she pulled out her warrant card. 'That'll be Detective Constable Singh to you. Speak to me like that again and you won't be spending the rest of the day on that bench.'

The man squinted at her under his eyebrow. His single eye looked her up and down. The other side of his head was crumpled, as if he had been struck a terrible blow and the skull had never been repaired. He raised a long, filthy nail and scratched at the empty eye socket. 'Should've said, darlin'. What's a bloke to think when a girl comes up to him dead bold?' He sniggered. 'Wants to know how much, dun' he?' He collapsed into snuffling giggles and pulled hard on his roll-up, making his thin face cadaverous.

From behind Lizzie came the unmistakable tones of Lee Marvin singing something about a star. Furious, she swung round to face Foster. 'Turn that bloody music off now, Adam, or I'll …'

Foster stared at her, grin fading fast. 'What? It's funny! Do I really sound like this?'

'Now.'

He put away his phone and strode up to the bench, pushing his face into neutral. 'Need any help here?' he asked, his damaged vocal chords adding useful gravitas to his youthful voice.

Before Lizzie could respond, the middle one of the three, an older man, swiped out a wiry arm and pinned one-eye to the back of the bench. 'Now, now, Spike, that's no way to speak to the officer.' He smiled mildly at Lizzie. 'He didn't mean no offence, miss. It's just that he's a tosser. What can we do for you?'

Lizzie controlled her anger. Ugly Spike was clearly off his face. Charging him for his behaviour seemed a bit pointless, although tempting. She took a breath and focused on the middle guy. 'Have any of your friends gone missing in the last day or two? Bloke about fifty, grey beard?'

One-eyed Spike lurched to his feet and clucked at his dog. Lizzie stepped back. 'Need a slash,' he muttered, and staggered off towards the public toilets.

The middle man watched him go, then turned back to Lizzie. 'Probably better if he's not here, miss. Likes the craic a bit too much, if you get my meaning?' He raised a hand and tugged at his beard, ginger shot through with grey. 'We all get a bit beardy after a while on the road, but it could be Moose you're talking about. He was here Saturday, but I haven't seen him since Sunday afternoon.' He nudged the dozing figure next to him. 'Dimp, wake up. D'you reckon it's Moose that has gone missin'?'

Dimp opened an eye, registered the strangers, and closed it again. 'Dunno,' he said.

Foster rolled his eyes and put his hands on his hips. 'We're not talking about someone having gone missing,' he said. 'The guy we're talking about is dead, burnt to death in a bonfire on Monday night. Any useful information would be very helpful.'

He leaned down into Dimp's face, and recoiled at the stench. 'Whoa, been hitting the cider early, haven't you, mate? You'd better hand me the bottle, it's illegal to drink on the street.' He held out his hand then heard a clearing of the throat from behind him. He looked round. 'What?'

'Sorry, he's a bit keen,' Lizzie said to the older man. She didn't add, 'and a tosser'. She edged Foster out of the way. 'What's your name?'

The man smiled with a mouth surprisingly full of teeth. 'Paddy will do. Has someone really been burned to death out there?' He stared hard at Lizzie, no sign of drunkenness in his manner.

'Yes, it's true. Do you know anything about this "Moose" person? His background? Family? Where he came from?'

Paddy shook his head slowly and stared off towards the war memorial in the middle of the square. 'Burnt to death, you say?

That's bad.' He looked up at her. 'He was in the Marines, so I hear, but nothing else comes to mind.'

'Okay, thanks for that.' She handed him a card. 'Here are my contact details. Will you call me if you can think of anything else?'

Paddy squinted at the card. 'Doubt anything else will occur, but I'll keep it in here.' He opened the front of his coat and put it in an inside pocket.

Foster stood in front of Dimp. 'Give me the bottle, or I'm taking you in for drinking on the street,' he said.

Paddy nudged the younger man. 'Give it. Don't be a tosser.'

With reluctance, Dimp handed over the bottle, a sneer on his face.

Lizzie grabbed Foster's arm. Ugly Spike was on his way back with the nasty-looking dog. 'Come on, DC Foster, we haven't got time to hang around here all day. Thanks, gentlemen,' she said, and strode off across the square, leaving Foster with the only option of following her. He emptied the bottle of cider, still almost full, down the nearest drain, and threw the empty bottle into a bin, ignoring the jeers coming from the bench.

Lizzie kept walking until she reached the pool car and had calmed down a bit. Adam was such a bloody irritant. She'd been mentoring him for months, but he never learned when to shut up. He was just the sort of copper that got them all a bad rep. Sticking his nose in, interfering. Pain in the backside. She rounded on him.

'How are you going to build people's trust in us if you go after every petty misdemeanour like you're the bloody pope?'

Foster leaned back against the car, a half-smile on his face. 'Keep your hair on, Lizzie, I was just doing my lawful duty.'

'No! No, you weren't. What you were doing was focusing on the side issue, not the major issue, and that's what gets me mad. Obviously, I saw him stash the bottle away, I could smell the cider on him, but that wasn't what we were there for, was it? We've got a cooperative bloke, Paddy, and you hassling his mates won't keep him that way.' She blew air through pursed lips. 'Adam, they'll just go and buy another bottle. Leave that stuff to the local force.

We've got bigger things to think about, like murder. We're the murder squad.' She searched his face for understanding, but saw little. Only resentment. Lizzie banged her head on the roof of the car. 'Give me strength,' she muttered, and turned back to him. 'So, what have we got to go on?'

Foster looked away. 'Moose, possibly ex-marines,' he said.

'And what do we have, less than three miles away up the coast?'

His mood lifted. 'Marine Commando base. Let's go.' He pulled open the car door and threw himself inside.

'Yes, let's go,' she said, sliding in next to him. 'Back to the station where I'll get on the phone and speak to someone.' She shook her head. 'Sorry to disappoint you, Marvin, but you won't get to play with the marines today. They're not the sort of places where you just drop in.'

'You're just having a go at me because Spike had a go at you,' muttered Foster, arms folded tightly across his chest.

Chapter Ten

The white of the overhead fluorescent lights bleached the faces looking up at him around the table. Dan sipped his coffee and waited for the current roll of thunder to pass over. Rain threw itself in bucketloads at the windows. The thunder rolled round again, followed by a flash of lightning. Appropriate weather for the bombshell he was about to drop. He shuffled through his notebook, found the right page, and glanced at the clock. He'd like a reasonable finish time, but it wasn't looking likely. 'Sam?' he shouted into the post-thunder quiet.

'Coming, boss. Just got the CCTV stuff.' Sam pushed his chair back, struggled to his feet and brought a memory stick with him.

Sergeants Bennett and Larcombe sat back in their chairs, chatting to Lizzie Singh and the civilian researcher, Paula Tippett. Foster seems to be on his own, thought Dan. He hasn't gelled with the team yet, isn't relaxed. Must chat to Sally about him.

'Right,' he said, 'let's crack on. I have some bad news.' He swivelled around and clicked towards the TV screen. Four photos in full colour filled the screen.

'Are they what I think they are?' murmured Bill Larcombe.

'If you think they're stills from the fire, you'd be on the money. Have a good look, I haven't had a chance since I got in this afternoon. They're from two short videos taken at the scene.'

'Who told us about them?' asked Lizzie.

'Social media surveillance team. They were just on the lookout for trends, new stuff, the usual nightshift trawl. Got the shock of their lives when they realised what they'd got. They were on the phone as soon as I got back from the PM. These were taken from Instagram. They were posted around 5pm yesterday afternoon.'

There was silence as the team studied the images. Only he and the flowerpot men had seen the body after it had been retrieved from the fire, and none of them had seen it burning.

'Good God, who'd do that to another human being?' asked Sally.

'Sickos, that's for sure,' answered Larcombe.

'Okay, let's focus. Picture three shows faces round one part of the fire. Sam, any way we can enhance these images to get a clearer view?'

Sam squinted. 'I might be able to, but if they've already been photo-shopped, I'm not sure how much use I can be. I can get them to the lab in Bristol, though. They're the experts.'

'Do it. Anything else anyone can add?' There was no reply.

'Right, there's more.' He clicked again and brought up a lurid website home page. 'I guess because they had nothing better to do, the team then found this for us too. I might owe them a large drink.' The screen showed a shadowy black image of a woman's figure being consumed in fire. Above, in words dripping with flames, was the title: 'Fire Goddess – find the way to purify your soul'.

Foster coughed out in disbelief. 'That's it? It's going to be this easy? All we have to do is find the website owner and we've got them, boss.'

Lizzie pulled a face at him. 'He would never have figured that out for himself, Adam. Thank God we've got you to state the bleedin' obvious.'

Foster subsided, cheeks burning.

'Never mind, Marvin,' muttered Bennett, patting him on the hand.

'The surveillance team have been on it half the night, but the track-back is old and convoluted and encrypted. They can't find the host, as yet. We're awaiting an update. Sam, I need you on the website provider search with them soon as: who's hosting this site, and can we have the details?

'In the meantime, what else have we got? Lizzie, what did you and Adam find out?'

Lizzie waved at Adam. He got up and wrote the name Moose, followed by ex-marine – with a question mark – on the incident board, and stood, pen poised.

'We had a nice chat to a guy called Paddy in Exmouth,' Lizzie said, 'who said Moose was a marine, so I called the commander at Lympstone training centre, a Colonel Mike Allport, and asked about anyone dismissed for drinking on the job in the last few years. Turns out it's remarkably common in marines who have seen active service, and he's happy to help. He's got his secretary trawling the court martials and dishonourable discharges for the last ten years for us.'

Adam wrote the name of the colonel on the board and waited.

'So, the victim wasn't staying in the hostel in Exmouth?' asked Bill Larcombe.

'No,' said Lizzie, 'but it was a good lead, Sarge, thanks. I … we've made a good contact there.'

'That's good work, you two,' said Dan. 'Soon as we get DNA through, we should be able to identify him if he's been discharged. Sam?'

Knowles got up, plugged the memory stick into the side of the whiteboard, and brought up a section of video that covered the centre of Exmouth town on the night of 31 October. 'It's poor quality, but I got this.' He pressed the forward button and grey images crossed the screen from right to left. Many of them in Halloween costumes. Sam concentrated for a couple of seconds then paused the picture. There was a group of three people walking with purpose across the square. They were clearly not drunk, nor were they joking or messing about.

'I just had a feeling about this lot,' he said. 'Almost eleven on a Sunday night, and they don't look like they're going home from the pub. No Halloween costumes as far as I can tell. The nightclub doesn't even open on Sundays in the winter, so they're not heading there. Thought they could be heading for the beach.' He pressed fast-forward then stopped at another shot. 'This is from behind the big hotel on the front. See, there's a tall guy, long black coat, guitar case. Two shorter figures, possibly females, wearing hoods. No attempt to hide their faces, but, to be honest, it's such poor quality film, they don't need to.'

Dan gave a whistle of appreciation. 'Sam, that's not bad at all. Thank you. Maybe it's not too far-fetched to think we might match these three up with our fire attendees? Or should we call them worshippers? Or cult members?

'Show it all again. The rest of you, eyes like hawks. What else can you get out of these tapes? Anything, don't be shy. We'll give it twenty minutes then see what we have.'

For several run-throughs, there was only the muffled slurping of coffee, the occasional 'stop, rewind' comment, and the grumbling appendix of the storm above their heads. Dan watched the team work. He watched Foster, who wasn't glued to the screen like everyone else. Foster was sneaking a look at Lizzie's notebook, then peering at the screen. I bet he's short sighted but won't wear his glasses, Dan thought. He snorted, and buried his face in his mug, swallowing the dregs of his coffee.

'Okay, enough for now.' He gestured at Sam to stop the tape. 'What have we got?'

'Three young people,' said Bill Larcombe. 'But no one looking like he's the right age to be the victim. This lot look young – going by their walk and stance. Where are the victim and the other two people? That's assuming every stone round that fire had a bum on it, of course.'

Lizzie asked about the long, dark coats. 'It's not some sort of uniform, is it?'

'Could be – they do look a bit Goth,' said Sally. 'I had a coat like that in the early eighties.'

'You're suggesting that they might be an organised group?' asked Dan, scribbling in his notebook.

'Just a thought, what with the videos.'

Dan indicated to Adam Foster, still standing next to the whiteboard, to write that down. 'Bill, what did your trawl of the pubs come up with?'

'Nothing concrete; loads of youngsters were around town on Sunday, some dressed up in Halloween costumes. Impossible task to identify any one group really.'

'But, what if we're looking for Moose, possibly well-known to local landlords, and just one other person? A person buying him drinks, and leaving with him at the end of the night?'

'Sam and I will get onto it straightaway, boss,' Larcombe said.

'No, you two stay on CCTV. Sally, will you and Lizzie go down to Exmouth and chat to the landlords, please?

'Anybody else got anything to say?'

Foster said, 'I think we need to seriously consider the Halloween angle.'

Dan watched outrage sweep across Lizzie's face. That's what he'd been doing – pinching her ideas.

'Why?' he asked.

'Err ... well, because it might have made a gang of teenagers a bit stupid. I mean, what if they were on legal highs and didn't realise what they were doing, or something?' he said.

Lizzie closed her notebook and rested her pen on top of it. 'I had that idea too,' she said, turning her back on Foster. 'But my angle is that it could have been organised; not a party gone wrong, but a ritualised killing for Halloween.'

Dan couldn't stop a grin from spreading across his face, even though he knew she was deadly serious.

Foster sniggered. 'Got our own Buffy the Vampire Slayer,' he said, and raised his eyebrows at Sam across the table. 'Buffy the tramp burner ...'

'Okay, enough,' said Dan. 'We have a boot that belonged to the deceased, and quite a lot of evidence has gone off to the crime lab for DNA testing today. Finally, there was a small torn-off bit of music paper in all the rubbish we picked up, and that may link to the guy with the guitar. That's not a bad start. I expect to identify the victim within a couple of days. Now let's see if we can get closer to the perps.

'A bonfire doesn't just build itself,' he continued. 'People have to collect wood. That takes time, unless there are loads of them doing it, and we think there were only maybe five people there. So, at some point in the day, somebody piled up wood into a bonfire shape. Who?'

'We could ask dog walkers, boss,' said Foster. 'Maybe one of them saw somebody.'

'Great, get down to the beach and ask. Try mornings and evenings, see if anyone remembers anything unusual.'

Foster jotted a note in his pad. 'It would only be the walkers who head off down the far end towards Sandy Bay, and only when the tide is out, won't it? I'd better check the timetables.' He scribbled away.

Dan sighed, they didn't have much to go on at all, really. 'Okay, write up anything useful, and I'll see you tomorrow.' He refilled his mug and stared out at the rain, while the team shuffled and bustled behind him.

His phone rang, interrupting a particularly ropy bit of reporting from the sergeant in Team One. He grinned when he saw the caller ID. 'Neil, mate! Not heard from you for weeks. How's it going?' He listened for a minute or two. 'You made Professor of Archaeology? That's amazing. Good on you. Yeah, let's meet for a drink. Not tonight though, already booked, what about Friday?' He wrote down the time. 'I'll see you there, Lord Professor Pargeter. Curry and a pint on you, I reckon.'

Well, he thought as the phone went back into his pocket, Professor Pargeter, now, was it? What elevated circles he moved in. As long as it wasn't ever going to be Professor Pargeter in the library with the candlestick, it couldn't happen to a nicer bloke.

Chapter Eleven

Apart from a vague feeling that he ought to be out on the streets doing something practical to move the case on, Dan's afternoon had been productive. He ploughed through his outstanding paperwork and signed off on the Team One case at last, pleasing his sergeants, and updated Superintendent Oliver on where they were so far. He was determined to finish on time, and slipped out of the station at 5.35pm without bumping into anyone who could stop him.

Dan drove the short distance to the quayside and his flat, lost in thought. Was he mad to imagine that there might be a ritual element to the killing? It seemed unlikely that anyone would deliberately set someone on fire as a method of murder: it was inefficient. But not everybody would know that. The public believe fire destroys evidence; reality shows fire leaves a great deal behind. So they were not dealing with professional gangland killings, or a personal attack, it would be too difficult to build a fire and get the victim to attend, never mind getting them into the fire. No, it seemed more likely that all five of the watchers were somehow involved in the victim's death, that some aspect of order or ritual might be involved. Who on earth could he ask for help on this? It was way out of his experience.

Dan pulled into his parking space and glanced up at his kitchen window. There was a light on in the flat coming through from the living room. He thought about his quick visit the previous evening and was sure he hadn't left a light on. Odd. He took the stairs two at a time and paused outside his front door. No sign of breaking and entering; the lock looked intact. The only other people who had a key were Claire and his mother. But he was picking up

Claire to take her round to his mother's for dinner, so why would she be here? And who else knew where his mother kept the key? Cautiously, he opened the door into the small hallway. There was music coming from the living room and the heating was on full. Angry now, and sure of his intruder, Dan threw open the living room door and shouted, 'What the hell do you think you're doing, Alison?'

His sister shot off the sofa, spilling her drink on the rug. She was white with shock and was shaking. 'Oh, you frightened me half to death,' she said. 'Dan, it's not ... I wasn't ...' Her eyes filled up.

'Don't do the tears,' he growled, staring at the growing brown stain on his white rug. 'They don't work on me.' He switched off the music. 'What are you doing in my flat?' He stormed into the kitchen, took a cloth from the tray, wet it, and scrubbed the spilled tea from his rug and floor. He didn't look at her.

Alison stayed where she was.

'I asked you a question,' he said, but he went back into the kitchen before she could speak, rinsed out the cloth and took a couple of deep breaths. It was better to be calm, he knew, but she pushed all his buttons just by being alive, never mind by what she did. He put on the kettle and made an instant coffee. The milk was off. He poured it down the drain and added a half-spoon of sugar to his black coffee to disguise the bitterness. Then he went back into the living room and sat on one of the chairs he'd never sat on. He always sat on the sofa, but he didn't want to now. Finally, he felt able to look at her. 'Sit down. Tell me what's going on.'

Alison slid down onto the sofa and clutched her tea between both hands. 'I didn't mean any harm, Dan. It's just ... Well, can you imagine what it feels like to be living at home with your parents at thirty-eight years old? It's awful. I mean they're kind and well-meaning, but Mum won't let me do anything useful, and Dad keeps staring at me, waiting for me to start shooting-up in the kitchen or steal the family silver. Or worse, his golf clubs.

And today they said you and Claire were coming over for dinner, and would I mind going out for the evening? And, I thought …'

'You thought I wouldn't be back tonight, so you'd take over my flat for the evening? Just took the key from the house?'

'Yeah.' She slipped the key from her jeans pocket and placed it on the table. 'I wouldn't do anything bad. I'm not going to wreck the place or anything. I just haven't got anywhere to go since I came out of prison. I haven't got any straight friends, and I'm staying away from the others because I really want it to work this time.' She tried to catch his eye. 'I'm clean, Dan. Really, I am. Not touched anything since I was let out in June. That's nearly six months.'

Dan drank his coffee and wished he had a whisky to go in it. Alison screwed with his head. It was good that she was clean, and he believed she was, now. Her dark hair had a shine to it, her eyes were clear, and she had put on enough weight to pass for attractive again. A small part of him felt sorry for her that she didn't have any friends, a house or a job. The rest of him knew it was her own fault, caused by her own bad decisions, and he had no responsibility for her whatsoever.

He glared at the coffee table for a minute then allowed a familiar mood of resignation to settle on his shoulders. Here we go again. Blood will out, as they say, and he couldn't just turn her out into a cold night to wander the streets. If she went back to her old druggie ways he wouldn't be able to stand it, and neither would his parents. He drank his coffee and let her stew while he thought about it. There was an option that might suit both of them, if he was prepared to take the risk.

'What if,' he started, thinking hard. 'What if I let you move into my flat, rent-free, and you keep the place clean and tidy for me?'

He could barely look at her face as she crumpled into more tears. She put her mug down and sobbed into the bottom edge of her jumper. 'Really? You mean it? I could stay here?'

Dan located a box of tissues under the table and passed them to her, waiting until she had cleaned herself up before continuing.

'You would need to stay registered at Mum and Dad's, as I'm not allowed to sublet this place, but it would give you some independence.'

Alison gulped down breaths. 'Yes, thank you. Thank you. Oh, my God. I don't know what else to say.' More tears flowed. 'It's more than I could ever have hoped, to have a place of my own, and not be … you know … '

'Totally off your face?'

She managed a little smile, and rubbed her arms where the marks of her past mocked her. 'Yeah. Or in a hostel or a B and B.'

'I want you to look for a job,' he said. 'You could do voluntary work at a charity or somewhere, to get a bit of experience, then see what's available. You still got a social worker?'

'Yes,' she came back eagerly. 'And I get benefits, which means I could travel to work. I can buy food. Make sure you've got milk in for when you do come back.'

She stood up, took a deep breath, and went into the bathroom. 'I just need a minute,' she said.

Alone, Dan questioned whether or not he had made an enormous mistake. But that was always the case with every decision concerning Alison. The dinner that evening with his parents had been arranged to talk about this very problem. What could they do about her? So, something had been done. For better or worse.

While she was in the bathroom, he pulled out a suitcase and emptied the wardrobe of three suits still in their wrappers from the dry cleaner's, added a drawerful of underwear and socks, and as many shirts as he would need for a week at Claire's. He made a space in one half of the wardrobe and gave Alison the empty drawer.

What else? Jeans and T-shirts, his Timberland boots, trainers. He'd have to leave his cycling gear for now. No way all that would fit into Claire's little house. 'You're making a big, big decision, Daniel,' he muttered, but there was lightness in his heart. Two big decisions.

He looked around the bedroom and wondered if he would ever sleep in there again. He also wondered if Claire and he were really ready to set up home properly. 'Ah, well, one way to find out,' he murmured, and selected three ties to match his suits.

Back in the living room, Alison had gathered up the mugs and was standing with her back to the window, waiting for him. She clocked the suitcase and suit carrier and grinned. 'You really mean it, don't you?'

'I do for now,' he said. 'Just don't cock it up, all right? Look, come back home around ten tonight, give me time to explain what's happening to the parents. I'm sure Dad will help you move. I'm in the middle of a murder inquiry, so you're on your own.'

'Yes, that's fine. Whatever you say.' She stood, awkward suddenly, arms at her sides, but he turned towards the door. They hadn't reached the hugging stage yet, although he knew that was what was called for. 'See you later, then,' he said, and pushed open the door into the hall.

'Oh, Dan,' Alison called after him, 'can I put some cushions on this sofa?'

'No smoking in the flat, Ali. Use the balcony. All right?'

Claire stared at him. 'You're really going to give the keys to your precious flat to your sister?' she said, so incredulous that she stopped getting dressed, with only one leg in her jeans.

Dan looked sheepish. 'I know I said a lot of stuff about her, and it was all true. But she is my sister, and I feel a bit sorry for her, I suppose, especially as she's making a real effort to straighten herself out.' He looked up at her. 'What I haven't done,' he said, patting the bed and shifting over for her to sit next to him, 'what I haven't done is ask you if it's all right for me to, you know, move in on a more permanent basis.' He nuzzled her neck. 'Can I stay?'

Claire appeared to think about it, which made him nervous.

'Just teasing,' she said, 'I've been wondering if you were ever going to bring it up. I was damned if I was,' she said. 'No one's accusing me of putting pressure on a bloke to commit.'

Was this it? Should he ask her now? Would she marry him if he asked? But the moment passed, and living together seemed to be acceptable to Claire for now, and it wasn't quite as terrifying as the alternative. So he squeezed her as tightly as he could, and murmured how much he loved her into her hair, which smelt, as usual, of jasmine.

The meal at the Hellier's that evening consisted of a roast chicken with roast potatoes and a mountain of veg. His mum's gravy was the best ever, so Dan made the most of it, and afterwards there was a trifle that was guaranteed not to contain less than three thousand calories per portion. They washed it down with an Australian Shiraz that Geoff Hellier had received as part of his regular quarterly box from the wine club. Geoff rolled the wine around his mouth and swished it through his teeth, making pretentious noises of appreciation, much to Claire's amusement and Dan's despair. Dan picked up a pile of plates and took them into the kitchen.

His mother, Carol, had wept on and off all evening since he had told them about his plan for Alison. She followed him in, clanking dishes onto the worktop. 'I'm glad I got you alone, darling,' she said. 'This means the world to me and your dad, you know, letting Alison stay at your place.' She took his hands in hers. 'I know it's hard, but she is ready to move on, and I've been so frightened of her going back to her old ways.' She turned away and wiped her face.

'Well, this is Alison we're talking about – anything could happen. But, for now, it's a solution. Let's see how it goes, eh?' He put his hands on her shoulders and kissed the top of her head. 'You and dad could do with the house back to yourselves again, too.'

Carol shrugged under his hands. 'He's never here,' she said. 'Since Alison's been back, he's always at the golf club. I'm a golf widow.'

'Maybe that will change, now.'

'Doubt it, but I still have a few years to go before I fully retire, so at least I get out of the house three days a week.'

The sound of the front door opening took them back into the dining room. Alison entered and stood in the doorway, in her coat, uncertainty clouding her face.

Claire got up and went across to give her a hug. 'I think you moving into Dan's flat is a great idea, Alison,' she said. 'You need a place of your own.'

Alison smiled gratefully at Claire and looked across from her to Dan. 'It's a fresh start for me. Thank you. I never expected, after all that's …'

Dan cleared his throat. 'Dad will help you to move over the next couple of days, and I'll be over later in the week to make sure you've got what you need. I'll let the neighbours know that they'll be seeing you, not me, and I'd better inform the landlord so I don't get evicted, I suppose.'

Chapter Twelve

On his way into work on Thursday morning, Dan was accosted as he got out of his car. Lisa Middleton, ginger hair blowing wild around her head in the blustery north wind, and her nose turning a shade of pink that did not suit her, grabbed hold of his arm as he went to take his bag from the back seat.

'Chief Inspector, could I have a word?' she said, and smiled at him as though they were friends.

Dan bristled. It was 7.35am. He wanted, no, he needed coffee, made strong and dark; he *wanted* doughnuts glazed with pink sticky stuff. What he did not want, ever, was this witch of a woman touching him. He looked down at her hand then across at her face, and she dropped his arm like it was hot. 'You can have a word, Miss Middleton, I have several I could think of that might be appropriate, but accost me in public again and you might get more than you bargained for.' He locked the car, pocketed the key fob and waited for her to have her word.

Lisa Middleton was made of tough stuff, he would give her that. Undaunted, she turned around and picked up a takeaway coffee and a paper bag that she had hidden next to another car. 'Thought you might need these,' she said. 'Strong, the way you like it. Oh, and an almond croissant. Costa's best.' She grinned at him. 'Go on, it doesn't count as bribery if it's before eight o'clock.'

Dan had to smile as he took the coffee and pastry. Canny cow must have been talking to someone on the team. He glanced up to the office window and could see Sally's face peeking down at him. 'Well?'

Middleton kept up her smile as she fished for her notebook in her bag. 'Well, it's three days since the body was found in the fire, and you don't seem to be getting anywhere on your own, so, I wondered whether we could, you know, work together to catch the gang?'

'I always expect the local press to support us in our job of catching criminals,' he said, and took a slurp of coffee. 'Sometimes it can take us a whole week to catch them on our own, though. On occasions, months. Rubbish, aren't we?'

'No, I mean we could set up an appeal. You know, like a mini Crimewatch or something, using the paper to get people to come forward. It could help.'

'And you would get what, from me, exactly, in return for all this generosity?'

'Aha,' she said. 'The bottom line. You tell me the news just before it goes to general press release.' She balked at the look on his face and made a patting gesture with her hands. 'I'm not asking for special treatment, Mr Hellier. Just a little heads up to, you know, give me time to get my article prepared and out before the big boys get to it. Give me an edge, so to speak.' She cocked her head to one side.

'You want me to help your career, Miss Middleton?' He shook his head. 'I have to admire your cheek. Tell you what, give me your card, stop interrupting me in press conferences, and I'll see what I can do, okay?'

He had to back away fast before she could kiss him, and he made it into the back stairwell before she could say another word. She was a piece of work all right, but a local press campaign could work well. He'd get Sally onto it, that would take the smile off her face – laughing at him from the safety of the nick.

He dropped in at his office, ate the croissant, which was delicious and warm and almondy, and took the coffee into the MI room, where he could feel the animosity radiating at him from the direction of his sergeant. 'What?'

'Did you just take a bribe from that woman?' demanded Sally.

Dan brushed his jacket front. 'Don't be daft, Sergeant Ellis, I just agreed to take her card. You can't accuse me of accepting bribes if there is no evidence,' he said, screwing up the paper cup and launching it at the bin. 'She wants us to work together, so that her paper can help us catch the perps. I know,' he said, 'why don't you and the lovely Lisa work up a little newspaper campaign this week? Might improve our press relations.' He threw the business card over to her.

Sally glared at him. 'You must be joking. I can't stand the woman.'

'No, I'm not joking. It's a good idea.' He frowned at the look of disbelief on her face. 'Are you refusing a direct order, Sergeant?' He watched the look on her face change from disbelief to outrage. But he really did need to do something about Middleton's snide comments about his team, and most of them were Sally's fault anyway.

Her eyes dropped to the table top. 'No, of course not, boss. It's just ...'

'Look, I know what she's like, but just meet with her once a week for the duration of the case, okay? Give her a little heads-up just before the press conferences. You never know, she might get picked up by some major London paper and buzz off and leave us alone.'

Sally buried her face in her hands. 'Beam me up, Scotty,' she muttered.

'Right, let's crack on. Any progress on the website, Sam?'

'I'm helping the online team to trace ownership. We have established the hosting company, but it's in America and we have to persuade them to let us in.'

'Data protection laws are good in principle,' said Bill Larcombe, 'but they make it difficult for us to get anywhere in the first crucial days.'

'Difficult? They're a pain in the backside. Still, at least we've got that line of enquiry open. Anything else on the tapes?'

Sam settled further into gloom. 'No, boss. Haven't been able to ID the last two members of the group at all.'

'I reckon they didn't come into the town centre,' said Sally, her colour fading back to normal. 'What if they drove straight to the beach, parked on the prom, and went straight to the bonfire? What if they got the vic plastered and he couldn't walk far, so they drove him? Who would see them?'

Sam perked up. 'There's one camera opposite the lifeboat station, I'll have a look at that this afternoon. Thanks, Sarge.'

Lizzie Singh tapped at Dan's door in the late afternoon. He stood up as she entered and switched on his main light, flooding the room with a dingy yellow glare that did little to lift his mood. He shuffled the applications for the DI role into an untidy heap and indicated that she should sit. 'Have you got anything to cheer me up, Lizzie?'

'Not likely. I've been studying these so-called fire cults and it's horrendous. I mean, they've been around for thousands of years, and I get that. Fire must have been amazing when we were still painting our faces blue.'

Dan smiled. '*We* were painting our faces blue; your culture was writing books, building temples, and making beautiful music, as far as I recall,' he said.

'You know what I mean. Anyway, I'm English on my mum's side. I'm like a hybrid.' She waggled her eyebrows at him, making him smile again.

'Okay, spill it.'

'There are modern fire cults.' She placed a sheaf of printouts in front of him. 'If what we have here is a cult, then they are following similar customs and rituals to others of the same type.' She counted on her fingers. 'The number of people attending the ritual; the use of pseudo-religious codswallop to convince people that they are doing the right thing; the promise that they're special, that they will be saved, that their leader is a god … et cetera, et cetera.' She nodded her head at the printouts, 'It's all in there.'

He placed a hand on top of the pile. 'Thanks for all this, but I need you to save me the job of reading it, Lizzie.' He didn't add:

because that's what I pay you for and because I know you will have formed some opinions and all I need to do is winkle them out. 'What do *you* think? Have we got a ritualistic murder on our hands and, if so, are we likely to have any more?'

Lizzie perched on the edge of the chair and thought. 'I think there might be something in it, but equally something's not right. It's almost too perfect, if you see what I mean.'

'They are following the "rules" too closely, you mean?'

'I think that's what it is. Most of these cults that end in murder, or mass suicides, have charismatic leaders who want to gather followers, so why is ours hiding their identity?'

'Because they're publishing literally incendiary photos on the Internet?' Dan said, watching her reactions.

Lizzie stared down at her hands and picked at a hangnail. 'Could be. Could be that they'll tell us who they are when they have finished the killings.'

'You think there'll be another one?' Dan sat up straighter. 'Go on.'

'If … if it's a fire cult, and they have to burn people to get their power or whatever, then why stop at one when you think you've got away with murder? And let's face it, sir, we've got bugger all to go on so far and it's Bonfire Night in a few days. Perfect opp for another go, I'd say.'

'Hmm. I hear what you're saying, but it's a long shot, isn't it? There are lots of people about on the fifth, it would be much harder to find a spot to do it in, surely? Jesus, I hope that's not what they're planning.'

Lizzie stood up. 'I know it's only a theory, sir, but I just …' she shrugged. 'Oh, I don't know.'

'You've got a gut feeling?'

'Yes, that's it. I think we're at the start of something bad. Just the start.'

'Okay, thanks Lizzie, I'll get the patrols to keep their eyes open.'

When she had gone, Dan stared at his wall. He didn't have a gut feeling at all, about any of it. He nudged the sheaf of paper she'd placed on the desk. There was no way he wanted to sift through it himself. Maybe he could read the headings.

And, there just might be a murderous cult out there, planning their next gruesome bonfire. Great day.

Chapter Thirteen

Friday's morning briefing was an uncomfortable half hour for everybody. No new leads and the press and social media going bonkers over the photos. Dan quickly called a halt and sent the team off. Sam Knowles was being supported by the online surveillance team. Dan hoped that meant they would have a lead back to the web hosting site by noon. He was floundering and he didn't like it.

The call from the marine commander's office came through as Dan was staring at the incident boards, sipping yet another coffee. He'd get the jitters soon if he didn't eat something. He listened, made a note, and said, 'We'll be right over.'

His three sergeants stared up at him from their desks, expectation on their faces. 'It's the marine base at Lympstone,' he said. 'Colonel Allport has summoned me.'

'Wow, if we can identify the body this quickly it'll be a record,' said Bill Larcombe. 'Fingers crossed, boss.'

'Yes, let's see what he's saying before we get too excited, though.' He beckoned Sally, who still wasn't talking to him, although he had heard her making an appointment to meet with the dreaded Middleton. 'Come on, let's go and see the colonel. He won't want to speak to the lower ranks.'

The journey to Lympstone would take a little over twenty minutes at this time of day. Dan had intended to spend it cheering up his sergeant, but instead she stared resolutely ahead and answered each question with a monosyllable. He didn't know what to do to make it better. At least Claire was talking to him. It made him smile ruefully to think that he had two women in his life whose opinions mattered to him so much. And then there was his mother.

He drove down towards Countess Wear, on to Topsham Road, and past the motorway bridge where he had caught Merlin Garrett a few months before. He slowed to look. Already, the little animal sanctuary had a desolate air about it. All the animals were gone, and the house and land were up for sale. Prime spot for new houses, he thought. The trial of the Garretts was scheduled for the following month. He had everything crossed that the evidence against Moss and his mother was secure, and that the courts would see fit to be lenient towards Merlin.

Colonel Mike Allport was a compact man with grey hair that was cut short, and steel-rimmed glasses that framed blue-grey eyes. The image of a soldier, thought Dan. Allport came around his desk, shook Dan's hand, and indicated to them where they both should sit. Ranks established, Sally sat to Dan's left, leaving Dan directly opposite the colonel.

'Thank you for coming over promptly,' Allport began, settling back behind the desk and fingering the edges of a folder.

'Whatever help you can give us in identifying the victim would be much appreciated, sir,' said Dan.

'This is a difficult matter,' said Allport. 'I will need a guarantee of discretion before you release any of this information to the press.'

Dan felt a sudden flutter in his chest. What on earth was the guy going to tell him? 'I'm sure you understand I can't guarantee long-term privacy, sir. Once the information gets into the public domain, in a court room for example, there's not a lot I can do. Unless to make it public would breach the Official Secrets Act, of course?'

Allport removed his glasses and ran a thumb across his eyes. 'No, hopefully nothing like that, Chief Inspector. It's of a more personal nature, I'm afraid.' He slid the file across the table. 'I think the person you are looking to identify might be ex-Sergeant Simon Ongar, who left the marines under a dishonourable discharge seven years ago.'

Sally picked up the file and opened it. Pinned to the record was a photograph of a tanned man of about forty years, with dark hair and dark eyes, wearing the blue beret with a sergeant's insignia on it. She turned the file so Dan could see it. 'When was this taken, sir?' she asked.

Allport thought. 'Probably just before he was court-martialled. He'd have been forty-two then. We're the same age.'

'You sound like you knew him,' said Sally.

'I did. Very well. Or at least I thought I knew him well. We came up through the ranks together, served in the same units, saw some horrendous things, but our ultimate aim was to get here and help train the recruits. That was always our dream.'

'Looks like it came true for you, sir.'

Allport curled his lip. 'If you mean I'm now in charge and Simon's dead, yes, you could say I'm living the dream, Sergeant.' He put his glasses back on, steepled his fingers and stared at the desk.

Dan took the opportunity to glare at Sally and point at her notepad. 'So, what makes you think this is our man?' he asked.

'It was something your sergeant said about tattoos that made me realise it was probably Simon. Lots of the men have tattoos, of course, but Simon's were all over his back, just like she said. I checked our records. He's also the only one of our men to have been discharged for serious drug abuse in the last seven years.'

'Really? I thought drug abuse ran through most services. In the police, it's mostly alcohol abuse, but we see plenty of drugs, too,' said Dan.

'Our training regimes tend to weed out the dodgy characters at the start,' he said, 'if you'll excuse the pun. Yes, we have some issues, but they rarely come to dismissal.' He met Dan's eye. 'Usually we can come to a mutual arrangement, if you follow me.'

Dan followed, it was similar in the force. After all, wasn't that exactly how he had come to be transferred back to Devon, rather than be out on his backside begging for work? 'So, how come this dismissal was done by the book?'

Allport gave a rueful chuckle. 'Because, Chief Inspector, Simon Ongar, under the influence of hard drugs and alcohol, put the commanding officer into hospital. Admittedly the man was a total idiot and had been sleeping with Simon's ex-wife, but Simon behaved abominably – as if all the petty annoyances had reached their peak one summer evening at a barbecue in front of all the officers and their wives.' He sighed. 'The colonel sustained serious injuries. It took three men to pull Ongar off and the colonel wanted his day in court. Simon served three years in prison for assault.'

'And then ended up on the streets. Did you know where he was?'

Allport shifted in his chair. 'I did, indeed. He hung around the perimeter a lot. We look out on to the estuary at the back, and the men go out there for physical training sessions. There's a public footpath running right alongside. He would stand and watch the teams training for hours, poor sod.' He looked away. 'We lock the gate to the little train station that serves the barracks just after midnight when the last train goes through. It may be that Simon had his own key and was sleeping in there, though.'

'Right. Did you give him the key, sir?'

Allport gave a small nod. 'I was looking out for him, I suppose. I didn't think it would do any harm.'

That was why they could find no record of Ongar in the homeless shelters. Dan watched Sally make a note while he thought. 'You mentioned his ex-wife?'

'It's all in the file. She now lives with the ex-commanding officer in North Devon.' He looked up. 'I suppose you will have to tell her?'

'I think I should, before it becomes public, don't you?'

Allport gave a slow nod. 'I suppose so. Such a shame when drugs take over your life to that extent.'

Sally cleared her throat. 'Sorry, sir. I understand why Ongar was dismissed, but you haven't told us why he got himself into the mess in the first place. After all, he could have been commanding his own unit by now, couldn't he?'

Allport appeared to battle with himself, then shrugged. 'Well, it's a simple story. He fell off that climbing wall just outside my office.' He pointed towards the window. 'He was leading a PT session. Fell flat on his back and never fully recovered. Not that we knew that at the time. He took a month off and was back at it. PT was his life. I think that's where his addiction to painkillers came from, then it just escalated to hard drugs when he needed more to keep going. We never knew.' He looked at Dan. 'We never knew how bad it was.' He rubbed at his eyes with the pad of his thumb, drying any hint of a tear. 'It's not easy, you know, to talk about such things.'

'So,' continued Sally, 'is there anybody here who would want him dead? Apart from the ex-commanding officer, of course?'

'Good God, no. He was a sad case, but much liked and respected for many years.' Allport got to his feet and stared out the window. 'Nobody wanted him dead, Sergeant. We helped him as much as we could.'

Dan got to his feet and offered his hand to the colonel. 'Thank you for all your help, sir,' he said. 'It must have been a terrible thing to watch a friend go downhill like that. There's just one more thing I would like to ask.'

'I was expecting this,' Allport said. 'You want me to identify the body?'

'Please. It's not as bad as you might think, his upper body was less … damaged than the rest.'

'I'll do it, it wouldn't be appropriate to ask his ex-wife. Just tell me when.' Allport shook Dan's hand and escorted him and Sally from his office.

It was a short walk to the back gate that led out onto the public footpath and the tiny train stop for the Exmouth to Exeter train. The duty marine unlocked the gate and waited for them. They crossed to the shelter, and there, sure enough, hidden under the metal bench, was a folded up sleeping bag, empty food containers and a bag of spare clothes.

'I can't believe he lived here,' said Sally. 'How do people live like this?'

'I guess he couldn't quite move on,' said Dan, 'and this was the closest he could get to what he'd thrown away. Poor bloke. He certainly didn't deserve to die for it.' He sent Sally back to the car to collect a large evidence bag, some gloves, and several small bags. This would all add to the evidence pile, but it still didn't give him a clue as to the motive for murder. Was there more to Ongar's attachment to the barracks than he'd been told? How much would Allport keep from the police if he could?

Chapter Fourteen

A night out with Neil Pargeter could turn into a session that Dan could not afford this early on in a new case. It usually involved music, beer, and an ill-advised curry eaten too late for it to digest before he went to sleep. Cue a bad night. After the fun, you have to pay, he thought. On the other hand, they had to celebrate both promotions, didn't they? Claire had gone out with a couple of her friends for a meal, but he'd asked her to text him at 11pm, before she went to bed, to remind him to go back to the flat and sleep before he lost the following day to a hangover.

Dan worked his way slowly across town, glad that the storm had passed over after two days of non-stop rain. Tonight, it was cold and clear. He drove into his parking space and reflected that it was probably one of the last nights he'd spend in his flat for some time. Was he being a complete idiot in keeping the flat on and letting Alison use it? It would be cheaper for him to pay to put Alison up in a shared house somewhere. But then he couldn't keep an eye on her so easily, and now she was on the straight and narrow, it would be good to keep her there where he had a key and access. Just until he was sure it was all going well.

He took a couple of minutes to knock on the doors of the three other flats that shared his landing, to tell his elderly neighbours about Alison. A small white lie was called for, he decided. He stuck to a story that she had been very ill, was recuperating, and would be staying there until she found her feet and was able to look for her own place. Satisfied, he dropped clean clothes for the following day on the bed, a pint of milk into the fridge, and a bunch of flowers from Claire to Alison into a measuring jug.

Flowers didn't enter his consciousness much, and buying a vase was beyond him.

Neil was waiting in the curry house and was halfway down his first beer when Dan arrived. He stood up to shake hands, but Dan moved in and gave him a hug. 'Congratulations, Prof. You really did it, then?'

'Ah, mate, it was like doing my viva exam all over again.' Neil gave a mock shudder and sat back down, pulling out a chair for Dan. 'Bloody terrifying. Let's order, I'm starving,' he said.

Onion bhajis came first, with poppadums and dips. Dan ate a mouthful: hot but not outrageous, tasty. 'Neil, I've got this new case …'

'Too right you have. It's been all over the Uni this week.' He mopped up mango chutney on a poppadum shard. 'You don't need me to look at the bones, do you? Can't be an archaeology slant to it, can there?'

'No, it's not that. We've ID'd him already. No, I'm stuck on the possibility of it being a ritual murder, and I know nothing about all that kind of stuff. No, I was wondering if there was anyone at the university who I could talk to about it.'

Neil chewed a mouthful of bhaji. 'I can put you in touch with Nav, I suppose. Professor Navinder Patel is in charge of the Ancient Religions courses. He might be able to help.'

Dan made a note of the name then forgot about the job and got to work on the lamb curry.

An hour or so later the table was a shambles of naan bread crusts, Rogan Josh sauce stains and empty beer glasses; both men leaned back on their chairs, loosening their belts.

'That was good,' said Dan, belching quietly and enjoying the flavour all over again.

'Few more beers should sort us out for the night I reckon,' said Neil. 'There's a band on at the arts centre we can drop in on. Just a student gig, I think.'

Dan checked his phone. Mercifully no messages from work, and it was still too early for his goodnight text.

'She's got her claws well into you, mate,' laughed Neil, nodding towards the phone. 'Have you had your late-night pass signed?'

Dan winced. 'Yeah, but she's fine about me having a night out. I can't blame Claire. It's me that's worried. Once I get beyond the fourth pint I lose all perspective, and I can't afford to do that at this point in the case.'

'No worries, we'll just have another one, and then you can stagger off and I'll watch the band, okay?'

The band may have been students but they were good. A great girl singer, with a husky voice and a good range, belted out everything from Annie Lennox to Aretha Franklin and the place was hopping. Dan stood at the bar and tapped his foot, watching the crowd enjoying themselves. On impulse, he'd rung and asked Alison if she wanted to come down for an hour. Currently she was leaping about with Neil on the dance floor. He was worried that they were getting on a bit too well, but he thought he'd done the right thing. He just hoped that not inviting Claire and her mates had been the right thing to do too.

Claire, spookily psychic as always, text him as he was having that thought. He text back:

Am sober and stuffed, watching band at Arts centre with Neil and Alison. Thought she needed night out. Sleep tight. Love you. Xxx

The song finished and his two companions, dripping with sweat, pushed their way back to the bar to find him. Alison's eyes were shining. So were Neil's. Dan battled with himself. He hadn't foreseen this, but who was he to stop them enjoying themselves if they wanted to? Who was he to say to Neil: stay away mate, she's such bad news? Wasn't he old enough to find that out for himself? Dan had already told him enough to frighten off any sane bloke. He still felt uncomfortable seeing them together, though. He needed to talk to Claire about it. She'd give him some sound advice.

'I'll get the round in,' he said, as Alison disappeared to the ladies.

'It's okay, mate,' said Neil as they waited to be served, 'I can see the worry all over your face. I'm not going to get involved with your big sister. It's just nice to have a bit of female company and someone to dance with, all right? I mean, no offence, but you're no Justin Timberlake.'

Dan laughed. Cheek. At well over six feet tall, Neil's dancing resembled a flamingo in a mating ritual more than anything else. 'All right, but just be careful, that's all I'm saying.' He passed Neil his beer and left Alison's on the bar. 'Right, if you're absolutely sure you won't miss me, and you're wearing your chastity belt, I'm off home to my bed.' He gave Neil another hug. 'Congratulations, again, mate,' he said, 'you'll be a great professor. Shake the old buggers up a bit, eh?'

Chapter Fifteen

The five of them had built the bonfire during the day, carrying beach debris and shifting bits of tree, sticks and small logs from the back of Kegan's old Land Rover, right into the heart of the Dawlish Warren dunes. Then Kegan had taken off to collect the next 'sacrifice'. Jay Vine finished making the body-sized space, in the fire, that the guy would be pushed into. He was finding it hard to keep panic and desperation at bay.

He moved away into the shadows and sat quietly against a tree smoking a spliff, watching the scene unfold. Scarlett and Amber were off in the dunes locating six big, flat stones to set around the unlit fire. Not far away, a train rattled along the track back to Exeter and made him jump. Tana was using the last of the light to paint her face in the black and red swirls she seemed to find necessary.

Nobody was talking to him since he'd walked out on them in the cafe and had refused to attend the evening meeting. He felt invisible. Insignificant. Why didn't he just get up and run? Dropping his head onto his chest, he admitted to himself that he was scared to stay but even more scared to run. Kegan would kill him if he ran. He was sure of that.

It was hard for him to comprehend that they were actually doing it again. Going along with Tana's crazy plan. Willingly. Scarlett and Amber were just as into it as the other two. Their eyes slipped past him as Tana called them over to sit on the stones.

Even at 6pm fireworks whizzed and hooted up into a sky shot through with colour and noise. Across the estuary, Exmouth glittered as more and more people arrived for the lighting of the grand bonfire and firework display.

Tana was standing in a small circle of stones, holding a torch that lit her face from underneath, staring up at the sky. Wearing black from head to toe, and with her wild red hair and painted face, she looked every inch the fire goddess.

Amber was taking stills of her and shooting short videos as she danced and writhed near the fire. They were enjoying themselves. He hoped that the poor fool they had lined up for tonight was a better fighter than the old bloke last week had been, and that he might fight back and run off into the dunes. Then they could just have a fire and a drink and go home like the rest of the country on Bonfire Night. Not that that was likely. She wanted three sacrifices, so someone was going to die tonight. Or another night.

Jay got up and wandered off along the path towards the deserted holiday park behind the dunes. Kegan had set the bonfire in a natural dip in the sand dunes, where grass grew and they would be sheltered from prying eyes. Jay felt lonely without Scarlett; they hadn't spoken since the day after the last fire and she still wouldn't look him in the eye. She had changed so much. What had started out as a laugh had turned her into something else, someone he didn't know at all. He pushed on, over the grass, and followed the lane towards the main road to Exeter. Out there, in a pub somewhere, Kegan was getting the sacrifice drunk and promising him a great night out at a bonfire on the beach.

Jay was looking for a phone box, hoping that somehow, he might be able to get a message to the police before it was too late. He'd been very late the first time. It had only dawned on him as they were making their escape that there might still be a chance to save the man. He hit himself on the side of the head, hard. The man Jay was now snarled at the naivety of the boy he had been just a few days earlier. He walked faster, looking out for phone boxes.

If he could somehow mark out his route for later, and make a run for it as soon as Kegan arrived, he might be able to get to the phone before they realised he'd gone. A moment later he shook his head yet again at his own stupidity. As if he'd even get the opportunity this time. As if they'd take their eyes off him. And there was no sign of a payphone on this deserted, crappy beach, or on the road into Dawlish.

The nearest public phone, it turned out, was right in the middle of the town, and it had taken him twenty minutes to walk in from the beachfront. He stared at the phone box from the shelter of a shop doorway. Too open. Too many cameras around. No good. No, he would have to use his own phone then throw it away and pretend it had been stolen. It was the right thing to do and it was the only way to stop this madness. He should do it now, shouldn't he? He knew he wouldn't.

Scared and depressed, he turned round and trudged back, hopelessness settling like a noose around his neck. Damned if he did; damned if he didn't.

It was properly dark down in the dunes when he returned. Scarlett stood up as he arrived then sat down when she saw who it was. There were three places left. He took the one between her and Amber. They didn't acknowledge him, but got up as soon as he was seated and lit the fire. The smell of paraffin was strong on the cool air as the fire caught. There was a lot of smoke from wet twigs and branches, but the core would be wood from Kegan's shed, and that would be dry and ready to burn.

Tana walked around the inside of the circle as the flames grew, touching each of her followers on the shoulder and kissing them on the lips. When she got to Jay, he thought she stayed a long time holding his face in her hands and staring into his eyes until he had to blink or drown. Then they sat in silence as the fire took hold, only the cracking of logs, and sparks leaping illuminated their faces.

Eventually, against all Jay's hopes, Kegan drove up over the dunes and parked the Land Rover in the shade of gnarled and twisted trees. Scarlett ran across and helped bring the sacrifice out of the passenger seat. Jay stared as the guy staggered across the grass and sat, chuckling, on the rock. It was another homeless guy, but young this time. An alcoholic no doubt, like the other one. Was that supposed to make it better? Or just easier? The guy slid off the rock and leaned back against it, a can of lager dangling from his hand beneath a skinny roll-up held between two outstretched fingers. Idly, he picked up the smaller rock that nestled next to the one he was leaning against. The women tensed, but he dropped the rock back where it should have been and they went back to watching him. Jay didn't like the light in their eyes.

Kegan brought across a crate of lager and passed bottles around, giving the sacrifice another one, and laughing as the guy downed it in three gulps and threw the bottle onto the fire.

'Great, this, isn't it?' the sacrifice said, and groped Amber's ample thigh with his spare hand.

Jay watched her recoil and smack the hand away. Only Kegan pretended friendship. Jay was glad about that. If they'd all cosied up to the poor bastard, it would have been more than he could stand. The sacrifice had to be less than human, didn't it? Ready for death? Or what did that make them? He drank his lager quickly. Needed more, much more. With shaking fingers, he rolled another spliff and took a couple of draws deep into his lungs. Couldn't the sacrifice see there was no talking, no party? That everyone was staring at him? Did he even have a clue about what was going to happen?

The fire finally surged up, as the dry, thicker logs began to burn. They drank more lager, ate crisps and pasties, smoked more dope. The sacrifice got more drunk. Tana stared at the guy, drinking him in with a strange, lop-sided smile on her face that chilled Jay more than all her histrionics.

The heart of the fire glowed yellow, then red, then blue, then finally white-gold. Tana stood and began her wailing to the gods, an ululation of sounds and groans that made Jay's hair stand up from his scalp. She was great at this stuff. It was what had captured him in the first place – her knack for drama. Kegan filmed her from below, adding to the weirdness.

It was worse this time, far worse knowing what was to come. Jay watched the rapt faces of his friends as they cast their predatory eyes over the sacrifice.

When Kegan stood up, moved behind the sacrifice, and lifted the smaller rock, bringing it down two-handed on the top of the sacrifice's head, Jay screamed along with the terrified man. The sacrifice bucked and goggled at them as he tried to stand up and face his attacker, but the alcohol had done its work and he could only stagger and swear wildly, unable to comprehend what he had walked into. Scarlett stuck out a leg and tripped up the sacrifice and Kegan hit him again.

The sacrifice lay silent and bleeding as they pulled long fireproof gloves up to the tops of their arms, and donned masks to protect their faces. Jay stayed seated. They would have to do this one on their own.

Between them, Kegan and the girls hauled the sacrifice upright and pushed him into the red heart of the fire, deep into the hole that Jay had so carefully made.

For a few seconds little happened, then the sacrifice, not quite unconscious, woke up. He thrashed and yelled in earnest until he did finally die and the terrible noise stopped.

They stood in the face of the flames for a long time, and only Jay wept.

Tana stepped away from the fire at last and pocketed her phone. 'We can thank the gods of fire tonight. We have made the second sacrifice. You have been cleansed, my loyal followers, and have no need to fear anyone. It's all going according to plan. Let's meet tomorrow as planned. Go now.' She stepped up to Kegan, kissed him hard on the lips, and led him across to the Land Rover.

Jay buckled where he was standing and fell down onto the grassy sand, he didn't think he had the strength to move. He clutched the phone in his pocket. Didn't seem to be much point in ringing the police now. The guy was well dead.

He waited until they had all left then walked slowly back to the train station, careless of being seen, avoiding the others. Coward, he taunted himself. Coward. Tell the police, tell them everything.

They will be okay with you, right? Yeah, right. His life would be over, then.

The only brave thing he dared do was not go to Tana's for the meeting later. Let them find him if they wanted him. He wiped away tears as he waited for the train back to the city.

Chapter Sixteen

Sunday morning came in fine and clear. Claire brought Dan up a cup of tea and headed off to the gym for a step class and a swim, followed by coffee, cake and a chat with the girls. Reprieved, Dan went for a bike ride. Murder inquiries could just wait a day. He needed downtime, too. He'd given the whole team the same two-day break so they would be fit for Monday, and he'd have them all available. Even so, he knew Sam, Adam and Lizzie had pulled some overtime on Bonfire Night, which was fine by him. Thus far, there had been no news of any murderous fires, about which he was mightily relieved.

He'd had to pick up his bike from the flat, but he'd sneaked in and got it, only pausing to knock at the bedroom door and tell his dozing sister that he'd see her later. All had looked good at the flat. He could feel the stress and concern that surrounded Alison easing. Maybe he had done the right thing after all. Maybe people could change.

Picking up speed along Cowick Street, he headed out of the quiet city towards Dunsford and the Dartmoor National Park. There was little traffic about before 9am. He had an ambitious forty-mile circular route planned, including a couple of big hills and some great downhill stretches. It would take him up to Postbridge, past the prison, and back home via the quiet lanes. The day was cold, but it might warm up. He didn't care. He felt the surge of freedom that only being on a bike gave him, and put his legs into it.

He was snuggled into a corner of the bar in the Warren House Inn at Postbridge, enjoying a pint of Otter Ale and a bacon roll, when his phone rang. He groaned, took another swig to send the bite of sandwich on its way, and answered. It was Colin White, duty sergeant. 'Colin, what can I do for you on my day off?'

'You know I wouldn't bother you unless it was urgent, Dan, but you'd better get in, fast. There's been another one.'

'What, another burning?' His heart did a flip. The bloody ritual element after all. Lizzie, you were right. Deep down, after ploughing through all the ridiculous claptrap that the Internet had spewed forth about these fire cults, he'd known that.

'Yes, sir, Dawlish Warren. Nature Reserve ranger called it in. I've got the forensic team on their way and informed the coroner's office.'

Dan checked the time. 'Colin, I'm on Dartmoor, on my bike. It'll take me almost two hours to get home, and about the same if I cycle straight to Dawlish.' He banged the table in frustration.

'No worries, I can get Bill Larcombe down there to oversee the site. The local Dawlish bobbies are keeping it safe for you. Go home and get changed.'

'Aargh. No, it'll still take too long and I want to be there to see it for myself. Send me out a van big enough to get my bike in, and see if you can get Ben Bennett down there, too. Tell them I'm on my way.'

He explained where he was, and sat staring out of the window at the moor dropping away from the high road. There was very little he could do for the next thirty minutes, so he finished his sandwich, ordered a coffee, and had a good think. These were well planned murders, with easy victims. A serial killer cult in Devon? Really? Lisa Middleton would be wetting herself with excitement.

He rang Chief Superintendent Oliver and told her they needed to meet later. He tried in vain to recall the name of the guy that Neil had recommended he talk to about cults, but he had it written down in his notebook, which was at home.

There is nothing, he thought, nothing as frustrating as not being able to do anything.

An hour and a half later, Dan locked his bike to a railing, thanked the driver, and was happy to climb into a protective suit to avoid any unnecessary comments from his sergeants about his mode of dress. He could see the entrances to the dunes were blocked off with tape and gave a swift nod of approval.

A Dawlish PC stood with his clipboard at the outer cordon and insisted on calling Bill Larcombe to identify Dan, who had no ID on him at all. Left alone, outside the cordon, he felt suddenly vulnerable without the usual trappings of a suit and his warrant card. It rendered him 'civilian', and therefore, a nobody.

Bill Larcombe, glowing inside his protective clothing, bustled over and signed Dan in. 'Everything's under control, boss, no need for you to be here on your weekend off.'

'It's your weekend off as well, Bill, and I'm not staying long. I just need to see if it's the same MO as the other one, and then I'll let you get on with it. Who else is here?'

'Fox is off this weekend. We have a different doctor, and forensics has just arrived.'

'Okay, thanks.' They walked across damp sand and grassy stretches towards a natural dip in the dune landscape. You would need to be pretty close to see the flames, Dan guessed. He couldn't see any houses, or even buildings, except the deserted holiday park and the Nature Reserve hut. It was a good spot, and one that had to have been thought out in advance. Serial killer cult flashed through his mind again.

The forensic team waited for the go-ahead from the doctor, chatting to each other and preparing their equipment. Dan found Ben Bennett setting up his kit. 'Sorry to drag you out on a Sunday, Ben.'

'No worries, boss. You got me out of shopping for bridesmaids' dresses with the wife and daughter. Mind you, they have got my credit card, so I'm terrified, frankly.'

'She'll soon be off your hands, then?'

'Hallelujah. Last one to go, then it'll be time for me to take it easy.'

'Can't say I blame you.'

Dan walked carefully along the designated path, towards the site of the fire. It had burned down overnight to smoking, charred lumps of wood and ash. Possibly they had set it earlier than the last one. Six rocks were placed in a ring around the fire. Same as the previous one. Dan waited until he got the nod and approached the doctor. 'Afternoon, Doctor.'

A small, wiry woman with very short, dark, cropped hair, and heavy-rimmed glasses, shook his hand then led him round to where the body was in situ in the middle of the dying fire. No tide had come to wash away the evidence this time. The victim sagged across a partially burnt log, arms in boxer stance, but way too late to fight anybody. Clothes gone, flesh mostly burnt away.

'I'm Kate Porter,' she said.

'Nice to meet you,' said Dan. 'Had much experience with burns victims before?'

'Enough to know that it's a male. But there's not a lot to go on. Fox will tell you more next week, obviously. He'll do the PM.'

'Yeah, not much left for us to look at this time,' said Dan, shifting out of the way as the forensic team came in en masse and began the task of recording the site.

'It looks bad, but there will be some skin and tissue available.'

'Right.' He tried to get closer to the smouldering embers, inching towards the heat. 'I just want to see if he has any distinguishing marks.'

Doctor Porter blocked his movement with her arm. 'Actually, you'd better move back out of the way, DCI Hellier. Give people room to work. There won't be much for you to do here today, you know, it will take ages for the heat to die down properly and we can't do much until then.'

'I could go back to my weekend, you mean? Fat chance.'

'Give us a bit of space, though, eh?'

Dan backed away and left Larcombe in charge of the scene. Bennett would make sure they got much better samples this time, and maybe they would be able to ID the victim or one of his attackers.

He stripped off his suit and gloves, stuffed them into an evidence bag, and left them with the PC as he signed out. Then he got on his bike and pedalled back to the flat to collect his car, get changed and head into work. The team wouldn't be happy being called back in, but there wasn't a lot he could do about that. So much for a lazy weekend.

Dan sat in his office with the blind down to keep out the low afternoon sun, and watched the hits grow on the Fire Goddess Instagram site. She'd had this set up, hadn't she, knowing that the website would be taken down? It was such a ridiculous front page he was half convinced this was all the work of kids. Except for the bodies. But six kids could get an unconscious body into a fire, couldn't they?

He'd been waiting for last night's murder pictures to be posted. There didn't seem to be any reason why the 'Fire Goddess' would change her methods, and at 5.15pm, there they were. She'd used Instagram again, and no doubt every other platform she could get on. He sat up straighter and enlarged them. Two videos and two stills, more or less the same as the last lot, but with a much more immediate impact on the waiting and watching world.

He rang through to the MI room, where Sam Knowles acknowledged the call. They were on it.

The front desk had been inundated all week with the press on the phone and in person asking whether the first lot of pictures were fake or real, and what the police were going to do about them. He'd been tempted to tell them they were fake. Make it all go away for a while. After today, there would be no pretending that they didn't see a pattern emerging.

He screwed up the briefing notes he was preparing for the press conference scheduled for later in the day, threw them in the bin, and pulled a clean sheet of paper towards him. How do you calm everyone down, tell them nothing, but make them feel like they are getting a story? It was more than he was trained for.

He didn't raise his eyes as Chief Superintendent Oliver entered and took a seat opposite him.

'Earth to DCI Hellier.'

'Sorry, ma'am,' he muttered, and closed the lid on his laptop. 'Thanks for coming in on your weekend. I can't stop watching, and neither can the rest of the world it would seem. How can such a ridiculous premise cause such havoc?'

She stretched jean-clad legs in front of her and ran a hand through her bobbed hair. 'Social media runs the world now, you know that. How long before they're taken down?'

He shrugged. 'There's no way to get these media sites to work quickly. They deliberately make it difficult for people to complain if they don't have an account with them. I've got Bill Larcombe out getting a warrant signed by the magistrate – not easy on a Sunday.' He checked his phone. 'He should be back soon. Then we can email it to the USA and we may get them taken down later today. Then we'll do the same for any more sites she decides to use.'

'Hmm, okay. Now though, the public knows that the images are real, and it's moved on from last week. What shall we tell them? That all this attention is messing with our case, and will they please push off and let us do our job? It's not that they even care about some homeless guys being killed, it's the fire cult angle that's got them all worked up,' she growled. 'So frustrating. Anyway, take who you need from Team One to top up your numbers. The tactical support group is ready, and I can send in a forensic psychologist if you need one for a bit of profiling.'

'Thanks, ma'am, I'll need them all at this rate. We're keeping quiet about it being a possible serial killer, then?'

'Yes. I'm damned if I'll say that to the public yet, although they're all speculating. I've spoken to ACC Bishop, he agrees this investigation takes priority over anything else we've got on, but that we "play down" the connection between the two murders.' She raised her eyebrows at him as she made quote marks with her fingers.

'Play down? Right. They're exactly the same in almost every way except location, but we play it down.' He stared at the blank sheet of paper in front of him. 'I should get Bishop to write this briefing.' He threw down the pen. 'The press aren't idiots.'

'That's why I'm here, and press liaison will be in before the end of the day, now that we've located her. Let's work on it together. I reckon we've got an hour before the hammering at the door becomes too much to avoid.'

They both turned at an actual knock on the office door. Sam Knowles stood outside, his tall shadow looming.

'Come in, Sam,' Dan called.

Knowles hovered in the doorway. 'Sorry to interrupt. I've contacted the host site and they've given me the name of the account holder – a Conor Reilly.' He flushed as both senior officers cheered. 'It doesn't mean we've got the murderer, though, just whoever started the website.'

'Still, that's great news. Right, get off everything else and focus on getting us some contact details.' Dan grinned as his junior officer left the room. 'They might think they're clever, but let's see them wriggle out of this.'

Oliver looked more serious. 'We'll see. At least I can tell the press we have a genuine lead at last.'

Chapter Seventeen

By 7pm on Sunday evening, the whole team had been rounded up and were gathered around the screen in the MI room looking at the images. The room was stuffy, with Dan's own team, the press liaison woman, three civilian researchers, and the duty DI present.

'Sorry to cancel your weekend, everyone, but we have a lead and this may kick off quickly. Sam, put the pictures on the large screen and get all eight up at the same time, please.'

Dan waited until the shuffling had settled and the officers could all see the screen. 'There is less blurring, and better focus this time,' he began.

'You can see the guy being thrown on the bonfire in that one. Gross,' said Adam Foster. 'These are amazing,' he added, leaning in for a closer look.

Dan glared at the younger officer. 'You finding all this exciting, Foster?'

Foster shrank back into his seat. 'You have to admit it's pretty bizarre, sir,' he said.

'Can't argue with you there. And aimed at kids and other thrill seekers on the net.' He looked out, over Foster's head, at the darkening sky. Was that where they were really heading? Kids?

'Young people,' said Sally, 'kids who are on their phones the whole time; students.'

'Yeah, they'll be lapping this up.'

'As the pictures are clearer, are they more confident this time?' offered Lizzie Singh. 'Because they got away with it once?'

'Yes, could be. Better use of the camera, certainly. Or less worried about being seen, and therefore less hurried,' said Dan.

'The location of this one was deep into the dunes at Dawlish Warren – a much more difficult place to spot a fire.'

'They must know there'll be lots more forensic evidence without the tide washing it away.'

'I know, Lizzie. Why take so much care on the first one, and so little on the second?'

'Maybe this is the last one?'

'Maybe.'

Sally pushed her reading glasses down her nose and peered over the top of them. 'I can count four people over the four pictures, meaning the photographer is the fifth, and the vic is number six.'

'Exactly the same MO as the last one,' agreed Dan. 'Single male victim. No information about how he was incapacitated yet, but I'll bet my breakfast he was hit over the head with a rock.'

'Have we got a serial killer, boss?' Adam Foster's eyes grew round. 'Wow.'

'Serial killers,' corrected Sam Knowles. 'They're all as guilty as each other.'

'Even more wow,' said Adam.

Dan avoided rolling his eyes. 'Sorry to disappoint you, lads, but until there are at least three deaths, it isn't a serial killer according to the ACC. Okay? Back to the pictures. What else can you see?'

'The faces aren't as well disguised. Not as much make-up this time, boss,' said Sam. 'I may be able to get the face recognition software to analyse these more closely than the other set.'

'Do it,' said Dan. 'This investigation takes priority over anything else they've got on.'

'Very little to see regarding their clothes,' said Lizzie. 'Bit tatty, bit hippy. Students? There was that one with the guitar and long coat in the first set of pics.'

'Good, that's what I've been thinking, too. This could well be the work of a group of young people, possibly students. That's your line of enquiry. Get down to the university tomorrow and see what you can find out. Take Foster.'

Foster's mouth dropped open.

'I know there are thousands of students there, Adam. They'll all be talking about this, won't they? Just see what jumps out at you, okay? I'll be there anyway to see the professor of Ancient Religions, if I can find his name. He might be able to help us narrow it down a bit.' He riffled through his notebook and placed his finger in the page with the professor's name on it.

'Okay, currently, Sergeant Bennett is still at the scene with Dawlish police, and forensics are all over the site. The good news is that it was dry last night and the sea is too distant to wash away all our evidence, so I have high hopes for DNA this time – from the bottles and food cartons. And … DC Knowles has discovered the name of the website account holder.'

Sam grinned, jumped up and wrote the name Conor Reilly on the whiteboard, taking a bow at the smattering of applause.

'So, we have a direct line of enquiry at last. Let me know as soon as he answers his phone, Sam.'

He took a moment to watch the small image of a woman being consumed by fire in the bottom corner of the screen, and willed it out of existence. What were they playing at? Why was it taking so long to stop it? 'As soon as that account is taken down, it'll go bonkers round here,' he said. 'There will be no possibility that these pictures are a hoax.

'We all have to be clear that no one, except Chief Superintendent Oliver or me, talks to the media. Sergeant Ellis will do liaison with the local press, and I'm hoping that might have a positive effect on the usual sniping we have to dodge. Okay?' He scrutinised the team. They looked with it – at least for a Sunday night.

'Right, let's divvy up the jobs and crack on.'

As he spoke, Bill Larcombe opened the door and waved at him. 'Warrant sort of served, boss, and the account should be closing any minute. Much more cooperative than the other lot, I must say.'

'That's because they understand that we are dealing with real murders, Bill,' said Dan. 'They don't want their reputation damaging, do they?'

The small picture in the corner of the screen winked off, to a cheer from Sally.

'Where's Jay?' Tana asked, as the clock ticked past 8pm.

Scarlett flicked a glance at Amber but the younger girl kept her eyes on her hands. 'We called at his flat but the lights were off,' she said. 'Maybe he's sick?'

Tana's anger bloomed as two red patches on her white skin. 'We all knew what we were doing. We have to be in it together or this will not work.' She looked at Kegan. 'Go and get him. I can't risk him talking.' She waited until Kegan had left the room then spoke to her remaining followers.

'They've taken down my website and knocked me off Instagram, the pathetic eejits. Just got a little Facebook surprise for them in a day or two. Don't worry,' she said, flicking a hand at Scarlett who had let out a gasp of surprise, 'the accounts are all registered under false names and there won't be any way they can trace it back to us.'

Scarlett subsided onto the sofa with a frown. The trouble was, she knew who Tana had stolen the Facebook access from, and she wasn't at all sure it was a safe enough prospect to avoid tracking back to a rather stupid girl who would give them away in a second. 'It's just that I thought you weren't going to use Facebook as they're much stricter now, and it's easier to trace back if it's not done right …'

Tana stared at her. 'If you know something I don't, you'd better tell me. Don't just sit there, gawping like a fish, silly bitch.'

Scarlett stared back, mouth open. Bitch? 'No, there's nothing specific,' she said. Bitch, was it? 'Just asking.' She glanced at Amber, who was sitting quietly on the floor with her head down, and wondered if Jay had been right, and Tana was using them all for some reason of her own. Had she been a total idiot? She looked with clearer eyes around the room, and understood for the first time that if anything went wrong with Tana's planning, it would be them carrying the can, not her. Their friends' accounts had been hacked or borrowed, not hers. Tana knew all their real names, they didn't know if she was even called Tana. Jay had said Tana meant fire.

Tana waved a hand at her. 'It'll be fine, I have everything covered. Stop worrying.' She brought up the photos on her laptop. 'Come and have a look. You did a great job out there, Amber, these are really clear. And it's going crazy on social media.' She scrolled through Twitter. 'Look, trending all over the world. How satisfying is that?'

She sat quiet for a few minutes, staring at the laptop, and Scarlett wondered if Tana was ever going to tell them anything about why there had to be three murders. She wasn't stupid, she knew the cult stuff was a cover for something darker, but she hadn't a clue what it was.

Tana closed the laptop and pushed it to the corner of the bed. 'Now, the third and greatest sacrifice is almost ready. It was supposed to be at the end of the month, but we'll bring it forward to next week and call it a late All Souls day – when the dead come back to visit the earth before they go on to greater glory. That's a good one to hang our hat on, don't you think?' She grinned at the girls and rolled a cigarette while they took in the change of plan.

Scarlett had to ask, even though she didn't want to be singled out again. 'Why have you really brought it forward, Tana?'

Tana looked at her through black eyelashes, as she ran her tongue along the edge of the cigarette paper and pressed the edges together. 'Let's just say I want this particular sacrifice fresh and eager, and I don't want him disappearing on me or getting wise to what's happening. That all okay with you, Scarlett?'

Scarlett was saved from answering when the door slammed back against the wall and Jay was thrown roughly into the room.

He stood in front of Tana, eyes wild. 'What's going on?'

Tana sat back against the bedhead and took a drag of her cigarette, removing a thread of tobacco from her bottom lip. 'You were late. Kegan gave you a lift.'

'I wasn't planning on coming. I'm sick. I need to be in bed.' He dragged his hand across his eyes.

Tana stared hard at Jay, as if she really wanted to understand.

Scarlett could see his face was white, with black circles around bloodshot eyes. He looked terrible. Was he really taking this so hard? Two tramps?

'Fair enough, you do look a bit peaky,' said Tana. 'But your mum's not here to sign your note. Just sit down and shut up while we plan the next one. Then you can go back to beddy-byes.'

Kegan dragged Jay to the floor and sat next to him. 'All for one and one for all, mate,' he chuckled.

Scarlett reached down in front of her to where Jay had sat on the floor, and squeezed his shoulder. She pulled him back so he was resting against her legs and kept her hand on him. If he went doolally on them now, she wasn't at all sure that he wouldn't end up being the next sacrifice. Or she would. She was going to have to be very careful indeed to get out of all this unscathed.

Chief Superintendent Oliver called Dan up to her office a little after 9pm; he was surprised she was still there.

'Come in and take a seat, I've made us some coffee,' she said, and passed over a mug of dark stuff. 'No milk until tomorrow.'

Dan swigged it down without – he needed the caffeine.

'The press gave us a mauling, didn't they?'

'I was expecting it, to be honest,' he said. 'We've not got a lot to give them, have we? Not British policing's greatest moment when the bad guys just seem to be able to do exactly as they like, when they like. They have a point, I feel totally useless.'

'You'll get there. You have the website holder to interview, and I think you're spot on focusing on the university. You just need a break, and it will come. Chin up.

'I've been thinking, let's say they are students, and they've been watching too many cheap horror films.'

'You being serious?'

'You must have watched all the *Friday the Thirteenth* and Chucky schlock when you were a student, surely?'

'Hmm. Didn't make me plan to murder anybody though.' He winced. 'Well, there may have been a couple of people on the list ...'

'Psychology of a psychopath, Daniel: when someone has crossed over the moral taboo that humans have about committing murder, or child abuse, or hitting the wife, or whatever, and they've gotten away with it, they will do it again and again until they are caught. It becomes a compulsion. They do it because they can, and they have no need to justify to anyone what is so clearly a "right action" in their own eyes. What if the person behind these murders feels entirely justified?'

Dan chewed the end of his pen and thought about it. 'A clever student with access to willing volunteers who are out for the excitement, and a secret mission they must accomplish?'

'Could be a student. Or a lecturer. Easy to hide in the middle of a crowd.'

Dan stared out at the black sky over her shoulder. It was a feasible idea, and it made a bit of sense – better than he was coming up with anyway. 'I think you're onto something, ma'am. We'll focus the team on the university on Monday and see what we can find. Thanks.'

Oliver stood up and collected both mugs in one hand. 'Do you think there'll be another one, now that the website and Instagram site have been taken down and they know we're after them?'

'I don't know, depends on what this is all about, doesn't it? If you read the blurb on the website, it says something like: one for the cleansing, one for the power, and one for the something else. Maybe there's the third to come.'

'Maybe they're planning it as we speak,' she said.

Chapter Eighteen

'The problem with students is that they get up really late, especially on a Monday morning. We're just wasting our time,' said Adam Foster, stirring his cappuccino with a stick taken from the counter.

'La la la,' sang Lizzie, with fingers jammed in her ears. 'Deaf to the complaints today.' She grinned at him and blew cappuccino froth in his direction. 'Actually, most of the students will be in lectures at the moment.'

'Or still in bed.'

'Or still in bed, right. But you know, there must be courses here that attract the more weird type of student – arty or a bit eastern. Anyway, the boss is in with the dean as we speak, explaining what we need and alerting security so we don't get hassled. He might have a better idea about what we're doing when he's talked to the professor guy. For now, I suggest we have a chat with anyone who's around, about the pictures on the Internet, anything strange they've seen or heard, any people acting weirdly. You know, get the feel of the place.'

'And there are how many students on this campus?'

'You don't have to talk to them all, Marvin. Just get a feel of how the murders are sitting here, that's all. Put feelers out. Are they shocked, scared, excited?'

'I'll go to the student union,' said Foster, 'see if it's open yet.' He muttered 'waste of time,' under his breath as he walked away.

Lizzie drank the rest of her coffee and took a moment to have a think. She was almost certain that students were at the bottom of this, but why they would make the leap from Halloween prank to murder, was more than she could get her head around. There had to be a compelling reason to put their own lives and liberty at risk. Surely, they must know they would be caught sooner or later? There was no way it could have been a prank that went wrong. Not after the second murder. There had to be a link between the victims and the gang, and she hoped she'd find it here. She threw her empty cup into the bin and headed off towards the library, no wiser for her thinking session.

Dan sat in a chair, opposite Professor Navinder Patel, and waited until he had finished his phone call in which he appeared to be cancelling a tutorial to make way for an 'important meeting'. Dan observed that, even though it was cold outside, and he was quite comfortable wearing his coat and scarf indoors, Patel had a line of sweat on his top lip and was finding it hard to meet his eye.

Patel finished his call and smiled at his visitor. 'Sorry, I needed to cancel one of my senior students in order to accommodate you. So, what can I do for the police? The dean mentioned that I may be able to help you with your inquiries.'

Dan watched him closely. The professor was giving off all sorts of signals, if he could only read them, so he relaxed back into the chair, undid his coat, and adopted an open position with his hands relaxed on top of a closed notebook. 'Thanks for agreeing to speak to me, sir. You'll have heard about the murder that took place on Halloween?'

'I have indeed, terrible business. What a truly frightful way to die.' He used his forefinger to wipe the sweat from his lip.

'And, of course, the second murder on Saturday night, Bonfire Night, you'll have seen that all over the press as well?'

'Yes, yes, of course. You're wondering if this is a serial killer?' He nodded sagely as if he had worked all this out himself and was giving Dan new information. 'Sadly, I cannot help you, Inspector. I thought you had criminal profilers for this kind of crime?'

'We do, and we are building a profile, but I wanted to ask you for some details about these fire cults. One of our DCs has done a bit of investigation and suggests that they are alive and thriving in some less well-developed areas of the world, but not here in the UK.'

'Well, yes, they are. Fire is seen as a cleansing agency for disease of the body or the spirit. Nowadays people may sacrifice an animal in place of a human, but it is true that there are cultures that still sacrifice their own members for various reasons. In fact, the British culture still follows the traditions of sacrifice.'

'It does?'

'Why yes, when you cook a turkey or a goose at Christmas, it represents a sacrifice to propitiate the gods, so there will be a spring and you can continue to farm and live. We dress it up, but we are all savages underneath, praying for godly intervention whether it be for good or evil purposes.'

Patel had relaxed into lecture mode. Whatever he had been frightened of at the start had faded, as Dan dutifully took notes like one of his students. 'I can see that you're an expert, Professor, thank you. So, if I was a student, how could I find out more about such areas of interest?'

Patel clutched a hand to his heart. 'Dear me,' he cried. 'I hope you are not suggesting that any of my students might be caught up in these terrible murders.'

And there we have it, thought Dan. That is indeed what he's frightened of. 'I'm just making inquiries at the moment, sir, but you do have to admit it would be the best place to learn about such matters. So, tell me about your courses.'

Patel's face turned red as he stared at the table top. With extreme reluctance, he said, 'In fact, we do study the rise of cults. We focus on the cults in the USA such as the Charles Manson one, the Waco Texas tragedy, and others.'

'You run a course that focuses on cults?' Dan's heart did a little leap. Closer. 'Who teaches it?'

Patel looked even more uncomfortable. 'I do. I have a lecture this afternoon, in actual fact.'

'Brilliant. I need a list of names and contact details for everybody on that course at the moment, everybody who has taken it over the last three years, and anyone else who helps you teach it.'

'I am not at liberty to divulge that information.'

'Well, get the liberty, because I'm not leaving this room without the lists. This is a double murder investigation, and I'll arrest you for wilful perversion of the course of justice if you prevaricate. Do I need to get a warrant, or will you help us with our investigation?' He took out his phone. I think I just invented a new criminal offence, he thought as he scrolled through the list. But it should definitely be one.

'You have to understand that I can't just hand out personal information without permission. This is unacceptable bullying on your part.'

The redness in Patel's face extended down his neck and under his shirt. Dan didn't want to give the man a heart attack, but he needed the intel, and now. Why was he so reluctant? Did he have an idea who the cult members were? Why would he try to hide that? Protecting his own arse probably. You'd struggle to keep your job if it turned out you were harbouring, and indeed teaching, a bunch of murderers.

'I do understand that, Professor. I'm not trying to bully you, I'm trying to hurry you up. It's urgent. We need to stop any more murders. You do get that? Please go and get permission to release those details, now.' He waved his phone. 'Or shall I get that warrant and have a word with the dean? She seemed like a very nice woman and offered us full cooperation.' He checked his notebook for the dean's number.

Patel shoved his chair back and stormed from the office, shouting at his secretary in the next room.

Phew. Dan got up and had a nosy on Patel's desk. It was messy, and full of crumbs, and half-marked papers on interesting topics. What on earth did you do with a degree in ancient religions? Not that he'd found much use for his geography degree so far, he'd have to admit.

Right at the bottom of the pile on the desk was an A4 pad on which Patel had written something then scribbled it out until the paper had worn through to the page underneath. The guy was clearly under stress, and it might not take much to get him to blurt out what he knew. Another little push might just break him. Cruel, possibly, but Patel was such a pompous git that he didn't feel too bad about it. He felt sorrier for the two men who'd been burned to death.

He stood by the window, watching the sky turn grey with the promise of more rain, and got ready to tell Professor Patel that he would be taken into the station for an interview later in the week, then he sent a text to Lizzie and told her to gather the team in the cafe. They were in for a busy afternoon as soon as he got the list of names.

Chapter Nineteen

Scarlett Moorcroft and Amber Northrop sat at the back of the lecture theatre as Professor Patel gave a lecture on the Mayan civilization and their sacrificial rites. Scarlett checked her phone for the umpteenth time and flicked a glance at Amber. Nothing from Jay at all. They all tried not to miss lectures, as Patel always noticed and told their tutors. Scarlett was on a warning already and her last assignment was late. But it was hard to concentrate when she was alternately hot and cold with excitement, then fear, then excitement again. They had done it, twice, and got away with it. Maybe she didn't need to worry about Tana having a go at her. Maybe she was right and they were all idiots, the straight people. Her exchanges with Tana had really bothered her last night though. She was worried that she had seriously underestimated Tana's madness and Jay's weakness. Both of them could land her in deep shit if she wasn't careful. She sat quiet as a mouse in the top corner, staring down at the prof doing his thing with a slideshow of these long-dead people and their burning sacrifices, and did some thinking.

'It's different, now, isn't it?' whispered Amber. 'You can feel what the Mayans experienced when they did it, can't you?' She shuddered. 'Wow.'

Scarlett smiled. 'Makes you feel powerful, doesn't it? Invincible.' She clamped her hand over her mouth to prevent a snort. 'If we don't get an A on the next assignment, there's something wrong,' she said.

A few minutes before the end of the lecture, Patel stopped talking and three people she hadn't noticed sitting on the front row stood up and turned to face the class.

'Good afternoon, everyone,' said the good-looking one in the grey suit. 'I am Detective Chief Inspector Hellier and these are my colleagues, DCs Singh and Foster.' Scarlett sat upright in her seat in order to see more clearly. What was going on?

'Professor Patel has kindly agreed to give us the last part of your lecture time to talk about the recent murders that you will no doubt have seen on the Internet.' He waited until the noise had died down. 'Nobody here is being accused of anything – far from it. What I need is your help and expertise in an area about which we know very little; can you tell us anything about these murders, or about anyone who may have been behaving a little oddly recently?'

He stared around the room and Amber instinctively shrank down into her seat. 'Oh my God,' she whispered to Scarlett. 'What do we do?'

'They don't know anything, they're just asking questions. Stay cool and tell them you don't know anything.'

Scarlett took Amber's hand and squeezed it. 'It'll be all right,' she whispered. 'Stay strong. Remember where we were and who we were with. Tell them nothing else. You know nothing else.' I'm glad Jay isn't here, she thought. I'm not sure what would happen. She held on to that thought. She'd see him later, talk to him.

The main policeman continued. 'So, there are twenty-four of you, and we're going to split you into three groups. As soon as we have finished you are free to go. It shouldn't take long.' He glanced at the piece of paper he was holding. 'We'll do it alphabetically, by surname. If you are A to G, please make your way to the front of the room, with DC Foster.'

Scarlett and Amber were with DC Singh. 'She doesn't look too scary,' said Amber.

They stood up. 'I'm going to channel that obnoxious whiny girl in my philosophy class,' said Scarlett. 'That should put PC Plodess off the scent.'

Lizzie waited in the top corner of the lecture theatre for the last two of her little group to come and be interviewed. She noticed that they'd held back until the end, and positioned herself so she could get out and give chase if they ran for it. After some intense whispered chat, though, they sat and waited in line.

She smiled at the first one. 'Please, take a seat, this won't take long. Your name is?'

'Scarlett Moorcroft.' Scarlett was a large, young woman, with dark hair and make-up and black clothes. Bit retro, Lizzie thought. 'Scarlett, we're trying to establish any connection between your course on cults, and the murders that you've probably heard about. Can you help us with that?' Lizzie watched the girl's face closely. 'For example, are any of your fellow students a bit too interested in how these things work? Anyone you're a bit worried about? Behaving oddly? That kind of thing.'

Scarlett stared off into the space over Lizzie's left shoulder, then shook her head. 'Not that I can think of,' she said slowly. 'Well, apart from the usual loonies that you get at uni, of course. But they get everywhere.' She gave a little laugh and twirled a strand of black hair around her finger.

The girl's voice was at odds with her size, clothes and demeanour, Lizzie noted. She was all breathy, and high-pitched like a child, and that set up a disconnect that made her suspicious in a way she hadn't been with the other six people she'd interviewed. Scarlett opened her eyes very wide and mentioned the name of a girl Lizzie had already spoken to.

'Oh! I shouldn't say anything, she's just a bit weird, really,' she said, and giggled again. 'Not that I think she could set fire to someone, of course, but she does like the occult.' She sat back in her chair and continued to twirl her hair.

'And where were you on Halloween and Bonfire night?'

'I was with a group of friends at the organised firework display in Lyme Regis, and on Halloween, I just went to the uni bar with a group of the girls from the house.'

That seemed very easy, almost rehearsed. 'You seem to be very confident about where you were. Could other people confirm that?'

Scarlett gave the little laugh again. 'Oh, you can ask any of my friends, we were together all night.'

'And you didn't hear anything about a rather different type of fire from any of these friends?'

'No. If that's all?' she said, and gathered her bag and coat from the floor.

Lizzie checked that the contact details she had were correct and let her go. That one was definitely worth following up. Cocky, she was, and a bit odd.

Amber Northrop took the seat vacated by her friend, and Lizzie watched the closeness between the pair as they passed each other. All her spider senses were tingling. These two knew something. Amber was a shorter, podgier copy of her friend.

'Amber, is there anything you can tell me about the Fire Goddess website? Anything you have noticed about the other students? Any of them particularly interested in fire, for example?'

'I have no idea, I'm sorry. I only took this course because my friend was doing it. It's interesting, finding out about all this weird stuff, but it's not my thing.'

'Which friend? Scarlett?'

The girl blushed. 'Err … yes, Scarlett. We share a house, that's how we got to know each other.'

'So, you can't think of anyone who might be able to help us with our enquiries?'

'No.'

'That didn't take you long to think about. I would have thought this sort of course might attract people with a slightly different outlook on life? Your friend suggested someone we could talk to.'

'She did?' Amber looked surprised. 'Right. Well, I have no idea about anyone. I don't really know them.'

'Where were you on Halloween and Bonfire night?' Lizzie was unsurprised when the girl gave the exact same answer as Scarlett. She checked her details and let her go.

While she waited for the others to finish, she rang the station and asked for a check on both names, but, as she expected, they had no criminal record of any kind. So what was it? The alibis, easily tripping off the tongue; the whispered conversation before the interviews? Yes, all of that. She tapped her pen on her teeth impatiently and willed Adam to hurry up.

Dan walked up the steps and sat beside her on the back row. 'Anything?'

'Yes, I think so.' She gave him the girls' details. 'I'd bet my lunch that these two are hiding something. Just something about their cockiness, and lack of interest in what's been happening. Neither of them asked a single question about the murders. I dunno, gut feeling I guess you'd call it.'

'Well, we've trusted your gut feelings before, so we'll follow that up later. I had one missing, a Jay Vine. One of the students says he's ill, you should follow him up later, too.' He passed over the student's details then stared down the theatre at Adam, still chatting away. 'How's he doing?'

Lizzie had been dreading the question. Much as she wanted to drop the idiot in it, she just couldn't. 'Oh, you know, sir, he's Adam. About as sensitive as the chair I'm sitting on, and still like a bull in a china shop, but he'll get there, eventually.'

'You're doing a good job from what I hear from Sergeant Ellis, but, you know, we're not running a charity. If he can't cut it as a detective, he has to go back into the pond and that's all there is to it. I'll put him in his first post-mortem with victim two this afternoon. That should clear matters up a bit. See if he's up to the job.' He grinned. 'Do you remember your first one?'

Lizzie studied her pen. 'I haven't been in one, except during training. I think Sergeant Larcombe's protecting me.'

'Is that right? Well, brace yourself, when there's another one, you're going in.'

Below them, Foster started on his last interview. 'I think his review comes up in January, or thereabouts; I'll expect a report in by then.'

Lizzie's face dropped. 'I know, thanks for reminding me and ruining Christmas.'

Dan laughed. 'Cheer up, we may have a lead with these two girls you interviewed.' He scanned the almost empty room and watched the professor wringing his hands and fidgeting with the projector. 'The professor's really jumpy. Could his students really have concocted a series of murders? Can't see it myself.'

'Are you fancying the prof for it?'

Dan smiled. 'Doesn't seem very likely, I know, but my own gut feeling was all over him. He's scared.' Dan scanned the list the professor's secretary had passed to him. It looked like they had seen all of the students except Vine. It was still very cloudy in his mind, but there was something here with these kids, he just knew it. Hellier's psychic sleuthing: rates to suit all wallets …

Lizzie clapped her hands together. 'Great. I love it when we start to break open people's grubby secrets.' Then she gave a little cheer. 'Yay, Adam's finished at last. Can we have some lunch, I'm starved?'

Chapter Twenty

Jay sat on the floor in the corner of his room, out of sight of the window. He'd hidden out all day, avoiding lectures, waiting for the cover of night to make his move. If he could just get away before all this blew up, he'd be okay. He would get his passport from his parents' house and disappear. Plenty of people did that every year. He'd blocked the door with his chair and abandoned his phone on the bed. He was writing a note, to explain to his flatmates that he'd gone home to stay with his parents because he was feeling ill, when the front door to the shared flat reverberated to the hammering of a fist.

'Open up, Jay, let us in. We just need to talk mate, that's all. Get this all sorted, yeah?' There was more banging. 'Come on, mate. We know you're in there. Let us in. There's people giving us funny looks out here.'

Jay recognised Kegan's voice; he assumed the other person would be Tana. He didn't for a minute imagine that talking was what they had in mind. At best, it was a warning. At worst? He'd known they would come. He punched himself in the side of the head, eyes watering at the shock of the blow. Too slow. Always too slow, Jay. Stupid, stupid, stupid. He swung over onto all fours, wiped his sweating palms on his jeans, and looked round for some means of escape. On the bed, his army surplus kitbag was packed, ready for the train to Bodmin. A sob escaped before he could stop it. His time at Exeter had been fantastic for two years, and now, here he was, almost finished, about to walk away with nothing except, when it all went tits up, a life sentence for accessory to murder. Two murders. He banged his head back against the wall, hard. What had he been thinking when Tana approached him? What had they all been thinking?

Kegan stopped banging on the door. Jay listened to the silence and counted enough steps until he thought they would be round the back of the house. It was what he would do: break in at the back where it was quiet. He crept to the door of his room, removed the chair, and opened it. Nothing. They hadn't broken in yet. Quietly, he edged towards the front door. His only plan was to get the door open and run as fast as he could until he lost them.

He cracked open the front door and was bundled instantly back against the hall wall before he could utter a word. Kegan shuffled Jay along the wall and into the small bedroom, held his arm across Jay's neck, and punched him hard in the stomach. Jay vomited bile, and the rank smell of old coffee, all over Kegan's trainers.

'Not that clever after all, Jay,' Tana said, and stepped around the vomit into his room. Kegan pushed Jay after her and ripped the kitbag out of his hand.

'Planning a holiday?' Tana asked, pleasantly.

Jay said nothing. He didn't think it mattered what he said. He would agree with everything she asked and run away as soon as she'd left. If he still could. He needed to get home, and then keep running.

Tana perched on the end of the bed. Kegan sat Jay down hard in the single chair, and stood behind him, blocking the door.

'So, Jay,' she began, 'are you running out on us before the great work is finished, little man?'

'I just need a break,' said Jay, striving for a normal tone, not the terrified squeak that came out. 'I was only going to my parents for a couple of days, honest. I will be back for the next ... the next one. I'm sick, you can see that I'm sick.' He tried to twist round to look at Kegan, his eyes swivelling wildly. 'Sorry about your trainers, mate. I'll pay for a new pair, no worries.' Aware he was babbling, Jay put his fist into his mouth and bit down on it.

Tana frowned at him. 'But I need to know that you are loyal to us, Jay. We can't afford a weak link at this stage, when it is all nearly complete. You get that, don't you?'

He nodded, over and over. 'Yes, I do get it. It's fine, you can trust me, Tana, I won't tell anybody.'

His phone rang, loud in the silence. Tana picked it up and looked at the screen.

'It's Scarlett, answer it. Put it on speakerphone.'

Jay answered the call. 'Scarlett? What do you want? I'm not well.'

'At least you answered at last, I've been trying to call you for the last two hours. The police have been in to uni. Came in to our lecture with Patel and interviewed us.'

Tana and Kegan locked eyes. She shoved Jay in the shoulder to make him respond.

'Right … What did you say?'

'I don't think they suspected us. We were cool. My one was a bit dim I reckon. Anyway, they'll probably be coming to see you, so be ready, okay?'

'Okay. Thanks Scarlett. I've got to go now.'

'No probs, hope you feel better soon.'

Jay put the phone back on the bed and stared at Tana. 'Now what? They found us, like I knew they would.' He slumped under Kegan's hands. There didn't seem much point in resisting any more.

Tana sat very still. The only colour in her white face came from the usual two red spots on her cheeks. She looked up at Kegan and nodded. 'There is only one thing we can do, Jay, and that is to make it safe for us.' Tana took latex gloves from her bag and handed a pair to Kegan.

Jay panicked. As soon as Kegan removed his hands from his shoulders, Jay made a dive for the door. He almost made the handle before Kegan's fist connected with his temple and splayed him out on the floor.

'What shall we do with him?' Kegan asked. 'He's gone to pieces.'

Tana shrugged. 'As I said before: he's depressed. Everybody says so. Let's do it.'

'Jesus, Tana, I was hoping we could just have a word with him – threaten him a bit.' Kegan rolled Jay onto his back. 'He's one of us.'

'I think things have gone too far for that. He'll blab to his parents or the police, and then where would we be? No, this is the safest way for all of us.' She dug into her bag and brought out a bottle of whisky and three packets of paracetamol. 'On his empty stomach, these should get to work quickly. Go find me a jug or something.'

Kegan slipped out and into the kitchen down the hall. He found a jug and took it back to the bedroom. 'We've not got long,' he said. 'The other students will be back soon.'

'Let's get on with it, then.' She crushed the tablets as best she could with the bottom of Jay's boot on the fake wood floor, and added them, along with the whisky, to the jug. She gave the mixture a swirl with her finger.

Kegan propped Jay against the wall and shook him until he came round. 'Here, drink this,' he said, and held Jay's nose closed and his mouth open as the boy spluttered and choked a little of the mixture down, and then coughed it back up again, eyes wide and rolling.

'Careful, eejit, he needs to take most of it if it's going to work.' Tana held the jug and poured, while Jay used every ounce of strength to wriggle free from the strong arms of Kegan.

But, no matter how much he flailed and fought, he began to slide into sleep as he took more of the mixture. Soon he would swallow enough for the drugs to do their job. Against all his instincts, he let eyes roll back into his head, stopped fighting Kegan, and fought for control of his breathing instead. Kegan let him slide to the floor. 'He's unconscious,' he said, and felt the boy's neck. 'Pulse has slowed down a bit.'

Tana judged the remains in the jug. 'I hope that was enough to do the job. Let's get out,' she said, 'before anybody comes.' She gathered her bag, crushed Jay's phone under her heel, and shut the door behind them.

Stillness crept into the room, interrupted by irregular breathing and snuffling from the floor. Jay, almost too terrified to show he was still conscious, made the move that would save his life. He rolled over onto his stomach, stuck two fingers down his throat, and vomited until there was nothing left to bring up. On his hands and knees, he stared at the mess. Had he got most of it out?

He staggered to the bathroom and cleaned himself up under the tap, scrubbing at his hair and face until they felt raw. He set his mouth into a straight line. Try to kill him, would they? They should have made a better job of it. The bravado lasted a few seconds before it dissolved into tears in the bathroom mirror. Run …

He drank as much water as he could get down and ate some stale bread. Run … Clearly, they knew nothing about the mechanics of death by pills and whisky, otherwise they'd have hung around a bit longer to check him out. Unlike Jay, who had attended his elder brother's funeral for the very same reason, and had looked at suicide sites on the Internet, obsessively, for many months after his brother had died. Run … A pillow across his face would have sorted him out quickly enough – if they'd had the wit. He suppressed a shudder at what it would have done to his parents if Tana had succeeded, and then remembered that whatever happened, he had already broken their hearts.

He ran away, into the afternoon gloom, to catch the train to Bodmin.

Chapter Twenty-One

Lizzie Singh faced the boy, whose name was Luke, on the doorstep of the flat that Jay Vine shared with several other final year students. He didn't want to let her in to see Jay's room, that much was clear. Sam Knowles stood behind her, hands on hips, enjoying being out of the office for once.

'Look,' Luke said, 'I've banged on the door and there's no answer. The guy's not there, okay? I can't just let you in because you want to go in, can I? Be reasonable. As if I'm gonna let the fuzz just wander in. It's like letting vampires over your doorstep: you just don't do that. Okay?' he said, and attempted to close the door in her face.

A punch of anger exploded in Lizzie's chest. She shoved the door back so hard that it crashed against the hall wall and sent the young man spinning into the wall. 'No, you look, Luke. There are two dead men lying in the mortuary down the road. They've been burnt to death and I want to talk to your mate about that. We're not messing about here. So, let me in, or I'm coming back with a warrant and I'm going to take the whole flat apart. Get it? Every room, every little stash you've got hidden away, every bit of porn you don't want your mum to know about.' She took a step towards him. 'So, it's up to you. We can do it now, with just the two of us in Jay's room, or later, with a forensic crew crawling over everything.' She cocked her head to one side and ignored the dig in her kidneys from Sam.

The boy flattened himself against the wall and allowed the officers to squeeze past. 'I'm gonna speak to someone about this,' he said.

Knowles bent down and stuck his face very close to Luke's. 'Seriously? And bring all that crap down on your head? Be sensible, just hang about until we gain access to the room, and you can go.'

Luke passed Knowles a key he took from the top of the door frame above Jay's door and disappeared into his own room with a theatrical slam of the door. Sam laughed. 'Bloody hell, Lizzie, I didn't think you had it in you.'

She shrugged. 'You don't get out much, Sam. Doesn't work with most of the people we interview, so there's no point wasting it. If you're going to bully someone, make it count.'

The door wasn't locked. Lizzie pushed it open and recoiled at the stench of vomit coming from a patch just inside the door. 'Stop,' she said.

Sam stared over her shoulder. 'Phew, stinks. Bit of a mess. Doesn't seem to be anybody in there,' he said.

'No, but that vomit smells of whisky and there are three empty paracetamol packets on the floor.' She craned her neck to see the rest of the small room. 'Someone got a guilty conscience? Has he attempted suicide, do you think?'

Sam widened his eyes. 'It's not like you to ask my opinion, Lizzie,' he said, scanning the small room, 'but yes, I'd say Vine took some stuff, but he was either well enough to get away or someone took him. Brought most of what he took back up again by the looks of the mess on the floor.'

'So, where is he now?' Lizzie asked.

'He could have run away. If he has, that makes him a suspect.'

'Right,' she said. 'This could also be a crime scene, couldn't it? I'll ring it in.' She wandered into the shared sitting room and stared out of the grubby window until she got through to Sergeant Bennett. She listened, and walked back to the bedroom doorway. 'We'll need to stay here and secure the scene until the boss arrives. Says he wants to look at the room himself. Thinks we may have a lead.' She closed the bedroom door and found a kitchen chair to place in front of it. 'We can be a nice welcoming committee for the other students.' She drew out her notebook and plonked herself on the chair. 'There are three more students living here, besides Vine and the charming Luke, let's see what they have to say for themselves, shall we?'

Dan arrived at the student house with Ben Bennett in tow. He had no idea if this was a crime scene, but he didn't want anybody else collecting evidence, whatever the case was. He spared a swift 'hello' for his DCs, who were interviewing the other residents in the spacious sitting room, and changed into his protective clothing in the hallway. Suited up, he and Bennett stepped over the vomit. Bennett pulled down the window blind, against the blackness of the night, and started the photo evidence collection, working his way from left to right around the edges, then into the centre of the room. Dan drew a plan of where everything was in the room. He could see the smashed remnants of a phone, and there was a note on the bed. In the corner stood a guitar case. Now, what self-respecting muso would leave without his instrument? One in a hurry. The old wooden wardrobe stood open, and there was little in it, but that didn't tell him much. He picked up the note and slipped it into an evidence bag, smoothing it out so he could read it:

Hi guys, feel like crap, reckon it's the flu. Going home early for Christmas. See you in …

And that was all. Perhaps he had been interrupted while he was writing it. Had he had a visitor?

Bennett finished photographing and scooped up some of the vomit into a plastic vial. 'Do we need fingerprints, boss?' he asked.

Dan shrugged. 'If this is like any other student's room, there'll be tons of them, all untraceable. No, we should have a good one or two from the note, assuming Vine wrote it. Let's leave that until we need to do it. Currently we don't even know if anything untoward happened here. We're plucking at straws, aren't we?'

'Don't say that. We have a suspect with a guilty conscience. Let's see if we can catch him.'

Lizzie stuck her head around the door. 'Sir, the flatmates seem to know nothing, and I believe them. Jay was studying completely different subjects. Their paths hardly crossed. They could only suggest a girl I interviewed today, Scarlett someone, as being his friend, which is a good link. We've got Vine's mobile number but I have a feeling that those ruined bits of plastic were his phone.'

Bennett bent down towards the floor, huffing as he got to his knees. 'Hold on, someone smashed the phone, but there's a sim card in it, we may still have a lead.' Using tweezers, he extracted the card, placed it into a small bag, and hoisted himself to his feet, beaming. 'Intact. Now that has to make you smile, boss!'

Dan gave half a smile. 'Let's see what's on it first. Okay, Lizzie, let them go. We should seal this room for now. Threaten them with a night in the cells if they step over the doorway, and let's get the team on door-to-doors. Did anyone see him leave, or did he have a visitor today?'

He let Bennett finish and sat in his car. He had Jay Vine's details in front of him; it wouldn't do any harm to contact the boy's parents and let them know he wanted to speak to him.

The front of the Exeter Road station was quiet at 8pm on a Monday night in November, and Dan was thankful. The reporters had given up on getting any new, juicy stuff and had gone home. He'd quite like to go home too, but they needed a debriefing before he could let anyone go. He parked on the front, in a proper parking space for a change, and walked round to the side entrance, head so full of what he had to do that he almost fell into Adam Foster, sucking on a cigarette. 'Taken up smoking, Adam? Or trying to get rid of the smell?'

Adam threw down the cigarette and stamped on it. 'I don't even smoke any more,' he said, 'it's just …' He shuddered.

Dan suppressed a grin. 'Yes, your first PM today. Fun, was it?'

Adam gave a rueful laugh. 'I'm not sure I'll ever sleep again, but it was okay.' He hesitated, and said, 'What were you like on your first one?'

Dan punched in the code and led the way along the corridor and up the stairs to the MI room. 'I fainted clean away as soon as they took out the woman's heart. Thunk, straight onto the floor. Glad I was unconscious, because apparently they wet themselves laughing at me.' He stopped at the doorway. 'Let them have their laugh, Adam. It won't do you any harm and it will help them bond with you.'

He opened the door and headed for the drinks corner, ready for his usual fix of Italian dark roast. Sally Ellis leant against the counter, arms folded, wearing a scowl he recognised only too well. 'What?' he asked, as she moved grumpily out of his way.

Sally flicked her eyes across the room to where Adam was sorting out his notes, and whispered. 'He, the little shit, bought cream cakes today for everyone except me. If that's not having a personal dig, I don't know what is. I'm doing this for all of us, you know.'

Dan pressed the button and watched black liquid drip into his mug. 'I'm not fighting those battles for you, Sal. Either give him a bit of time to bed in, or sort him out. You can manage that, can't you?' He gave her a slight smile, added milk to his coffee and changed the subject. 'Did you hear about him at the PM?'

'No, been out interviewing people in Exmouth all afternoon.'

'Up-chucked twice, passed clean out the third time. A natural.'

Sally couldn't stop the grin. 'You've made my day.' She straightened her shirt over her skirt and turned into the room. 'I'm just off to catch up with Sergeant Larcombe, and see how the PM went this afternoon,' she said, loudly enough for Foster to hear. 'Back in a minute.'

'Okay, let's get started.' Dan waited until the team had gathered. They looked tired. On the whiteboard he wrote: Suspect: Jay Vine – where is he? Home? Sim card. Possible connection to Scarlett Moorcroft. Suicide attempt? Next to that, on the victim board, he added the best description they had for burns victim two: six feet tall, ginger hair, tattoo on right arm, possible eagle. 'What else we got?' he asked. 'DC Foster, preliminary notes from PM?'

Foster shuffled his pages and stood up next to Dan at the whiteboard. 'The post-mortem revealed that this man was between thirty-five and forty years old, but was already showing signs of cirrhosis of the liver. Judging by the state of his teeth, it is likely he was another homeless person.' He cleared his throat. 'Although death was caused by burning and asphyxiation, the victim was incapacitated by a blow to the back of the head, in the same manner as the previous murder.'

Bill Larcombe put up his hand, a smirk barely concealed on his broad face.

'Sergeant?'

Larcombe turned to Foster. 'Did your gut tell you anything, Adam? Or were you otherwise occupied at the time?'

Foster flushed.

'I hear the hospital does a great job in keeping the floors clean,' added Sally. 'You could take a nap on them, they're so pristine.'

'Okay, you two, enough,' interrupted Dan. 'I bet you can all remember your first PM with vivid horror. Well done, Adam, you survived to live another day. It does get easier,' he said, as Foster slid back into his seat. Dan drew an arrow across from vic one, Simon Ongar, to vic two.

'Do you think they might know each other, sir?' asked Lizzie Singh.

'I know bits of tattoos don't really tell us much, and there wasn't enough skin left to tell us if he had similar ones to vic one, but he could have been a marine too, I suppose. I'd be interested to know if there is a connection between the victims. That could change things, couldn't it? Look into it tomorrow.'

Lizzie shook Adam Foster's arm. 'What was that younger guy called that we tried to talk to? You know, the one you took the bottle of cider off?'

'Gimp? Wimp? No, Dimp, that's what the older guy called him.'

'Yeah, Dimp. Sir, there was a younger man with the group of homeless men we interviewed. He fits that description. Shall I call the hostel, see if he returned there on Saturday night?'

'Do it, Lizzie.' While she moved to the other side of the room, Dan surveyed the boards. 'If Lizzie's right, are we looking at a homeless person serial murderer, or is this something to do with the marines? Or is it just that they were homeless and available?' He stared at the incident board for a minute, but nothing else came. 'And why would students be killing them? Assuming it is a student-led thing?'

'It's probably just a coincidence,' said Sally. 'If you need bodies for ritual killings, who better to choose than a drunk, who'll come with you for a few beers?'

'Hmm. And if your murders are rituals connected to this fire cult, maybe you justify them to yourself by saying that they are men with no family; they don't have a home and no one will miss them. Almost like doing them a favour.' Dan perched on the corner of the large table.

'Yeah, but you could get any student to follow you anywhere for less than that – once they've got a few beers inside them,' added Foster. 'Surely there has to be a reason why the homeless are being targeted.'

Lizzie sat back down at the table and slipped her phone into her pocket. 'Only the night manager is on at the moment,' she said, 'and the residents have another hour before they need to get back and the door is locked. I guess it will wait until the morning?'

Dan nodded and added it to his action list.

Sam Knowles, quiet up until that point, raised his hand. 'Sir, the website says nothing about the victims, except that they were willing sacrifices and have been purified so they can rest in peace.'

'Right. Okay, Sam, what else have you found out about the website for us?'

Sam's face dropped. 'You're not going to believe this, but the guy lives in Ireland, in Cork city.'

'I can believe that, Sam. He's got to live somewhere. Go on.'

'No, I didn't mean … oh,' he said, and shuffled his notebook pages. 'Conor Reilly, who is at this moment in Cork prison, serving eighteen months for tax avoidance, and, I quote, "gave the laptop away to a friend three years ago and hadn't even realised that he was still paying for the site".'

'Right. Probably a stolen laptop, then. Presumably he could remember the name of this friend?' asked Dan.

'Yes, sir, she was called Kathy Kelly.'

A ripple of appreciation went around the table, until Sam held up his hand. 'But, I can't find anything useful from that name. He had a brief fling with her then she disappeared. There are literally hundreds of women called that in Ireland, but those with a connection to Cork have been checked out by Paula Tippett, and none of them sound useful to us. Sorry, sir.'

'Wasn't she a singer in the sixties?' asked Bill Larcombe. 'Big, juicy red lips?'

'That was Kathy Kirby, you twerp,' said Bennett, tapping him on the head with his pen.

Dan thought about it. It wasn't great news, but it confirmed what he had suspected. 'This is a woman serial killer, isn't it?' he said. 'I thought it must be, because of all the fire goddess crap, but now I'm convinced a woman is at the back of it.'

'We need to find the Kelly woman, boss,' said Bill Larcombe. 'I'll get on to the Garda first thing in the morning, see if they can help us to track her down.'

'Thanks, Bill. We may need to get over there and interview this guy, Reilly, properly, and talk to the police. Sally, do you fancy a day in Cork?'

'Ooh, yes. It'll be like a little holiday.'

'That's not quite what I had in mind. Take ...' He scanned the table at faces that had perked up considerably at the thought of a trip away. 'Take Lizzie, and get there and back in a day, okay?'

Sally nodded, and smirked at Lizzie.

'You do know you're not going to Ibiza,' he said, 'it's Ireland, in the winter?'

'Guinness, log fires, folk songs ...' murmured Sally.

'I've always wondered what craic meant,' said Lizzie.

Dan held up his hand before the rest of his team could complain. 'I don't want to hear it. Let's do actions for tomorrow and go home.'

Chapter Twenty-Two

Early morning on the river. Dan needed to think, and what better place to do it? Mist twisted the trees and obscured the first stirrings of the swans that lined the banks. He sank his hands deep into the warmth of his hooded coat and strode out along the path that cut past his flat on the other side of the water. He couldn't stop his eyes drifting up to the window, but, as he'd expected, all was dark and quiet. He wondered if he should give up the tenancy at the next six-month break the following March; Alison might be up to sorting out her own place by then. She may even have a job. He gave a wry smile. *Let's not get our hopes up too high, Daniel.*

Should he and Claire buy a house together? It made sense to put the money he was throwing away on supporting his sister towards a home of their own. Was it time to ask her to marry him? They'd been together almost six months and it was fantastic. He was even warming to the lump of a cat that had attached itself to her. He could kick himself for missing the chance the other night, but what if she'd said no? He stopped and stared across the weir – the water full and flowing – and allowed himself the luxury of thinking about kids. Taking a son or daughter along the canal, showing them the cygnets in spring, playing pooh sticks on the bridge. It was such a tempting dream, and maybe, with Claire, he could achieve it.

Warmed by the thought, he struck out along the path while thinking about the case and why they weren't any nearer to identifying the woman. Someone must be hiding her, and they were no closer to working out who that was. There was a huge amount of planning in these murders. It couldn't just be a bunch of students having a bit of fun. Just couldn't. But students *were* involved in the murders, even if they didn't plan them. He felt like having another go at the professor, but first he wanted to talk to Jay Vine's parents, and then Scarlett Moorcroft, his friend from uni that Lizzie was suspicious of.

And he had to make sure that the second victim wasn't a marine like the first one. It would take the investigation in a whole new direction if there was a link between them. He checked his phone, Sal and Lizzie would be landing in Cork within the hour. It was time to get to the office.

Lizzie yawned. Catching a 6am flight had done little to improve her mood and she hadn't slept well. 'I hope this isn't a total waste of time,' she grumbled as the small plane came in to land at Cork airport.

'What happened to enjoying a day away?' asked Sally. 'You just think you might miss something because you're over here with me, and you're terrified Adam will do something right and steal all your thunder, aren't you?'

'No, course not.' She examined her fingernails. 'Well, maybe a bit. I like to be where the action is.'

'Well, if we meet the bloke who set the murderer up with her website, you might be closer to the action than you know, so cheer up, we're here, let's make the best of it. I hope they've sent a nice, handsome Garda to meet us ...' She waggled her eyebrows at Lizzie.

The home of Conor Reilly stood forlorn and neglected on a street of tidy terraced houses not far from the centre of Cork city. Fin O'Malley, the detective assigned to Sally and Lizzie, slowed the patrol car as they drove slowly past it.

'I thought you might like to see the house of the guilty as we have to go straight past it.'

'It's still empty?' asked Sally.

'Our Mr Reilly is a very successful thief. He owns the house, and several other student houses in the city. He was a terrible difficult man to catch, so he was, but, just like Al Capone, we got him on non-payment of tax. Ever. He'd never paid a penny in thirty years! Can you believe that now?'

'Sounds like the Irish tax office is a bit slacker than ours,' muttered Lizzie. 'They get my dad before he's even made any money.'

O'Malley chuckled as he turned the car in to a car park that looked like it belonged on a condemned building site. Solid metal two-metre-high railings surrounded a single-storey, wire netting-covered sprawl that hardly featured in the flat landscape. 'Welcome to Cork prison, spa and sauna currently under repair.'

Once out of the car the view was no better. 'This is horrible,' said Lizzie. 'What a depressing place.'

O'Malley winked at her. 'Ah, well now, we don't give the inmates a soft life like you Brits do. This is better than it was, ladies. Before the EU interfered, even the rats wouldn't stay long. Come on, I'll introduce you to the charming Reilly.'

They showed their badges and were escorted to an interview room, which was so like an ordinary interview room at home that Lizzie relaxed and took a normal breath.

'You all right?' Sally asked, as O'Malley went off to sort out the prisoner. 'It's hardly your first time in a prison.'

'Sorry, Sarge, I think it's being in a foreign country. I know it's only across the water, but it feels different, doesn't it?'

'Let's focus on the interview. I want all that this guy's got about the mysterious Kathy Kelly, so let's be very nice. At first.'

On first glance Conor Reilly was handsome, thought Lizzie. He had black hair that was going grey around the sides, ridiculously blue eyes, and a half grown-out beard. Mid-forties, she would guess. She instantly warmed to him when he gave her a huge smile as he sat down. He wasn't handcuffed, she was pleased to note. He was only a tax avoider after all, not a master criminal. Fin O'Malley sat near the door, folded his arms across his stomach, and nodded at Sally.

'Thanks for seeing us, Mr Reilly,' said Sally, after the introductions had been made. 'We are going to record the interview so we can take it back with us to the UK. Is that okay with you?'

'No problem. Fire away,' Reilly said. 'This will make a pleasant change – chatting to you two ladies instead of looking at these arses all day.' He sat back, put his arms behind his head, and spread his legs wide.

Lizzie frowned. *Try classic male domination posture on me, would you, mate?* She sat up straighter and set her mouth in a straight line. No one was going to intimidate her that easily, twinkly eyes or not.

'Tell us about Kathy Kelly,' said Sally. 'In your own words. How did you meet, and what was your relationship?'

'Ah, Kathy. Live wire that one. Met her about, oh, five years ago. She came to live in one of my student lets, over towards the university. Was studying there, I assume.'

'You assume? I thought you were friends, or even lovers?' Lizzie watched his eyes as he turned towards her.

'Did you now? Well, I suppose you could call it that, although we were never official, if you know what I mean? More just occasional lovers, you could say.' He closed his eyes and scratched at his scalp, shifting his rear on the seat. 'Oh, yes, a live wire, that one, she was.'

'You obviously knew her well enough to give her a laptop, Mr Reilly,' said Sally. 'Why did you do that?'

'Ah. Well, it may be more that she stole it from me, but I didn't report it to the Garda.'

'And you didn't do that because it was already stolen, I presume?'

'Not just a pretty face, your sergeant,' Reilly said to Lizzie. 'Got it in one.'

'So, if you were only occasional lovers, as you suggest, why did you carry on paying for a website, hosting her domain name, not getting anything in return once she had gone away?'

To Lizzie, the air, already stale, turned still and sticky.

Reilly put down his hands on the table and laced his fingers together. 'I can do a favour for a friend, can I not?'

'You can indeed,' said Sally, 'but somehow that doesn't strike me as your style, Mr Reilly.'

He grinned. 'Sharp as a knife. There are five or six friends sharing my hosting facility. I've been stuck in here for the last year. I just let it run, and pay up once a year. All happens through online banking. No mystery there, Sergeant.'

Lizzie nudged her sergeant's foot. 'Can I ask a question, Mr Reilly? Are you still in touch with Kathy Kelly? Is she still living in the city?'

He stared hard at Lizzie. 'I am not in touch with that woman. She stole from me. I'm here helping you find her, aren't I? I have nothing to do with her any more, and I think she's moved over the water. She hasn't contacted me for three or four years. Isn't that why you're here?'

But she may still have something to do with you, Lizzie thought. Something you don't want to share. Oh, no, she didn't believe for a minute that Kathy Kelly had gone from Reilly's life. Maybe Kelly had something over him she could use. She flicked a glance at Sally, who was looking through her notes. Time to press on.

'Mr Reilly, is Kathy Kelly blackmailing you?'

Reilly rocked back in his chair and bellowed a laugh. 'What? What are you talking about? Blackmailing me? That little tart?' He shook his head, chuckling to himself. 'You don't look stupid, girly,' he said, 'but I guess you must be.' He snorted once more.

Fin O'Malley got to his feet. 'That's enough, Reilly. Don't you be losing your manners with the officers from England, now, or you'll be back in your cell and no time off your sentence for helping the British police.' Reilly subsided, crossed his arms over his chest and stared at the table top.

'Thanks, Detective O'Malley,' Sally said. 'So, Mr Reilly, you have no idea at all of the whereabouts of this Kathy Kelly?'

'No.'

'Could you describe her for me?'

'Medium height, black hair, long. Dyed, I guess. Thin. Too thin.'

'Age?'

'Young, early twenties.'

'Eye colour?'

He shrugged. 'No idea. She had 'em closed most of the time.' He gave a rallying smirk and glanced at Lizzie from under long, dark eyelashes.

'What about her university courses, her family background ...'

Reilly stared at Sally. 'You haven't really got the story, have you, Missus? I hardly knew the girl. I've got nothing more to say to youse.'

Conor Reilly waited in his cell for the click and clunk of the lock drawing back and the precious hour of 'association' time to begin. It had been a very long ten minutes. His agitation was almost under control, but until he checked in, there was no way of knowing whether or not the game was up. The British police. He never would have given them the credit, but they'd gotten as far as him. He just hoped Tana hadn't left them too many clues to follow. She wasn't a professional after all.

He leapt from his bed as soon as his door was unlocked and ran to the nearest payphone – shoving the young lad who was about to lift the receiver himself out of his way. 'Later,' he said, and waited until the lad had slunk away. 'Brendan, it's me,' he said when the phone was picked up. 'The British police have been in to see me about Kathy Kelly.' He listened, nodding. 'No, I think I convinced them that I hardly knew her. Have you heard from her?' He frowned. 'Okay, keep me posted. Have you got her in sight? Good, good. It's been a long time coming and we're not throwing it away now.' He replaced the receiver and banged the wall hard with his fist. To be stuck in this place now, of all times, and on a tax dodge, was an irony not lost on him.

Back on the outside, in the grim car park, Sally thanked Fin O'Malley for taking them in.

'It was nothing, glad to be of help. Where to now?'

'I'd like to go to the university and check out their records. Then see what your search has come up with, as far as records go, for any Kathy Kelly registered in these parts between one and five years ago. We could go back further, but we have to assume she moved to England at some point in the last few years, as Reilly claims not to have been in contact with her for three or four years.'

The university record keeper, Una McKeever, was a gently spoken woman of sixty or so. She held the archived records for every student who had studied at the university for the past hundred and sixty-two years. During the timescale they were interested in, three Katharines and one Kathryn Kelly had studied there.

'Of course,' she said, 'the usual spelling of the name is with a C not a K, after St Catherine, you know. We've got dozens of them. The K is more unusual.' Una spread out copies of the appropriate documents on the table in front of her. 'I found four names: one studying medicine, one in the law, one in Celtic and art studies, and the last one in food economics. They all graduated ...' She stopped and scanned the record of one girl. 'Oh, Jesus, Mary and Joseph, no they didn't.' She looked up at Sally. 'I remember it now, one of the Kathy's died in her first year here, a terrible death.'

Lizzie held her breath. Oh, please, let it be. 'Did she die in a fire?' she asked.

The woman stared at her. 'Now, how on earth would you know that? She did, 'twas a terrible thing, I can tell you.' She clasped a hand to her mouth.

Sally took her arm and led her to a worn wooden chair. 'Here, have a seat, Una. I think we've found our Kathy Kelly. Can you tell us what you remember, please?'

Una fanned her face with the document while Lizzie resisted the impulse to rip it out of her hand.

'I remember it well. It was in November, about five years ago. Almost to the day, I'd say.' She stared at Lizzie again and grew even paler. 'I remember it now. There had been a spate of arson in and around the city. Most unusual for Cork, and then one night the first-year girls' dormitory went up. All the students should have been at the Christmas ball, but Kathy Kelly, a postgrad researcher who looked after the younger ones, had the most awful toothache.' Una searched her pockets for a handkerchief while the two detectives hovered. 'She was in bed and had taken quite a lot of painkillers it seems – from the newspaper article. Didn't stir an inch, poor mite. She was found the next day when the fire was out, still in the very bed.'

Una got up and returned to her record drawer. 'Here, you can have this as well. It doesn't matter now.' She passed Sally a newspaper cutting and sat back down on the chair, dabbing at her eyes. 'None of it matters any more. We're going over to the computer and I'll be on the scrapheap soon enough.'

As soon as they felt able to leave her, Sally and Lizzie shot out into the corridor. They scanned the article. It was exactly as they had been told, but the picture of Kathy Kelly, although in black and white, showed a plump, fair-haired young woman with the sort of open expression that made Sally's heart go out to her. Just a youngster – twenty-two years old. And that fire could easily be laid at their suspect's door, couldn't it?

Sally held the piece of yellowing newsprint. 'Are you thinking what I'm thinking?'

'Kathy Kelly's dead. It puts us right back at the start, doesn't it? We've got nothing.' Lizzie folded her arms. She was cold, and tired, and fed up.

'Well, that wasn't quite what I was thinking, grumpy. Our serial killer isn't Kathy Kelly, is it? The suspect probably stole Kelly's ID and certificates after she was dead, and, if she had Kelly's ID, she could have applied to Exeter as her, couldn't she?'

Lizzie wouldn't meet her sergeant's eyes. 'We're still nowhere. She could be anybody. We only have a name. A common name. And there was no Kathy Kelly listed as being part of Patel's course.' She kicked the skirting board.

'Now, don't get all depressed on me. We know she's smart enough to fake an ID and persuade a tough guy like Reilly to do stuff for her. We know she's now in Exeter. She's Irish. She probably started killing before she came to England. Although this one could have been an accident, I suppose. We have a description, of sorts. We know loads more than we did a couple of hours ago; certainly enough to make it worth getting up early for. Come on.' She nudged Lizzie's arm.

'Okay, sorry. I just got excited for a minute that we may have found her.' She reread the article. 'Let me have a look at what Kathy Kelly was studying,' said Lizzie. She looked at the girl's record and punched the air as she followed Sally back to the car. 'Yes, there's our connection. Kathy Kelly was studying Arts and Celtic Studies here in Cork. The Ancient Religions course at Exeter fits perfectly with postgrad research. I knew that professor was hiding something. I reckon he knows exactly who we're asking him about. Maybe it's time we were a bit less polite.' She stopped and held both hands in front of her to break Sally's stride. 'Or, or … what if the killer has something over the professor, too? What if she made him take her name off the register?'

Sally's eyes glittered. 'Good, good, good. Heh! She could still be at the university. We're coming to get you, whoever you are,' she said to the ceiling. 'Let's get the police records from our little friend Fin, and I'll ring the boss. We're doing all right, Lizzie, and if we get finished here quickly, we may even get a pint in an Irish bar before we catch the plane home.'

Chapter Twenty-Three

Jay Vine woke slowly, savouring the familiarity of his bedroom, the smell of bacon frying downstairs, and the feeling of being safe that home always gave him. His throat was raw from throwing up the corrosive, acidic bile that was laden with crushed pills. Was that only yesterday? He shuddered and dug deeper under the duvet. What to tell his parents? His mum had picked him up from the station, eyes all shiny because he was home for Christmas, but she had recoiled when she smelt the whisky and saw the dregs of vomit on his clothes. He'd just stood in the drizzle and tried not to cry. It was a bad moment when your own mother didn't want to touch you. And as soon as she found out what he had been part of, she would never be able to touch him again. Unbidden, tears slid into the pillow. He must have been mad, totally crazy to ever get involved with Tana. She was a witch. She enticed him, drugged him with all her spiel. Tricked him. If they caught him, he would say he had to run, he was frightened for his life. Yes, that was all true. That was the story he would tell if he got caught. When. When he got caught.

He pushed away the duvet and staggered into the tiny en suite that his parents had installed for him while he'd been away. The shower would wash it all off him, and the washing machine would do the rest. Then he would pack, and slip out the door. First stop would be money, then the train to Plymouth, foot passenger on the ferry to Jersey, foot passenger to France, and he'd be gone. He turned the hot water up high and tried to drown out the sound of his weeping under the water's steaming flow.

Dan drew up to the solid grey stone house just off Bodmin's main street. The Vines were shopkeepers in Bodmin, and had owned the greengrocer's until the latest supermarket had taken their last customers and closed them down. He scrolled down further. The father now worked for a heating engineer and the mother was a teaching assistant. Jay's sister and brother were older than him but the brother had committed suicide. That was tough on a family. Dan could see no signs of life at the house, but he got out of the car and banged on the door anyway. Pressing his ear against the wood, he could hear the sound of a radio playing at the back of the house. After a minute or so he walked to the end of the short terrace, took a left, and counted down the gardens until he was outside the back of the house.

As he unlatched the gate, a small woman opened the back door with a pile of damp washing in her arms. She gave a yelp when she saw Dan and dropped the washing onto the path.

'Ooh, you gave me a fright. Where did you pop up from?' she gasped.

'Here, let me help,' he said, and retrieved several items from the concrete path. 'I'm Detective Chief Inspector Hellier, Devon and Cornwall Police, Mrs Vine. I'm sorry to have startled you.' He piled the clothes back into her arms. Men's black jeans, black socks, even black underwear. Jay's washing?

Linda Vine calmed when she saw his badge. 'What do you want? We haven't done anything wrong, have we?'

'No, of course not. It's Jay I want to see. He may be able to help us with our enquiries.'

Mrs Vine cocked her head to one side like a bird. 'Is he in trouble? Only he was in a terrible state when he got home last night. Proper distressed he was. I had to send him straight to bed, and then get this filthy washing in the machine first thing this morning. God only knows what he's been up to, some awful end-of-term party I shouldn't wonder. You know what students are like. And then he's faffing about, saying he wants a lie-in, but I could hear the shower going.'

Dan glanced at the upstairs windows. 'Can I speak to him now? It is a matter of some urgency, Mrs Vine. I could go and call him myself if you'd prefer. Might be quicker?' Dan moved towards the open back door, but Mrs Vine beat him to it.

'No, no, I'll go up and tell him. You wait in the dining room. My husband's at work, you see, and I'm going in to work myself this afternoon. It's all such a nuisance, isn't it?' She thumped up the stairs and banged on the door. 'Jay, open up, there's a policeman here to talk to you.' She banged again but got no response. 'He's not answering. I don't think he can hear me because of the shower.'

From the foot of the stairs, Dan asked, 'How long has the shower been running?'

Mrs Vine glanced at the mantle clock. 'Goodness, at least twenty minutes. Our Jay's not that clean,' she said, and banged on the door again.

Dan ran up the stairs, swearing under his breath, and rattled the door. Locked, but it was an old wooden door with an old-fashioned lock. 'Have you got a newspaper, and something long and thin, like a chopstick or a wooden spoon?'

Worried now, Mrs Vine brought up her husband's morning paper and passed it over. She held a wooden spoon out in front of her like a small sword. Dan spread the paper on the floor, pushed it through, under the door, and used the spoon to poke the key out from the inside. It dropped onto the paper and he carefully pulled it through. 'That'll save me breaking down the door,' he said to her pale face. 'Stand back, and let me go in first, please.'

The room was steamy, warm, and empty – just as he had suspected. He checked the wide-open window, but he knew he was too late. The couple of moments he had taken in the car to read the information on the family, and the chat to Jay's mother, had probably been enough to alert the boy and he'd disappeared through the bedroom window before Dan had even got into the house. Damn. He turned off the water in the shower. 'Your son has done a runner, Mrs Vine, which is most inconvenient as I want to question him about his possible involvement in two murders in Exeter.'

'Murders? Jay? No, you're mistaken. He would never hurt anyone. Not Jay.'

'Then why did he run? And where might he run to?'

She could give no answer.

'Will you check what he's taken, please? Passport, computer, phone, all that stuff.'

After a quick check, Linda Vine confirmed that Jay had taken his passport and a bag full of clothes and toiletries. 'He's gone, hasn't he? My boy? What has he done? You may as well tell me.'

'I think he's been involved in the murder of two men in bonfires. You may have seen it on TV? It's been all over the news.'

Linda Vine sank onto the bed and let out a mewling sob. Total incomprehension made her mute.

Dan wished, and not for the first time that morning, that Sally was there to help him out with this part. He rang the local nick and spoke to the duty sergeant, who dispatched a PC to sit with Mrs Vine until her husband came home. Then he alerted all patrol cars to be on the lookout for Jay Vine at train and bus stops. The best picture his mother had of him showed a fresh-faced lad of eighteen, about to go off on the biggest adventure of his life to university, and now he was a suspect in a murder investigation. You never know what life's going to throw at you, thought Dan, as he copied the picture on to his phone.

'If he contacts you, Mrs Vine, you know what to do. If he hands himself in now, to the local police station, it will be much better for him.' He handed her a business card. 'Here's my number, call me any time at all. Also, I haven't got time to wait until your husband gets home, so tell him he can ring me to talk, too. Okay?'

He drove away as soon as the young PC had made herself and Mrs Vine a cup of tea. Bloody elementary mistake – coming out on his own to interview suspects. Superintendent Oliver wouldn't be impressed. She'd offered him more bodies to assist than he knew what to do with. He turned onto the A30 and put his foot down, allowing the Audi to cruise up to seventy as soon as he got out of town. He desperately wanted to talk to Scarlett Moorcroft before she decided to disappear as well.

Chapter Twenty-Four

Exeter sprawled to his left as he rounded the motorway bend and came off at the Sowton junction, foot tapping on and off the accelerator as he waited in the inevitable queue to get off the roundabout. Bill Larcombe had assured Dan that Scarlett wasn't in lectures that afternoon, and that she had a job in the local coffee shop at Pinhoe.

He turned right, onto the street, and parked behind a delivery van outside a small row of shops. It was vital that he didn't scare her off. Dan stood outside and pretended to take a call so he could look through the window. He could see Scarlett, black hair tied up now, making a sandwich in a small kitchen. There were three customers inside, none of whom looked like any of the students they had interviewed already. He pushed the door open and kept his head down until he was at the counter. Damn, the back door to the kitchen was open. It was a quick getaway if she ran. Shrugging, Dan flashed his badge at the woman on the till, said, 'Excuse me, please, I need to speak to Scarlett,' and pushed past her into the steamy kitchen.

Scarlett's mouth dropped open. 'You can't just walk in here, you know …' She stopped. 'You're the policeman,' she said. 'What's happened?'

Dan stood between her and the open door, but she looked calm, rather than ready to run. 'Your number is on Jay Vine's phone,' he lied. 'When did you last see him?'

Scarlett finished buttering a roll and filled it with egg mayonnaise from a plastic tub. 'Probably at the weekend,' she said. 'He was sick. I checked yesterday and he said he was feeling bad.' She patted the top of the roll onto the bottom and slid it on a plate. 'Give me a sec.' She took the sandwich to a woman sipping a coffee and returned to lean back against the counter and stare at Dan. 'You don't think he's involved in these burnings, do you?'

'He might be. What makes you think he isn't?'

She laughed and ripped off the blue food preparation gloves she was wearing. 'He's a bit of a wimp underneath that Gothic exterior. Has the soul of a poet, if you know what I mean? I couldn't imagine him hurting a fly.'

'Did he sound depressed when you spoke to him?'

'Depressed? What d'you mean? Oh God, he hasn't tried to top himself, has he?'

'Now why would you think that?' asked Dan.

Scarlett folded her arms across her chest and stared at the floor. 'I don't, it's just that he's still not answering his phone and I'm a bit worried about him, that's all.'

A voice called through the open door. 'Scarlett, one cheese toastie, one ham salad, thanks.' The woman poked her head around the door and glared at Dan. 'We are busy, you know. She's got a break in thirty minutes, why don't you come back then?'

Dan turned his back on her. 'You carry on, Scarlett, we'll talk while you're making the food, okay?'

Scarlett looked worried for the first time since he had entered the cafe. 'Is Jay okay?'

'He's run away, Scarlett. I was hoping you might have some idea where he's gone.'

'Run away? From uni?' She pushed away a strand of escaping hair and buttered more bread. 'No, he'll have gone home early for Christmas, that's all. Lives in Cornwall somewhere.'

'Look, Scarlett, I'm not messing about here. Jay has run away from home and we really need to speak to him. Why is he so frightened? Please would you call me if you have any contact with him at all? It's urgent and important.' He placed his card on the counter.

Scarlett glanced at it. 'Sure, no problem.' Her eyebrows contracted to make a deep furrow between her eyes.

'Is there anything else you can tell me, Scarlett? To help your friend?'

She shook her head and refused to look at him again.

Frustrated, Dan left the cafe. He'd been intending to buy a sandwich, but something about Scarlett had put him off. He thought back to what Lizzie had said after the university interviews. Her instincts were, as usual, spot on. There was something about this girl that rang false, and the news that Jay had run away had certainly rattled her.

On impulse, he diverted round to the back of the cafe and hid himself behind a large bin. It didn't smell too good. If Scarlett was in it up to her eyeballs, she would need to alert the others that he had been to see her. Of course, she could be completely innocent. He leaned against the wall, ignoring his rumbling stomach and the eight calls he'd received, and placed his phone on silent. After twenty minutes, he was ready to give up when he heard someone come out into the back and light up a cigarette. He heard Scarlett's voice, talking on her phone.

'Pig, yeah, same one as at uni the other day.' A snort. 'Not a clue. I told you not to worry, Tana, he's just a plod like the other one. But, yeah, looks like Jay has done a runner. He's not been right these last two weeks. Yeah, he knows that.' She went quiet.

Dan held his breath as Scarlett wandered down towards the gate, shoulders up round her head like she was being told off. Tana?

'No, course he's not dead. What made you think that? At least I don't think the pig would lie straight out, would he? No, he said Jay was missing, and did I know where he might have gone? Hey, calm down. It's fine, isn't it? Tana? You said it would be fine.' Scarlett stared at the phone, silent in her hand. 'Bitch,' she said, took a last drag on her cigarette and turned back to the cafe door.

Tana, thought Dan. Unusual name. He made a note in his book. Were they finally onto something? Could Kathy Kelly be called Tana now? He slipped quietly out of the yard and back to the car. It was time to put a tail on Scarlett Moorcroft. He felt positive for the first time in almost two weeks.

Jay slowed down as he reached Fore Street, and bent low over his knees to get his breath back. Too much weed weakened your lungs. He thought he had fooled the police guy into thinking he was still in the shower. There was no sign of him anyway. Jay wasn't stupid, he knew that by running he had made himself more than a suspect, it was just that he was scared of what would happen if Tana got to him first. She wouldn't make a mistake a second time.

He needed cash, and almost emptied the savings account his gran had opened for him twenty years ago. He'd promised to leave it in there until he graduated. Couldn't be helped. The girl in the bank had raised her eyebrows at him, and he had blustered and said something about a new car. He could feel sweat pooling under his arms, even after his long shower, and kept to the quiet roads as he made his way to the bus station via the local superstore.

He had no idea how to get to Jersey, but he knew he couldn't afford to fly, so he had to go by ferry. It would attract less attention if he did that anyway.

Bodmin Parkway station was quiet after the rush hour and he felt a bit conspicuous with his height and his backpack. He stood in front of the timetable board and tried to work out where to head for. Exeter? But everything in him rebelled against it, he'd just escaped from there – from being almost murdered.

He fingered the cheap phone he'd picked up in the supermarket. If there was free Wi-Fi he could fire it up and check out the ferries. He bought a coffee and sat on a bench. The signal was weak, but good enough to cause him to break out into a rash of swearing and muttering. He had to go to Poole to get a ferry. Where the hell was Poole? It would take hours. Jay put his head in his hands. He knew if Scarlett had been with him he could have done this. They could have run together and it would have been fine. She was just good at all this stuff, and he wasn't. But there they were. He texted her, to give her the new phone number, and said he was okay. Signed off with two kisses. Wondered if he would ever see her again.

The journey to Poole took four hours, and, of course, he had missed the last ferry for the night. Lost in a town he had never visited, he gave in and booked into a youth hostel. His money would dwindle fast at this rate. And there was an ache in his stomach that had nothing to do with drugs and alcohol swallowed. His brain was all too clear now.

Dan stared out of the large window. The major incident room behind him was almost full. The light faded from the sky and cars strobed their headlights across the ceiling as they filtered into the evening traffic. Time for a briefing before he let them all go home. He shoved the last bite of a sausage roll into his mouth and strode towards the whiteboard and wrote the word Tana next to Fire Goddess. He saw that someone had updated the Jay Vine board to say he had fled.

'Right, we have, at last, got some sort of a lead on three possible members of this so-called cult.' He looked at the team and the extra bodies gathered around the table. 'Thanks to Team One, we have a round the clock surveillance available to start this evening on Scarlett Moorcroft. She is, I'm convinced, one of the gang, and she was talking to a person she called Tana, who I think, assuming it's a woman's name, may be the leader of the cult. She also referred to the young man we know as Jay Vine, so I think it's safe to assume that they are the people of interest.'

He paused and allowed a low whistle to escape from Adam Foster's mouth. 'And, Scarlett had no idea that Jay Vine had tried to take his own life. But, the person she spoke to on the phone asked whether Jay was dead. Now why on earth would they think that, unless they'd had a hand in trying to make it happen?'

'We're getting somewhere, aren't we, sir?' asked Adam Foster, face alight.

'We are. I need to hear from the house-to-house enquiries about who was seen in the neighbourhood on Monday afternoon.

And I'm thinking we need to bring in the two girls Lizzie picked out, Scarlett Moorcroft and Amber ...' he checked his notebook. '... Northrop, for questioning under caution.'

'And we shouldn't forget the professor, should we, sir?' asked Foster.

'No. We shouldn't. Why don't you and Sergeant Bennett arrange to have all three of them brought in tomorrow morning.'

Dan gave them a moment to work out who would do what, then cleared his throat. 'It's not all good news. I lost Jay Vine this morning. He had gone home, just as I expected, but he got out of the window and legged it while I was trying to persuade his mother that I really needed to talk to him.' He coloured slightly. 'Bloody rookie mistake. Don't ever let me catch you doing such a simple arrest so badly, Adam.

'Anyway, alerts are out at all the stations, ferry points and airports. I doubt he's got the cash for a major disappearance, but he could be heading abroad, I suppose.

'Just one more thing before you toddle off home; what if they're planning a third one, and, if they are, how can we prevent it?'

Chapter Twenty-Five

Dan waited in the major incident room for the enlarged team to assemble. He'd put the briefing back until 10am to allow the three suspects to be placed in separate interview rooms. And he'd wanted Sally and Lizzie to get a decent night's sleep before they gave their reports. He quieted a flutter in his chest. They were getting somewhere. Maybe.

He added Scarlett Moorcroft and Amber Northrop to the whiteboards next to Jay Vine and Tana. The alert had gone out to local and port forces to arrest and detain, but he had no idea if they would even recognise him. It was only a hunch that he would try to go abroad, he could just as easily go to Ireland or Scotland, or even London, if he wanted to disappear. Dan sighed. No point in worrying about it, better to concentrate on the ones he'd got downstairs.

'Morning all,' he said. 'Time to reflect on what we have so far. These have been carefully planned murders, with victims that were easy to get to the location. Someone, we suspect Tana, has spent a long time on this. Why?' He looked around the room. 'Assume for a minute that they were targeted, rather than randomly selected. Why did she want them? Two homeless men? What did these two guys do to her? Or is it men in general she wants to hurt? Why not a woman? And, she has an obsession with fire. Why and when would she have developed such an obsession?' He paused. 'Or is all this stuff a cover-up for a serial killer who gets her kicks setting fire to people? Can we look more deeply into the psychology of these crimes, please? I've asked for a profiler to come over from HQ to help us out, but we have to wait until next week for one to be assigned. Who knew they were so in demand?

'Meanwhile, we'll help ourselves, shall we? As usual. Right, what do we know?' He pointed at Foster. 'Adam, what did you get from the homeless hostel?'

Foster flipped open his notebook. 'The manager of the hostel, Jane Poole, said that one man, name of David Hamworthy, hasn't been back for a week. I've got people checking out his background, but it looks like he's our man.'

Lizzie interrupted, eyes wide. 'Did you speak to Paddy while you were in Exmouth? I bet vic two is Dimp after all.' She looked at Adam. 'Is it Dimp, do you think?'

Adam exhaled. 'It could well be him, Liz. Right age anyway. And no, Paddy hasn't been at the hostel for a few days either. Couldn't talk to him.' He stopped talking and stared at Dan. 'Wow. Do you think those three tramps are being targeted?'

'Sir,' said Lizzie turning back to Dan, 'if vic two *is* Dimp, then Paddy could be the intended third victim. Oh my goodness, I've just realised; he's Irish as well as the Fire Goddess woman. What if he's gone missing because she's already got hold of him?'

'Welcome back Lizzie,' said Dan, holding up his hand to slow her down. 'Just take it easy, that's a lot of conclusions to leap to. The homeless move on all the time. Just because Paddy wasn't at the hostel, it doesn't mean he's missing. He isn't one of their long-term residents, is he? Or did I miss something?'

Lizzie stared at Dan, face aghast.

'I'm not saying you're wrong. Get out to Exmouth as soon as we're finished interviewing, and find out.' He took a breath as she and Foster scribbled furiously in their notebooks. Blimey, the enthusiasm of youth. 'No leads at all for weeks, and now we've got more than we know what to do with. Don't worry, we'll get round to all of them.'

He slid off the table and made a note on the whiteboard: David Hamworthy equals Dimp?

'Sally, report from Cork, please.'

'Conor Reilly, what a piece of work,' said Sally, casting her eye over her notes. 'He knew our main suspect as Kathy Kelly, a girlfriend who persuaded him to pay for her website, but it turns out that Kathy Kelly died in a fire in her dormitory at the university five years ago. We think our suspect stole the dead girl's ID and used it to blag her way on to a postgrad course at Exeter. Kathy Kelly was a postgrad student studying Celtic and Ancient Religions at Cork.'

'What we don't know,' added Lizzie, 'is whether our suspect caused the fire that killed Kelly. Suspicious, though, eh?'

'So,' Sally interrupted, 'she could have begun her murderous career years ago in Ireland, then registered on a course here, and gathered the supporters she needed to help her carry out these murders. It is beginning to look like she was targeting those men in particular, isn't it?'

Dan scanned the room. 'Paula, have we got those class lists from the university to hand?'

Paula Tippett nodded. 'There's nobody registered as Tana, or Kathy Kelly, on the lists, I've checked. It doesn't mean she wasn't on there, sir. Her name could have been removed to protect the professor?'

Adam Foster thumped the desk. 'I knew that professor was lying, boss. Knew it.'

'I think everybody's lying, Adam,' said Dan, 'and they all know something about it. The question is, has our main suspect got a record over in Ireland? Can we get an ID from them?'

Lizzie wriggled her shoulders. 'Our contact, Fin O'Malley, in the Garda, couldn't find anything similar to our case in their records, with a female protagonist. It *could* just be a coincidence.'

'But you don't think it is?'

'No, sir, I don't. Whoever she is, this woman has manipulated a known criminal, a respected professor, and a group of intelligent students to behave in completely outrageous ways. She's …'

'A psychopath?' asked Adam.

Lizzie cast a glance at her sergeant.

'I believe we are dealing with someone who has overstepped the normal boundaries, yes,' replied Sally. 'Psychopath? I'm not qualified to make that judgment.' She stared hard at Foster to include him in her gaze. 'Are we?'

'Okay,' Dan said. 'Thanks very much. Looks like the trip to Cork was necessary after all, which is good as I have to justify the expense.

'So,' he ticked off points on his fingers, 'if we are right in our assumptions, Professor Patel knows far more than he's telling us, like the identity and whereabouts of Tana, and we need to persuade him that it will be in his best interests to talk to us willingly.

'Second, Scarlett Moorcroft talked on the phone yesterday to a person she called Tana, and I think Sam will tell me that Tana is also a name connected to fire: an alias. Scarlett is in this up to her neck, and I want her to talk, so no frightening her off. We can't tell her how I got Tana's name, of course, as it was overheard, but we can ask her about someone called Tana – that's fine.

'The other girl, Amber, will be easier to break as she's already looking terrified.'

He stared around the room. How to split this up? He knew he should be in the communications room, observing all the interviews, but he was desperate to have a go at Patel himself. 'Right, we'll have Sally with Adam to talk to Scarlett, Sam with Lizzie in with Amber, and I'll take the prof with …'

'Me observing,' came a voice from the door. Chief Superintendent Oliver entered and pulled up a chair. 'Sorry to interrupt, but Assistant Chief Constable Bishop is concerned that our dealings with this highly respected member of the community, pillar of the inter-faith forum, and member of the same wine club, are carried out with the utmost discretion, so I'm in the comms room on obs; if that's alright, DCI Hellier?'

Dan nodded. 'Of course, ma'am. Sergeant Larcombe, would you accompany me?'

He stood. 'Let's make the best use of this time. Don't forget to offer them a solicitor, refreshments, and all that stuff at the start, and do it right. These interviews are under caution, but we're at the start of a long process, don't push too hard and do take breaks.' He checked the time. 'Let's stop in an hour anyway, and regroup.'

Chapter Twenty-Six

Dan nodded at Patel, pulled out a chair and slid into it. He got Larcombe to go through the introductions while he took a close look at the professor. Compared to the golden brown, round, unlined face that Dan had seen a few days before, Patel was grey-faced and sporting dark bags under his eyes. He looked hot and uncomfortable in his three-piece suit. Dan liked him that way – flustered.

Dan made the introductions, then read through Patel's statement while the others stated their names, and took a glance at the solicitor, a Harry Karpal Singh. Did he believe any of this? Karpal Singh was taller and thinner than his client, and given to stooping over Patel in a fatherly manner, which Dan found interesting as the solicitor was a good twenty years younger than his client. He hoped that meant Patel was ready to blurt.

'Right, gentlemen, this shouldn't take too long. Professor Patel, according to your statement you know nothing about the murders, and thought you were invited here to advise the police on the cult aspects of the investigation. Really?' Dan shrugged and placed the piece of paper back on the table. 'Do you have a young Irish woman called Kathy Kelly on your postgraduate course, studying ancient religions?'

Patel stiffened and looked at the lawyer.

'Come on Professor, you must know whether she's taking the course or not?'

Patel swallowed. 'I cannot answer that question.'

Dan sat back in the chair and stared at Patel. He looked at the solicitor. 'Did you tell him not to answer, Mr Karpal Singh?'

Karpal Singh shrugged. 'I have in fact advised my client to tell you all that he knows about this issue, but I cannot compel him to do so.' He pushed his chair back an inch from the table and crossed one long leg over the other.

'Right. Professor Patel, if you are withholding evidence that could be used in court, in the prosecution of a double murder case, it will be taken in a very dim light by the judge and jury.' Dan wanted to shout at the man: your friends can't save you, you idiot; talk! Instead, he forced himself to sit back in the chair. 'So, I'll ask you again: is a woman calling herself Kathy Kelly on your postgraduate course?' He waited for a minute. 'Nothing to say? Why won't you answer if you have nothing to hide?'

Patel's despair bubbled up and spilled out of his eyes. Karpal Singh passed Patel a handkerchief, and ran a finger around the front of his turban. 'Hot in here, Chief Inspector, could my client have a glass of water, please?'

Larcombe ambled out into the corridor in search of water.

Dan tried again. 'Professor, I understand how difficult this must be for a man in your position, to think that you might be harbouring a possible murderer and that she may have influenced your own students …'

Patel let out a sob. 'I … I can't. She …' He clamped a hand across his mouth and shut his eyes. 'No, no, no, no …'

'I think we need to call a halt,' said Karpal Singh, taking the glass of water from Bill Larcombe. 'Would I be able to have a few minutes alone with my client?'

Dan felt he could not refuse, especially as he had Oliver shouting at him down his earpiece to give the guy a bit of space. 'No problem, take fifteen minutes. Interview suspended at seven minutes past eleven.'

Frustrated, he banged his way into the tiny communications room and squashed into the space behind the desk, next to DCS Oliver, Ben Bennett and the young PC handling the recording equipment.

All was quiet as they watched the interview with Scarlett Moorcroft. Dan soon forgot his own annoyance. They had watched her for twenty-four hours and she hadn't done anything odd, or gone anywhere apart from college and work. She thought she was tough, this one.

Chapter Twenty-Seven

Interview techniques were an integral part of a DC's training, but Dan had not managed so far to observe Adam Foster in action. The young constable was perched on the edge of his chair, his arms open on the table, showing he posed no threat. Sally had removed herself slightly to the side to allow Adam some room.

Oliver turned up the volume.

'So, you must be really enjoying the course then, Scarlett? Oh, is it all right if I call you Scarlett?'

'Yeah, it's my name,' said Scarlett. She still looked remarkably composed, thought Dan, especially for someone who might have been involved in a double murder.

'I see that you take this elective course in the rise of cults,' said Adam, reading from his notes. 'Who else takes that course? Jay, Amber?'

Scarlett nodded. 'Yeah, both of them and loads of others, not just us.'

'But your little group, you've become good friends over the last couple of years?'

'Yeah, we're mates.'

'You hang around together, go out for drinks, all that sort of stuff, yeah?'

The girl shrugged. 'Yeah.'

'What about Kathy Kelly, is she involved?'

Scarlett's mouth dropped open. She disguised it well, coughing and pretending to change position, but it was clear that she hadn't expected to hear the name.

'Err … no, no, I don't think I've heard that name before,' she said.

Adam tapped his pen against his teeth. 'Odd. Amber says this Kathy Kelly is your tutor. I thought you might know her rather well, or do you know her as something else? Tana, perhaps?'

Scarlett pulled her jumper sleeves down over her hands and stuffed each hand up under the opposite armpit.

Sally sat spoke for the first time. 'Scarlett, we know you know who Tana is. If you can help us to find her we could prevent another murder. Please, can you tell us anything about the Fire Goddess cult, or where she is now? Anything?'

The moment it took Sally to ask her question seemed to give back Scarlett her inner core of strength. 'I have no idea who she is, or where she is, or what she's done, and I'm not saying anything else until I have a lawyer. And I don't believe Amber told you anything. The police just lie, everyone knows that.'

'You're the one having a problem with the truth,' said Foster. 'Can you at least admit that Kathy Kelly is your tutor? We do know that she is, so what have you got to lose?' He smiled at her.

Scarlett dropped her head to her chest and refused to speak.

Sally stood up and stopped the recording. 'We'll suspend the interview at eleven twenty-nine, until we have found you a duty solicitor. DC Foster will arrange for you to make a call to your parents, or a supportive friend, but you'll have to stay here until we complete the interview.' She stalked out of the interview room and into the corridor, grumbling.

'Back to the MI room, Sal,' said Dan, sticking his head out of the communications room. 'I just want to watch a bit of the Amber interview then I'll join you.'

Lizzie was already an experienced interviewer, but Dan had no idea about Sam Knowles. He hadn't actually allowed him away from the computer for weeks until this case. He was surprised to see that Sam was leading, and Lizzie, face like thunder, sat to one side, biting the top off her pen.

'So, you seem like a pretty cool person, Amber. What on earth have you been getting up to?'

Amber stared at him, lips curling in contempt.

Dan frowned. She'd looked terrified when Adam had brought her in earlier. She wasn't frightened of Sam though. 'This may work to our advantage,' he murmured.

Sam checked his list of questions. 'How long have you known Scarlett Moorcroft?'

'Three years.'

'So, you'd say you're good friends; hang out together, go to clubs, like the same things. You're mates, basically?'

Amber nodded and relaxed back into her chair. 'Can you tell me what I'm here for?' she asked. 'Has Scarlett done something wrong? Or is this about Jay? Not seen him for a few days.'

'No, Amber,' said Knowles, shaking his head. 'This is about you. Your involvement in two murders. Anything you would like to say about that?'

'Murders? You joking me?' She ran her tongue around her lips. 'Oh, the bonfire murders, right. It wasn't me.' She looked at Lizzie, who kept her head down in her notebook. 'I wasn't even there.'

'Really?' said Sam. 'What would you say if I said I can identify you from a CCTV video recording, as being present on Exmouth beach on the night of the first murder?'

Amber shot upright. 'You never ... you haven't got me. What are you on about?' She looked to Lizzie, who continued to stare down at her notebook. 'You haven't got me on any CCTV or anything. You can't have! You're lying.' Panic made her clutch the edge of the table then clamp her hands across her mouth, ignoring the tears that spilled out through her heavy eyeliner.

Sam leaned in. 'CCTV is my job, Amber. You'd be surprised what I can see. What were you going to say? You may as well tell us, you almost have anyway. What did Tana say?'

The girl stared in terror at him, said, 'Tana? Oh, God,' and broke down into such violent sobbing that Lizzie had to pass her a whole box of tissues.

Lizzie glanced up at the camera then turned to Sam. 'DC Knowles, I think Miss Northrop is too upset to continue for the present.'

Sam stared at the weeping Amber then stood up and walked out of the room, leaving Lizzie to quieten her down.

Dan looked across at his Superintendent, arms raised in defeat.

'It was effective,' Oliver said. 'The girl's broken all right. We may get a confession today.'

'No, ma'am, it wasn't effective in the long-term.' He stood up and grasped the door handle tight. 'I won't have it. He lied outright and broke her down too early before we got anything useful. It's duress, clear as. As soon as she has a solicitor we won't get anything out of her until the trial. I told them to take it easy. Lizzie would have handled it better. Amber is key to finding out what's going on here.' He banged the door frame. 'No, I should have interviewed her myself.'

He stormed into the corridor and pinned a surprised Sam Knowles into a corner, finger pointing at his chest. 'Do what I tell you, Sam, I do it for a reason. We're not messing about in there. You've blown it. That girl's a key witness or a key suspect, and you made her weep like a baby before you got anything useful at all. How are we going to get anything out of her now?'

Sam blanched. 'But ... but she was going to break. I nearly had her, sir.'

Dan lowered his arm, flexed his fingers, and tried for a deep breath. 'I said take it easy, take breaks. It's early days.' He took another breath. 'But I blame myself, not you. Lizzie is level three trained – she should have led the interview procedure and I should have made that clear.' He made a sudden leap of understanding: Sam was trying to prove himself in front of Lizzie, hence the out of character behaviour. 'If you want to impress anybody, Sam, do it by following orders, and let Lizzie lead where she is more experienced, okay? You got that?'

He scrutinised Knowles' burning face. 'You haven't done the training, that's why I paired you up with her. And you must have a grasp of PACE, surely? A confession acquired under duress will be knocked out of court by any reasonable barrister, and then we won't be able to use her evidence at all. Key evidence.'

Dan softened his voice, the bloke looked devastated. 'Look, take a break while we calm her down, and come back into the comms room. A bit of observation will help you, and I could do with another opinion in there, okay? I'll arrange the appropriate training once this is over.'

Sam gave a brief nod and sloped away.

Back in the communications room, Dan sent the constable away to get them coffee so he could speak to Oliver and Bennett. 'Ma'am, I've asked DC Knowles to join you in here to observe for the next session. He isn't level three trained but he couldn't somehow bring himself to let Lizzie lead. He's desperate to impress her.'

'Bless,' said Oliver. 'Maybe you need to get him out in the big world more often, let him loose from the computer occasionally.'

'I hear what you're saying, but he's just really good at the techy stuff. We can keep so much of that stuff in-house with his skills. No, I just need to get my staffing better balanced.'

'I can help with that, boss. Move the teams about a bit,' said Bennett.

'Okay, let's crack on. I'm going back in with Patel.' Dan stood, collected a coffee from the constable as she opened the door, and prepared to confront Patel. Perhaps he should let Sam have a go at him.

Chapter Twenty-Eight

Inside the stuffy room, Navinder Patel sat quietly next to his solicitor. Karpal Singh had a page full of notes in front of him.

Dan sat next to Larcombe and signalled for the recording to begin. 'I hope you're feeling better now, Professor Patel. It will be looked on favourably by the court if you tell us all that you know now, rather than hold back and have it exposed in a public trial by an adversarial barrister. You do see that, don't you?'

'I do understand, Chief Inspector.' Patel sniffed and blew his nose on his solicitor's handkerchief. 'It's just that this will mean the end for me. For my career, probably for my marriage, and, worst of all, for my reputation. So, I will cooperate, but only if you can give me some guarantees.' He gestured to his solicitor.

'My client wants an assurance that he will not serve time in prison for what he is about to say. He is cooperating fully with the police investigation, as he wants this criminal brought to justice as much as you do.' Karpal Singh looked up expectantly.

Dan pursed his lips and looked at Patel. 'You must know that we do not prosecute the cases, sir. Our job is to gather the evidence and present it to the Criminal Prosecution Service. You can't make a deal with me, and I won't promise you anything I can't guarantee. On the other hand, I will deal with you as fairly as I can, if you're straight with me.' He raised an eyebrow. 'Anything else?'

Karpal Singh ticked the first item on the list and opened his mouth to speak.

'She tried to blackmail me,' burst in Patel, unable to wait any longer for negotiations to finish.

'Did she, Professor?' said Dan, delighted to be out of the solicitor's hands. 'Why don't you tell us all about it?' He took a swig of coffee and opened his notebook.

'She – Katharine Kelly she called herself – came to me from Cork University with a testimonial and a very good degree. She wanted postgrad work to lead to a Masters, and then a doctorate.'

Dan nodded encouragement. 'Do you have copies of the documentation she brought with her?'

Patel shook his head. 'No, we just note that we have had sight of the appropriate documentation then hand it back. It looked fine. I had no suspicions, I'm telling you, none at all.'

'Okay, Professor, got it,' said Dan. 'She asked for a place and you just gave it. Is that usual?'

'Not exactly, no. But she had already done lots of work on ancient fire cults, and completed her Masters' thesis in a year. She was obsessed, Inspector. Do you hear me? Obsessed with fire.' He clutched the sodden handkerchief between his hands and stared at Dan. 'I ... I agreed to her idea of basing her PhD on the rise of cults. She had an idea that she could start her own and see how far people would go, how far she could use persuasion, auto-suggestion, reward and punishment. You know, the usual behavioural model.'

'So you allowed her to gather a group of young people around her, and bend them to her will?'

Patel nodded miserably.

'Did you really have no idea what messing with people's minds might lead to?' interrupted Bill Larcombe. 'Are you asking us to believe that you had no idea what she planned to do?' Larcombe scratched the top of his scalp with his pen, a look of bemusement on his open face. 'Come on, sir, we weren't born yesterday.' He shifted on his chair and threw a glance at Dan.

Dan moved in closer to the table top and rested his elbows. 'You did know what she was going to do, didn't you? That's why you were in such a state when I asked for your help, wasn't it? You thought the game was up, didn't you, Professor?'

Patel shrank back from the table. 'No, no, of course I had no idea, no idea at all.'

'Why, then, when I looked at the registration information on your students, the information that you were so reluctant to pass over, could I find no mention of a student called Katharine Kelly? She was with you for almost three years – where are her records?'

'Did you destroy them when you realised we were on to her, and then on to you?' pressed Larcombe. 'Were you covering your tracks, Professor?'

Patel nodded miserably. 'My secretary did it on Monday.'

There was silence as Dan stared at the top of Patel's head. Everybody lies. 'Have you lied to the police about anything else, Professor? Anything else you'd like to tell us?'

Karpal Singh intervened. 'It seems to me that you are either ready to charge my client, Chief Inspector, or you are fishing. Please decide which it is.'

'Just hold on a minute and you'll get your charge,' said Dan. 'I still have a couple of questions for your client.' He checked his notes, giving Patel time to calm down. 'You destroyed the records and told her she was off the course, according to your secretary.'

'I was distraught when I found out about the murder, and didn't want any more to do with it.'

Dan raised his voice. 'But you sat on the information that would have caught the guilty parties. You allowed another person to be murdered in the same grisly manner, Professor. What kind of a man does that?'

Patel's eyes filled with tears. 'You don't understand. She said she would tell you it was all my idea and you would believe her. That I seduced her and got her to do my bidding. She said …' He let out a strangled sob, 'she said I would go to prison for her, and I can't, I just can't … That's why I said nothing. I am not a bad man.'

Larcombe passed him a box of tissues and let out a sigh. 'Confession is good for the soul, Professor. You need to have a bit more faith that we don't just take someone's word for it, we do actually check what people tell us.'

'Is there anything else? Did she put any other pressure on you?' asked Dan.

Patel's bloodshot eyes swivelled around the room, avoiding eye contact. 'No.'

'Okay, so do you know where the woman calling herself Katharine Kelly, or Tana, lives?' asked Dan.

Patel shook his head. 'I don't know anything else about her. And I, well, I got my secretary to …'

'Destroy all her records?' asked Larcombe.

'Yes. I'm sorry.'

'What about the others who are in it with her?'

'I don't know who they are. She had pseudonyms for them as they were test subjects for her thesis. Brenna, Callida, Idris, Kegan, all names that mean fire in different languages. She never named them to me. For all I know they are nothing to do with the university.'

Dan couldn't help himself – he rolled his eyes. More lies. 'Come on, Professor, I think we all know that Amber Northrop, Jay Vine and Scarlett Moorcroft are the members, don't we?

Patel's eyes widened. 'Scarlett? Amber? I don't believe it. Such sensible girls. Jay? Possibly, yes. I don't know anything about anyone else.' He folded his arms across his chest and closed his eyes.

'Well?' asked Karpal Singh.

Dan listened in to his earpiece for a moment then nodded. 'I need to speak to my Chief Superintendent regarding the exact nature of the charges. I'm afraid you can't leave the building at the moment, and it is likely you will be charged and have to spend at least one night here before you can be seen by the magistrate to discuss bail.'

Patel sat up in shock. 'You can't keep me here.' He turned to his solicitor. 'Can he?'

'And you might like to alter some of the details in your statement,' added Larcombe, passing it back across the table. 'While you're waiting.'

'You won't contest bail, Chief Inspector?' asked Karpal Singh, brow furrowed.

'No, I won't contest it,' said Dan, 'but it doesn't mean I have to like it,' he muttered as he left the room.

Chapter Twenty-Nine

The communications room felt even more crowded with the lanky frame of Sam Knowles holding up the wall, thought Dan, as he closed the door behind him and leaned against it. 'That went well,' he said.

'Aye, well done, boss,' said Bennett, 'I reckon Patel's on for accessory to murder, and withholding evidence.'

DCS Oliver smiled at him. 'Well done, Chief Inspector. That's the way to do it. Now, about the two young women?'

'We'll have to wait until they at least have a solicitor, and I'm happy for a parent to be in the station to offer support while we're interviewing them, but they're all over eighteen, so they can be interviewed on their own. Ben, can you arrange for them to have a sandwich and a drink or something? The rest of us can meet back in the MI room and plan our next move.'

'Right,' said Oliver. 'Charge Patel. I will talk to ACC Bishop and ruin his day, but there's no way Patel is walking away from this.' She glanced at the camera, still showing the interview room, and shuddered. 'Odious man deserves what he gets.' She smiled at them and stood, requiring everybody to shuffle round to allow her to get out.

Back in the MI room, Dan pushed his mug towards the coffee machine and tapped Sam on the shoulder. 'Fill me up,' he said. There was a crowd around the machine. More accurately, he decided, there was a crowd around another plastic tray of cream cakes that had appeared in the last hour. They were disappearing fast. Dan sneaked an arm under Ben Bennett's and grabbed an eclair before they were all gone. He wedged it in his mouth so he had his hands free to add milk to his coffee, and only noticed Sally's face as he turned back into the room. He thought she'd had a change of heart, but her expression told him otherwise. Placing his coffee on the table, Dan took the uneaten half of the eclair out of his mouth and shrugged sheepishly at his sergeant. 'Might as well finish it now I've started,' he said, and devoured the rest in one mouthful.

Adam Foster smirked in the corner. The only people not eating cakes were Sally and Lizzie, Dan noted. It was an Adam stitch-up again. Sally needed to sort him out. It wouldn't usually take her as long.

'If you've finished stuffing your faces,' he said, 'Patel has confessed to knowing all about Tana's cult. It was for her PhD, apparently. He swears he didn't know she was going to murder anyone, and that he took her details off the university database because she was blackmailing him. But, he didn't tell us about Tana after the first murder, so, in a way, the second is on him, and for that he must pay.

'Bill, charge Professor Patel with withholding information.' He blew air out through his teeth. 'You know what? Charge him with being an accessory, too. We only have his word for it that he didn't put Tana up to it. We'll let the CPS sort out which one is most appropriate when it comes to court. At least we know he'll get three years. Can you get him processed for the night?'

Larcombe gave him a thumbs-up and went off humming to type up the charge.

'Right, Lizzie and Adam, get down to Exmouth and take the photo of the second victim. Can you get a proper ID? Is it David Hamworthy? Also, try to track down the homeless person known as Paddy. He may have gone into hiding if he thinks he's the next victim, or he could have simply moved on. We need to know.' He waved at them. 'Go on then, you can read the report on this afternoon's activities later. Oh, by the way, Adam,' he said to the departing detectives, 'good calm interviewing in there, well done.' He chewed the end of his pen and watched Sam Knowles flush to the bottom of his neck. Well, he could hardly expect to be praised, could he?

'Patel is now out of action and cooperating. Amber Northrop is very upset, as this morning's interview did not go well. But, we do need a confession out of both young women by the end of the day, otherwise, we have to think about letting them go. Despite what some people think, we have no clear IDs from any CCTV footage, so these two girls are being interviewed because they know Jay Vine and Tana, and their behaviour was … off, I suppose.' He gave a half-smile. 'Hardly a reason to hold them, is it?'

'I do really think they know what's going on, boss,' said Sally. 'Let me have a go at Amber this afternoon. I might be able to get her to talk.'

'She's yours. Tread carefully.'

Sally nodded her thanks, patted Knowles on the arm, and slapped her notebook shut.

'That leaves us with Scarlett Moorcroft – a much cooler customer. I have a feeling that if Scarlett thinks she may go to prison, and for a very long time, she'll drop the others in it to save her own neck. I'll take her.'

Chapter Thirty

Sally waited until Amber Northrop had settled herself. She had a new, young duty solicitor sitting next to her, pad poised for notes and wearing a smart skirt-suit and high heels that would be killing her before the end of the day.

The girl now knew she was not under arrest, and Sally was desperate to get something useful out of her before she had to allow her to go home with her mother, who was hovering in the reception area. 'Amber, I hope you're feeling a bit better now?'

Amber looked up at the camera that she hadn't noticed earlier. 'You recording this?'

'Yes, of course we are. We're hoping you can give us valuable information about Tana and her whereabouts. We'd like to speak to her before there are any more murders. Will you help us?'

'I suppose. I don't even know her real name. I'm not going to prison, am I? I didn't do anything wrong.' She plucked a new tissue from the box and screwed it into a ball.

Sally cocked her head to one side. 'Really? You know that's not true, don't you?'

'It wasn't my idea, I swear.'

'What wasn't your idea, Amber? Tell me a bit more and I'll see if we can let you go home with your Mum. If you didn't actually do anything, there's nothing to worry about, is there? We can eliminate you from our enquiries.'

Suspicion contorted Amber's tear-streaked face. 'You'll let me go? Just like that?' She stared at the duty solicitor, who gave her a reassuring smile.

Sally gave herself a mental kick. She could almost feel Dan glaring through the window, even though she knew he was in the other interview room. 'Not quite like that, no,' she amended. 'Amber, tell us the truth and I will do my best for you, I promise. Think of your mum out there waiting for you. What would she want you to do? I can see you're a nice girl. Probably got dragged along by your friends, didn't you?'

The girl looked up at her, grateful for what she saw as a chance to get out. 'Yeah, none of it was down to me. You do believe that, don't you?'

Sally smiled at her. 'So, were you present at the murder of a homeless man, Simon Ongar, on the thirty-first of October, at Exmouth beach?'

Amber swallowed. 'If I say yes, I'll go to prison, won't I?'

Sally shrugged. 'It won't be up to me, love. You're young; you have a bright future ahead. I don't know what the court will decide, but they will look more favourably on you if I tell them you have been helpful and cooperative, like the good girl you really are. So, will you answer the question? Were you there?'

Amber mirrored Sally's shrug. 'No comment,' she said.

'We're not on American TV, Amber.' Sally gripped her pen. Kids. Christ's sake. 'You need to give a straight yes or no, and I'd strongly advise you to think carefully before you do. Lying to the police is a serious offence.'

'I want to talk to my mum.' Amber looked at the solicitor again, but Sally jumped in before the woman could speak.

'That's not a possibility at the moment, but she's outside waiting to see you. If you tell the truth now, love, it will be much better for you later. Really. Think of your mum.'

Sally gave it two minutes of complete silence, while she stared at the girl who was sitting before her, her head down and her fingers lacing and unlacing in her lap. Come on …

Quick tears leaked from Amber's eyes as she made her decision. 'Yeah, okay, I was there,' she whispered, 'I saw what happened. But I'm not telling you any more. I can't. I didn't do anything, I swear.' She lost her brief composure, curled her legs up on the chair and bawled.

'And was Scarlett there, and Jay?'

Amber nodded her head.

'For the benefit of the recording, the suspect has nodded her head.'

Over her sobbing, Sally arrested Amber formally for being an accessory to murder, and asked the PC on the door to take her to be processed into the cells. They wouldn't get much of a chance to have another go at her. Still, not bad for fifteen minutes. Now we might start making some progress on this bloody case, she thought, and called Dan out of his interview to tell him.

Dan eyed up Scarlett Moorcroft through the window of the interview room. She was chatting animatedly to the duty solicitor. He sighed. Why was it always Vanessa Redmond for his suspects when he was on a murder case? She was guaranteed to wind him up just by breathing in his presence. But they had a confession from Amber, and he was good to go.

Bill Larcombe nudged his elbow. 'I reckon she likes you, boss, does our Vanessa. She keeps coming back,' he said, and yanked up his trousers at the front.

'You need your eyesight checking, Bill. I can feel those red talons poking my eyes out as we speak. Okay, here we go. Be still my beating heart,' he said, and opened the door.

'Chief Inspector,' said Redmond, looking up at him over her tiny tortoiseshell glasses, 'good afternoon.'

Dan nodded at her and faced Scarlett. 'Interview resumed at fifteen thirty-three, with the addition of duty solicitor, Vanessa Redmond. So, Scarlett, you have spoken to your mother and you have a solicitor. We have fed you and made sure your needs are met. Now, can we talk about the night of October thirty-first, please, and will you tell us what happened?'

Scarlett stared at her solicitor, unsure of her next move.

'You should tell the police all that you can about the murders, Scarlett,' said Redmond.

Scarlett looked horrified. 'But you're supposed to help me, to protect me. I don't want to go to prison …'

'I'm here to advise you of your legal rights. I always advise my clients to tell the truth.'

Dan sat back in his chair. She'd never once advised that in all the months he had put up with her.

'We know you were there, Scarlett,' said Larcombe, aiming for fatherly and kind.

'This is shit,' said Scarlett. She stood up and made for the door. 'I want my mum,' she said. 'You can't keep me here.'

Dan reached the door before her. 'We can if we charge you; Amber Northrop has just named you and Jay Vine as being there on the night of the first murder. And I reckon you were at the second, too. Sit down, you can't leave.'

Once again, Scarlett looked to her solicitor for help. Redmond waved her back down. 'If they are going to charge you, you have no choice but to hear the charge. At least then we'll know what we're up against, won't we? Come and sit here next to me,' she said, and patted the empty chair.

Reluctantly, Scarlett complied. Much of her earlier bluster disappeared and she appeared younger to Dan, more vulnerable. Here was the moment when he could break open the case. When the lies began to crumble and the gaping holes in stories became obvious. He let out a held breath and resumed his seat. 'We know you were there. Tell us what you know and we will do our best for you.'

She stared at him, eyes blue in black kohl rings. 'You can help me?'

'Why did you agree to do it, Scarlett, to help kill those men?'

And in that moment the girl saw her chance and grasped at it. 'We didn't know,' she said to the table top. 'We didn't know that she would really do it. It was just a laugh at first. You know, the bonfires, the chanting, making videos for Facebook and YouTube. I couldn't believe it when she …'

Scarlett stopped, and stared over Dan's head. 'I can't. It was … It was … horrible.'

'What was, Scarlett?'

She brought her eyes back to his. 'The smell, the fire. The screaming …' she dropped her head into her hands. 'What the hell have I been doing?'

Vanessa Redmond patted her hand. 'Well done, Scarlett. I think my client might be willing to write a confession, now, Chief Inspector,' she said, 'why don't you charge her?'

Outside, Dan waited until Bill Larcombe had handed him the signed confession, and taken a dulled and unresisting Scarlett to the cells. 'Thank you,' he said to Redmond.

She avoided his gaze. 'I have a daughter at Exeter, in the same year as these girls. Doing medicine, thank God.' Redmond folded her glasses and slipped them into a little case. 'I just thought, that if she was mine, and she'd done something so unutterably stupid, I would want her to come clean and face up to it. And I would want to keep her out of prison.' She looked at Dan. 'I suppose that's asking too much?'

'Way too much. Guilty, all of them. If both girls tell us everything, they know it might reduce their sentences, but they were accessories: they helped build the bonfires, they watched two men burn to death, horribly, and they did nothing. How lenient should the judge be? How lenient would a jury be?'

Redmond sighed and zipped her bag shut. 'I'll see you soon, then. Goodbye.'

Chapter Thirty-One

Lizzie chewed on an already ragged fingernail as Foster negotiated the shoppers' traffic in Exmouth town centre. She was still stewing over Sam Knowles's behaviour in the interview, and had to forcibly remove the scene from her memory before it became a headache. Silly idiot. What was he trying to prove?

Then she squirmed to think about Harry Karpal Singh. She'd almost bumped into him in the corridor leading to the interview rooms, and had to disappear into the toilets to avoid him. How embarrassing would that have been? Her father had never forgiven her for turning him down, especially when he became a solicitor – one of her dad's 'preferred professions'. But Harry was more like her grandfather than her cousin, and no way were her parents marrying her off like she was property to be got rid of. And Harry would want her to stay at home and raise babies, and that was never going to happen. She reckoned she was almost old enough for her parents to give up trying to match-make, and write her off as an old maid. Roll on, she thought.

'Do you think Paddy will be the next victim?' she asked Foster. 'I can see a pattern here quite clearly. I really hope he's in the hostel. Put your foot down.'

Foster gave her a swift glance. 'He wasn't there when I went in yesterday. Don't get your hopes up. At least,' he said, swerving round an old man pulling his wife and their shopping trolley across the road, 'at least if he has run, he might escape a nasty fate.' He pulled up outside the hostel, bringing the car to a halt using his handbrake.

Lizzie was out of the car before he'd undone his seatbelt. She ran up the path and rang the bell. This time, Jane Poole was ready for them.

'Thought it might be you lot again. Dimp hasn't come back, and neither has Paddy since yesterday.' She shrugged. 'They're not reliable, you know.' She looked at their faces as they stood on the doorstep. 'It is Dimp you're asking after? He's the dead one, isn't he?' She turned and led them down the corridor into the kitchen, and pointed them towards a long table with a bench on either side. 'Sit down.'

Poole sighed and folded her arms. 'What do you need?' she asked, all animation gone from her face. 'You know, I don't know what's happening here any more. Of all the people I'd happily murder, two homeless guys would not be my first choice.'

Lizzie passed across the post-mortem photo of the second victim, twirling it round so Poole could see it. 'Is this him?'

Poole studied the photo. 'Yes, that's him. Dimp. David Hamworthy is his real name. Poor sod. I just knew it was him when it was on the news this morning. Wait here a minute.' She sighed and went into a small room that Lizzie assumed was an office.

Minutes later she came back with a sheet of paper. 'Social Security number, and last known next of kin.' Her hand lingered on the paper. 'Do you fancy a coffee?' she asked.

'No, thank you, we need to try and track Paddy down,' said Lizzie, and passed the sheet to Adam. 'Can you phone the details in to Sam, please?'

Foster took the sheet then looked up at the careworn woman by the sink. 'Are there any other people staying here that Paddy would count as friends?'

Poole filled the kettle and flicked the switch. She turned back towards them and leaned against the worktop. 'They don't really make friends, our residents, not like you and I would think of friends. They have a sort of instant camaraderie, a sharing of the same horror and shame that has brought them so low, but they'd steal the other guy's last fiver to buy a bottle of cider without even thinking about it. They just get pissed, or high, complain about the state of the world, crash here and then go out and do it all again. Until they die.' She added a large spoonful of coffee and a small spoonful of sugar to a mug that told the world she was its best mum. Stirring boiled water into the coffee, she gave a little laugh. 'Jaundiced, moi?' she said, and came back to the question. 'Paddy is new here, he's barely been around in the last few weeks, but he seems a nice character. Nicer than some.'

Lizzie gave an involuntary shudder, certainly nicer than one of the three she'd spoken to. 'What about Spike? The guy with the staved-in head? He was with Paddy and Dimp when we saw them in the town centre last week.' The thought of having to look at that empty eye socket, and put up with the inevitable verbal abuse, didn't fill her with delight, but he might know something.

'Hmm, Spike is hardly around either, and he doesn't stay because he won't part with that dog, even for one night, although we have a really good kennel out back. And he's always high on something. No, if I'm on evenings, I'll give him a meal but then he goes off on his own.' She studied the wall for a moment. 'You could try the raised-up chalet huts down by the beach – you know,' she said to blank faces, 'the ones set back from the road, near the life boat station? They're all shut up at this time of the year, and I think Spike has a little den behind one of them where it's dry and sheltered.'

Adam gave a muted cheer as they emerged from the hostel. 'Positive ID on vic two. We're on a roll.'

'Yeah. Let's see if we can find Paddy and round off a successful day, shall we?'

Adam parked on Marine Parade. 'Don't want to alert him by sticking it in the car park,' he said.

'And you don't want to part with a quid, either, do you?' said Lizzie, fastening her coat against the gale bellowing in from a grey and frothy sea. They walked through the car park to the far side where a short path led up to the chalets. 'Right, you nip along to the far end of the chalets and walk back towards me. If he's there, shout.'

Adam nodded, and trotted off towards the last chalet.

Lizzie stared at the sea, quelling her nervousness at the thought of the big dog and its foul owner, then walked cautiously behind the first chalet. There was little to see. The chalets formed a wide semicircle; each of them faced the sea. There were no back doors and no designated outdoor space at the rear, just a narrow path and a low wall holding back the hill behind. She stepped over an abandoned bin bag and crept along the rear wall. It was at that moment she heard a muffled yelp from Adam. She stood on her toes to listen better. What was the idiot up to?

She moved on, past the next chalet, but froze as she heard panting. Dog panting. Heading straight for her. Cursing, she whirled and set off at a run to get out of the narrow passage. She was too late, the whole weight of the animal crashed into her and knocked her to the floor. The dog didn't stop, and neither did Spike, who came stumbling out and trod on Lizzie's hand in his haste to escape.

Adam bowled up a second later and shot straight past her. He didn't even check to see if she was all right – just swerved to avoid her and ran on. 'I'll get him,' he yelled.

It was her anger at Adam that forced a winded Lizzie to climb to her feet. Her left hand hurt like hell and was bleeding. She suspected that something was broken in there. Hobbling towards safety she almost missed a sound to her right, further along the row. She pushed back against the chalet wall and tried to control her gasping so she could listen. There it was again: a rustle and the sound of someone trying to move stealthily in the opposite direction. She placed her damaged hand into her pocket and went after the noise. 'Paddy! Is that you?' she shouted. 'Paddy, don't run. You're not in trouble.'

She shuffled past a spiky shrub until she was halfway around the development of twenty chalets. There was a small space at the apex of the buildings, into which two sleeping bags had been squashed. She moved on. The noise got louder, he wasn't trying to be quiet anymore. If it was Paddy, he was now running. Lizzie drew in a tentative breath, decided she was okay, and ran, shouting, 'Please, we just want to help you.'

There was no more scuffling through undergrowth. He must have reached the path. Lizzie stood up, gathered herself together, and shot off round to the front of the chalets. Her breathing was still wheezy, but she figured she was a hell of a lot fitter than a middle-aged alkie, and she was bloody well going to catch him. She spotted him heading down the parade in a shuffling stagger towards the beach where the first victim had been found. 'Stop, Paddy,' she yelled. Where was he going to go?

Then she saw him swerve left to head along the prom. There was only the steep path up to Foxholes down there. She grinned, he'd never get up there before she did. She started after him and was completely stumped when Paddy abandoned his shuffle and shot down the prom like an Olympic athlete. 'What the …?' shouted Lizzie. 'Stop,' she yelled again, but Paddy was already running. Thinking fast, Lizzie rang Adam.

He answered, panting. 'Lost him,' he said.

'Good. Come back and get the car, drive it up Foxholes to the top of the cliff path. Paddy's legging it to the road. Quickly!'

Lizzie took a better breath and set off up the nearer path behind the chalets: she wanted to head him off before he got to the cliff top. She was fit, but she was a good minute behind Paddy. She calculated that her path was steeper, but quicker than his, and she might catch him. She just had to take the chance that he wouldn't double back. She put her injured hand back into her pocket and ran.

The path was muddy and steep in places, but she kept her head down, passing dog walkers and proper runners. What she wouldn't give for a pair of trainers. She could see the top of the rise in front of her and knew the footpath would meet the road somewhere near there. Her breath was coming in short gasps by the time she reached the summit, and she had to stop, bend over, and get her breath back.

It was from that position that she caught a glimpse of Paddy's head as he clambered up the last few steps from the beach. Lizzie didn't think she had enough energy to stop him. But then, he wouldn't be in great shape after that run, would he? She crouched behind a shrub and waited until he was almost on her. He was looking behind him, probably wondering why she wasn't following. Lizzie rose to a crouch and sprang to her feet, knocking Paddy off his feet.

He crashed onto his side and, to Lizzie's relief, lay there wheezing and grimacing up at her, winded.

'Paddy! Why did you run? We're trying to protect you. You're not in trouble you know.'

'Dear God, I thought I was fit.'

Lizzie tossed her head in the direction of a wooden bench a few feet away. 'Come on, let's sit down over there, catch our breath,' she said. 'No one's going to hurt you, Paddy.'

Paddy sank onto the bench wrapped his arms around his chest and began to mutter, 'You've done it now, my boyo, done it now, you really have. So much for staying out of sight.' He stopped talking and stared. Lizzie had taken her injured hand out of her pocket. 'Did Spike do that to you?'

'Spiked by Spike,' she said, and summoned a pained smile. 'I think he broke a bone. Look at the size of it already.' Her hand had swollen into a puffy, filthy ball.

'You'll be needing to get that cleaned,' Paddy said.

Foster drove up the hill towards them at speed. Lizzie waved him over and he parked across the grass verge. 'Everything okay?' he shouted.

'Fine, but Paddy doesn't think we need to look after him. Could you get a patrol car to take him in?'

While Foster rang for support, she turned to Paddy. 'You're not under arrest. We think you're possibly the next victim for the so-called Fire Goddess. That's why we were trying to find you. I need you to come into Exeter Road Station so we can find you a place of safety for a few days until we catch her. That's all.'

'She can't possibly want me as she has no idea who I am,' he said, 'and I have no idea who she is.' But the shift in his eyes away from hers told Lizzie a different story. Paddy knew exactly what she was talking about.

'How do you know that?' asked Lizzie. 'We don't think these murders are random, you know. We think homeless men are being targeted — two of your friends so far. That's why we want you in custody, in case you can tell us who she is. So, have a think while you're sitting there.'

Paddy stared at her. 'Moose, and now Dimp?'

She nodded. 'And I think you're next.' Her hand was throbbing. She wasn't sure what else she should tell Paddy. He wasn't a suspect but, if he was Tana's next victim, he may hold the key to the whole mess.

Paddy sagged on the bench until he finally caught his breath. He gave a rueful smile. 'Well, it looks as if you've got me, but you won't want me, Miss. You really won't. But perhaps it's better if I come in at this point. Things having come to a head, as it were.' He rolled both eyes towards the sky and squeezed them tight. 'Ring your boss and say Poseidon 1824 to him, there's a good girl.' He took his phone, an up-to-date Samsung Lizzie noted, out of an inside pocket and sent a short text.

Lizzie stared at him. 'What do you mean, Poseidon 1824? Who did you just text? And why don't you sound like Paddy any more?'

'Just do it, please. I can't tell you anything, but you really do need to do it. Then it will all become clear. Go on, now.'

Frustrated, she rang Dan's number. He was delighted to hear that they had found Paddy, but not as delighted that she was going to need a tetanus shot and cleaning up at the hospital. 'But,' she said, eager to change the subject, 'Paddy wants me to say Poseidon 1824 to you, sir. He says it will all become clear very soon.'

She avoided Paddy's gaze, walked across to look at the view out over the sea, and listened. 'Not a clue, sir. He's undergone a personality transplant. Weird, and just a bit suspicious. I've got a feeling he isn't who I think he is. Anyway, I'm sending him in with a patrol car. Oh, they're here now. See you later.'

Chapter Thirty-Two

Two hours later, with Lizzie's hand cleaned and bandaged and both their stomachs full of food, Lizzie and Adam arrived back at the station where they were barred from entering the Major Incident room by Bill Larcombe, who stood, impassive, at the door.

'What's up, Sarge?' asked Adam.

'Is something going on?' added Lizzie, taking in the dark suits that seemed to be sitting at all the computers.

'You two are being waited for, upstairs in Chief Superintendent Oliver's office,' Larcombe said. 'Hop to it, you wouldn't want to keep the Chief Constable waiting, would you?'

Lizzie turned on her heel, fighting nausea. What the hell had she done? Was this about Paddy? Who exactly was he?

Adam hurried to catch her up at the stairs. 'What's going on? Is this about "Poseidon"?'

Lizzie ignored his question, heart hammering. 'I've never been in Oliver's office, have you?'

A slow dawning altered Adam's face. 'Blimey, no I haven't. How much trouble are we in?'

The door to the Chief Superintendent's office was open, and they could hear voices and the chink of cups on saucers from inside. Stella, DCS Oliver's secretary, came out of the office and beckoned the two DCs through.

They stood just inside the doorway, waiting to be noticed. Lizzie felt intimidated and she could feel Adam's nervousness radiating through his suit. DCS Oliver was standing near a huge beech-coloured table, which was heaving with sandwiches, cakes, and jugs of tea and coffee. She was chatting to the Chief Constable and a man Lizzie had never seen before. DCI Hellier was sitting to one side, talking to a woman dressed in army uniform. There were two more men in army uniform standing near the table. They were eating sandwiches. Lizzie tugged on Adam's sleeve and walked further into the room. She caught Oliver's eye. 'Ma'am,' she said.

Julie Oliver excused herself, wiped her mouth and came towards them. 'Come in, DCs Singh and Foster. Do you need a drink or a sandwich? I'm afraid Stella has somewhat over-catered.'

Lizzie stared at her boss, trying to read her expression, but the woman was wound up tight. 'Thanks, ma'am,' she said, holding up her bandaged left hand, 'we ate at the hospital cafe.'

'Right,' said Oliver, raising her voice to include the others. 'Shall we get started?' She indicated two seats for Lizzie and Adam, closed the outer door and took her own usual chair at the top of the table. 'Following your call to DCI Hellier, there has been quite a lot of frantic activity here at the station. Could you explain to the Chief Constable and these visitors exactly what happened this morning?'

Lizzie swallowed. Who on earth were these people? They were staring at her like she was the murderer, and three of them were standing guard at the windows and the door. 'Yes, ma'am. Err ... we had reason to believe that there was a pattern in the murders committed by the woman known as the Fire Goddess and her followers. We know the first victim, Simon Ongar, was an ex-marine, and have reason to think the second victim was, too. At the homeless hostel, we were able to identify the second murder victim as David Hamworthy, a missing homeless man. I thought there might be a link with the man we know as Paddy, as he was the friend of Hamworthy and Ongar.'

She noticed Dan nodding encouragement at her from the other side of the table, which made her feel a bit better. 'Jane Poole, the hostel manager, said Paddy had not been back since the previous night. He was friends with a man called Spike, and

Jane Poole knew where Spike slept – behind the chalets on the promenade. So, we went to see if Spike knew where Paddy had gone to.'

'I disturbed Spike and his dog, first, ma'am,' interrupted Adam. 'The dog knocked DC Singh over, and Spike trod on her hand as he made his escape. I pursued Spike towards the town until DC Singh asked me to bring the car round to escort Paddy back to the station.'

Lizzie took back control. She was quite enjoying herself now. They were all listening so intently she could hardly feel her hand. 'At that point, I heard more movement behind the chalet huts and suspected it might be Paddy. It was. He ran off but I apprehended him at the top of the path. He then told me to call DCI Hellier and say "Poseidon 1824" to him, which I did, ma'am. He then wrote a text on his own phone.'

'Do you have anything further to add, DC Foster?' asked Oliver.

'No, ma'am.'

'Right, thank you, both of you. You may return to your duties, and I'll need those reports written up before you do anything else.' Oliver checked her watch. 'Let's say half an hour, and email them straight to me. Okay?'

They jumped to their feet. 'Yes, ma'am.'

'Off you pop then,' she said.

They were quiet on their way into the corridor and on to the empty stairwell.

'It's MI5, isn't it, Liz?'

'I think you might be right. Or MI6. What the hell have we got ourselves into now?' She jumped down the stairs two steps at a time.

'Will you spellcheck my report before it goes in?' asked Adam, leaping after her.

'Of course I will, if you get the first round in later,' she said. 'I need a drink already and it's only three o'clock.' She stopped dead, swinging on the banister with her good arm. 'Oh no, I'm going to have to type it up with one hand,' she cried, shaking the offending splint. They rounded the corner and saw that the door to the MI room was now open. The room was still full of strangers, and the rest of their team looked up, mute and goggle-eyed, as they loped through the door.

Chapter Thirty-Three

A stranger sat at Lizzie's desk. 'Hi,' Lizzie said, but got no response. She locked eyes with Sally Ellis across the room. Sally shrugged and went to make a drink.

'They don't talk,' said Sam Knowles, who was leaning against the windowsill with his arms locked across his chest while his computer was being interfered with. 'Even though I've got a murderer to find,' he said to the woman who was downloading information to a memory stick, 'apparently *this* is more important.'

The woman finished, pulled out the stick, stuck it in her pocket and said, 'We do talk, just not to you. Okay everyone, if you're ready, let's go.' The others removed their own sticks and got to their feet. 'Thank you for your cooperation,' she said as they left.

Bill Larcombe was the first to explode. 'What the bloody hell was all that about? They come in here, lording it about, telling us what to do in our own station, interfering in our investigation …'

'Bill.'

'Not so much as a by your leave, please may we halt the unimportant work of catching an effing serial killer while we take stuff off your computers …'

'Bill.'

'Oh, "we don't talk to the likes of you", she says, stuck up …' Larcombe spun round to face Dan standing in the doorway. He turned an unhealthy shade of scarlet.

'Just sit down, everyone, please,' Dan said, 'then I can explain what has happened. It may actually help our case, Sergeant Larcombe, you'll be pleased to know.' Dan cleared his throat. 'Here's a sentence I never thought I'd say in a Devon nick: that, was MI5. To be specific, they were from GCHQ. A Commander Alice McCarthy was in charge. The Army reps were from Forty Commando Unit. When Lizzie said "Poseidon 1824", and Paddy sent his text, it set up an alarm and they descended on us.'

'By helicopter, sir,' added Sam Knowles. 'And how did they pick up the phrase from a police issue phone, I'd like to know?'

'Quickest way here from Gloucestershire, Sam, and Paddy texted them, I think.

'Anyway, it turns out Paddy was an undercover agent in Ireland during the Troubles. And he's still working undercover now, but it turns out he should not have been in Exmouth at all. Not a coincidence, I'd say, and very interesting.'

'Jane Poole said he only came to the hostel occasionally, sir,' said Foster, 'he wasn't a regular. Perhaps he does another job in between times?'

'But why was he hanging around with the two victims at this precise moment? That's what I can't get my head around. Who is he?' Dan got up and wrote Paddy's name on the board. 'Suspect? Victim? Who knows?'

'So, has he gone back with them?' asked Lizzie.

'Yes, they've taken him with them. I doubt we'll see him again.'

'But, we needed to question him about the murders.'

Dan threw up his hands. 'Not our problem, now. Let it go, Lizzie. At least we know he's safe – if he was the next target.'

'That leaves a hell of a lot of questions unanswered, boss,' complained Larcombe. 'Like, what MI5 are doing in Exmouth pretending to be tramps, and what that has to do with our investigation, and wouldn't it be polite if they mentioned that they were working in the area?'

'No point fighting it, Bill, we need to get back on with hunting for our Fire Goddess, and hope we have thwarted her next mission. The spooks will never share what they're up to.'

He turned to Foster. 'I believe you got a positive ID on Dimp, or David Hamworthy?'

'We did, sir, and I sent it straight along to Sam for research purposes,' said Adam, 'but I doubt he's been able to do much with it in the circs.'

Quietly, Paula Tippett, the civilian researcher, held up her hand. 'Sir, while those people were raiding the computers in here, I did a bit of work in the main office to help Sam. Turns out David Hamworthy was a marine, if only briefly. At Lympstone.' She smiled at the moment of silence that greeted her contribution.

'Bloody hell's teeth, there is a link with the military, after all,' said Bill Larcombe. 'Maybe it's not about the homeless?' He jumped to his feet and altered the whiteboard to show Hamworthy as victim two, and linked him across to Simon Ongar, victim one. 'Maybe you're right, boss. Maybe Paddy was supposed to be victim three, but we've put him out of the picture.' He gave a nasty chuckle. 'Now what are you going to do, Fire Goddess? You can run, but you can't hide …'

'Well, I know what I'm going to do,' said Dan. 'Sergeant Ellis, get your coat. We're going to speak to Colonel Allport again. He must have a clue what's going on, and I think it's about time someone explained this mess. The rest of you: reports. Don't forget DCS Oliver has to get all that paperwork in to the powers that be by the end of play today, so get on with it.' He nodded them back to work.

In the quietly busy office, Lizzie looked over the top of her computer at Adam. 'Is that it? Paddy says a code word, they raid us, and then it's all over?' She screwed up her nose. 'Nah, doesn't seem right to me. They came in a helicopter. There must be more to this—'

Bill Larcombe huffed. 'Bloody shut up, DC Singh, I'm worried enough already. Bet they've left bugs all over the place.'

At that, there was an uncomfortable silence, until Sam Knowles interrupted Larcombe's paranoia. 'We're the police, Sarge, everything we do is monitored by somebody.'

Larcombe raised an eyebrow. 'You are wise, Grasshopper. Long as they don't take my pension away, why should I worry? Right, back to it. Let's get reports written and everything updated by 4pm. And no whingeing, Lizzie, type it with one hand.'

Chapter Thirty-Four

'Are we not going to ring ahead?' asked Sally as she strapped herself into Dan's Audi.

'Not this time. He must have known who Paddy and Dimp were if he knew about Ongar. Must have. All three were mates and I bet they all hung around Lympstone, not just Ongar. Now why would they do that? No, I think he's been withholding information, and why would he do that? Have you got the photo of Hamworthy?'

Sally pulled it from her bag and studied it. 'He was only in his thirties,' she said. 'What do they do to them in that place?'

'Odd that three of them, all friends, or at least companions, should end up involved in this mess. All a bit too much of a coincidence, if you ask me.'

Sally stared at him. 'Do you think Allport might be involved? How?'

'No,' he said, slowly, 'I don't see how he could be, but he knows more than he's telling us. The CCTV and video footage shows nobody fitting his description. Although we still have no actual evidence about who the pseudonyms belong to yet, so I won't rule Allport out of the gang completely. I just can't see that he has a motive.' He shook his head. 'There's just something …'

'A bit irritating about his smug little "sticking by the rules" world?'

Dan laughed. 'Something like that. Could you get Sam doing a bit of research into his background for me?'

Sally texted, then laughed a minute later. 'Sam says Bill is getting paranoid about being bugged.'

'Judging by what DCS Oliver and the man in a suit were talking about earlier, he's got a point,' said Dan, pulling out into the traffic.

They had to wait for almost twenty minutes at the gate, even though it was the same guard they had seen on their previous visit only a few days before. Dan had a moment of longing to be one of those cops who barged down the doors of suspects and insisted on being seen immediately. He wasn't at all sure they wouldn't just shoot him if he tried that here.

He received a text from his sister saying she had an interview for a part-time job at a local charity shop. Minimum wage and only three days a week. She sounded excited and he was pleased for her. It had been quiet on the sister front since she had moved into the flat, and he'd only been back the once to check on her. Maybe miracles do happen, he thought, cheered by the news.

Colonel Allport didn't stand to shake their hands this time. He stayed behind a desk piled high with documents. His face was creased with worry. 'Keep it short, Detective Chief Inspector,' he muttered, 'as you can see, I'm busy.'

'Happy to comply, sir,' Dan replied, unconsciously falling into a speech pattern he would have used in a court room. 'Sergeant Ellis will show you a photograph of the latest murder victim, although I imagine you have seen his photo on the news already?' He watched Allport's face, but there wasn't a flicker of recognition.

'No idea who that is.'

'I think you do, sir,' said Dan. 'Perhaps you should look more closely. He was identified earlier as David Hamworthy, late of Lympstone barracks.'

'Hamworthy? Yes, I do remember him, obnoxious character. He didn't last long.' He took a closer look. 'Is this what he looks like now? I'd never have recognised him. Right, what do you want to know?' He put down his pen and gave them his attention.

'Think about it, sir,' said Dan.

'Are you trying to suggest that these deaths are linked with this facility? Two homeless men are killed and, because they happen to be ex-marines, the murders are linked to us? Don't be bloody ridiculous.'

Sally picked up the photo and stared at it. 'Hamworthy was only in his late thirties, sir, yet he was homeless and a hopeless alcoholic. I'm sure he didn't come in here like that, did he?'

'I don't like that inference, Sergeant.'

'And yet, the evidence is clear, sir. He entered as a keen recruit, and had such a bad time you threw him out, and now he's dead. We're just pursuing the line of investigation that points us to a link between the two dead men.'

'I know this is difficult, Colonel,' said Dan, 'but there may be a reason why ex-marines are being targeted.'

Allport steepled his hands in front of his face and closed his eyes. 'Hamworthy: potential was good, but his arrogant demeanour and unwillingness to accept military discipline meant that he was discharged after, I think, two terms on active duty.'

'Thank you. Did he ever serve in Northern Ireland in any capacity?' asked Dan. 'Only his and Ongar's service may link us to the man we think may be the potential third victim.'

'Who? Which third man?'

'We only know the man as Paddy. Northern Irish? Mean anything to you?'

Allport looked at Dan, 'I don't know anybody called Paddy.'

'But you do have Northern Irish recruits, don't you, sir?' asked Dan.

'Yes, of course, and to answer your question, I cannot tell you if either of those two men served in Northern Ireland. You would need permission from a very high authority indeed for me to reveal anything about our activities there.'

'Not even if I said "Poseidon 1824" to you?'

And there it was. Allport's eyes shifted away and off to the left. He's preparing a lie, thought Dan.

'Like the King of the Sea?' Allport laughed, glancing at his phone. 'No idea what you're talking about. Sorry I can't help.' He stood up, walked around them and opened his office door. In the outer room, a junior officer leapt to her feet. 'See them out,' he said, and slammed the door.

Sally put the photo back in her bag, ignoring the hovering woman. Dan pretended to check through his notebook. Sure enough, as soon as the Colonel got back to his desk he picked up his phone, but they couldn't hear what he was saying.

'We're in trouble now, boss,' muttered Sally as they hurried back to the car.

'Don't care. I knew it, Sal. It all links up. Allport does know Paddy.' He banged his hands on the roof of the car. 'It's so frustrating. I'm going to get it in the neck now for saying that word, even though it's a legitimate part of our investigation.'

He looked at the office window, where Allport stared back at them. 'You know, we may never get to the bottom of this case, Sal. If it's secret, it's secret.'

'Well, if that turns out to be the case, it's because of national security I suppose. I don't think they're being deliberately difficult.'

He stared at her in disbelief. 'You don't?' He unlocked the doors and slid inside, sitting quietly while she clambered in. 'Maybe not, and I do understand that we can't be told everything, but it doesn't help that none of the statutory agencies ever actually talk to each other, does it? We're trying to catch a murderer, not expose state secrets. And we needed Paddy.'

He was silent on the way back to the station. How did the two link up – the Fire Goddess and the marines? And how could he find out when they were all trying to block him? The marines, the students – even Professor Patel – were all lying to him. Where was this Tana, and was she ready to strike again, or could they relax now Paddy was safely out of the picture?

Chapter Thirty-Five

Tana waited until Kegan had chainsawed the young tree into short logs then helped him pile it all into the trailer that was bolted to the back of the Land Rover. She'd never had to do the hard work before, but it was all different since they had messed up the thing with Jay. The last sacrifice, the most important one, had to happen right, and she couldn't trust anyone else. Not with the police sniffing round. That old tosser Patel was bound to drop her in it. They had to move fast. She hugged a rough-hewn log to her chest and carried it over to the Land Rover. 'Are we nearly there?' she asked Kegan, who was carrying two logs at a time and sweating in the cool afternoon air.

He grunted. 'No, we'll need to collect more wood tomorrow as well to have enough. Should have asked someone to help.' He avoided her eyes and went back for more wood.

Tana pushed hair out of her eyes with her arm. Drizzle had stuck it to her forehead. She had to disappear, and Kegan wasn't bright enough to avoid the police. In fact, with his tattoos and muscles, he attracted attention; she had to go it alone and leave him to whatever fate decreed. She touched her newly dyed hair. Blonde suited her far more than she had thought it would. Out had gone the Goth make-up, and slowly, in came a persona she called secretary girl. As far away from Tana as she could get without having surgery. That would put the police off her trail for a while, especially as it made her look a lot more like the poor, dead Kathy Kelly on her passport.

She sat down on the tailgate and took a breather. On the outside, she hoped she looked her usual cool self. Inside, she had moths churning her guts. She had waited so long for this.

176

To revenge her darling mother and father and her beloved baby brother. To get to watch him burn. The last one. It was all she had wanted since she'd been eight years old. And afterwards, she would try to get away, but she didn't really care what happened to her. She'd been in a prison of sorts all her life. A shiver ran over her scars, rippling along her back and legs, down her arms to her fingers. It was nothing to do with the weather.

Kegan watched Tana through half-closed eyes as he finished loading the kindling. He pulled the tarpaulin tight over the load and climbed with relief into the driver's seat. She was pacing like a lioness, he thought; her blonde hair wild around her face, eyes no longer framed in kohl. It was cold in the woods, and wet, but she barely paid any notice to the weather – even when she wasn't consumed with planning her next murder.

She stopped to answer her phone and his heart constricted. Who did she talk to on her own all the time? Who rang her? Who else knew about what they were doing? Everyone was a liability as far as he could tell.

His hands hurt from shifting branches and twigs and cutting up old planks and logs. He worried about how much they had to do on their own to complete the next sacrifice. They couldn't set up this fire until the actual day. Too many nosy old gits around, and the tide had to be low enough to allow him to drive along the sand. At least with a trailer he could dump it all in one go, and get the fire lit while Tana brought the sacrifice. On her own. That was a worry as well. How the hell would she manage that?

He shifted in the car seat. The failed attempt to kill Jay had rattled her. Both of them, really. Kegan couldn't believe he'd just gone along with it. It was different seeing off tramps – they were no-hopers with no future – but a member of their own clan? That was bad. It felt wrong. He could see she had gone beyond caring though. It was this third killing that mattered to her, and she knew they must be close to being caught if the police had the girls in custody. If Jay went to the police, or was caught, and told them all he knew, all the planning in the world couldn't save him. Kegan had a record – from back when he was a stupid seventeen-year-old. A careless fingerprint would be enough for them to name him, and all three of the students could describe him. Kegan angled the rear-view mirror so he could see his face, and wondered what he could do to disguise his features.

The door rattled as Tana climbed back inside the Land Rover and shook out her mane. 'We have to move fast,' she said, 'there's very little time.' She reached across and took his hand in hers. 'Kegan, this next one is the most important. All the others have been practice for this one. I have to do this right. You get that, don't you?'

Kegan nodded. He'd worked that out for himself. 'What do you want me to do?'

She stared through the runnels of rain on the windscreen and chewed on a fingernail. 'I want to do the sacrifice on Saturday night. We must set the fire in the afternoon. The site is good and you can drive over the sand.' She stared out at the rain. 'It will be different this time. He has a girlfriend, and I think we'll need to get him in the pub they go to on Saturday nights.'

'A girlfriend? You never told me about this, Tana. I'm not killing a perfectly innocent woman.'

'Calm down. I'm not saying we should kill her, just get her away from the action.'

Kegan's heart stopped pounding quite so hard. This was getting ridiculous. All this stuff was making it harder than the last two, and they had no help. Think. 'Right. We could drug him. Put something in his drink at the bar. That should be easy enough. He won't recognise you, will he? But what do we do about her?'

'You know, we should drug them both, just to be sure.'

'How are we going to do that? Get two unconscious bodies out of a pub?'

'Leave that to me, I have an idea. Let's go back to your flat and hide the trailer.'

Kegan growled. 'You have an idea. But you're not going to share it with me, are you? I want this to be over, Tana. Do you hear me?' She stared out of the window. Frustrated, Kegan started the engine and they drove slowly down the back roads towards his Exmouth flat. 'Who was it on the phone?'

Tana threw him a glance and shrugged. 'You may as well know, now: my grandfather. We've planned this together, since I was a child. We're picking him up at his hotel and taking him down to Lympstone.'

'What? Why the hell would we do that? And why have you never mentioned him before?' He pulled over into a layby and stared at her. 'You haven't really told me anything about this, have you? All this planning you've done with your grandfather, all the secrecy. What's it all about, Tana? What are we doing this for?'

'It will all become clear very soon, Kegan,' she said. 'It's better for you if you know as little as possible. There are some pretty big fish in the pond here who would like to know more about my grandfather. Let's just leave it at that. What you need to know is that this is the most important sacrifice. What it's all been for – all this crap we've been spouting.'

She leaned across and took his hand. 'I may have to disappear for a while afterwards,' she said. 'Just until it all cools down a bit.'

'You? What about us? I thought we were going together?' Kegan tapped his breast pocket. 'Passport, euros, got the lot, and I'm ready to split.'

'Great, but I think we should travel separately for a while, just to put them off the scent, you know?'

Kegan nodded as his hands twisted on the wheel. 'Oh, I know. I totally get it now.' She was going to dump him after the last murder. He fought down the treacherous worm that said: 'and she'll let you take the blame'. After all he'd done, all he'd given up for her, all he'd risked. Anger burst in his head. 'I've walked out of my job, helped you with your "mission", been involved in all of this …' he struggled for a word, 'all of this nightmare, and you're dumping me?' He slammed both palms against the steering wheel. 'I don't believe you, Tana!'

Tana twisted in her seat to face him, blue eyes boring deep into him. 'I'm not dumping you, you eejit. I'm saving you. If Jay talks, if any of them talk, who are they going to give away? Not you, darlin'. No, they'll be after me, and I want to keep you safe. So, you run over to Spain for a few months and then I'll come and find you. You can get a cheap phone and we can keep in touch. Trust me,' she said, squeezing his large hand between both of hers. 'It will be all right, I promise. We just have to do this last one.'

He pulled his hand free. 'I'm not an idiot, you know. I know that all this cult stuff has been about this last one. You have to get him, don't you?' He waited for her slight nod. 'Then tell me about him. Why this guy? Why now? What did he do to you, Tana?'

She turned away from him. 'Better for you not to go there,' she said. 'I bear the scars for us all. Why now? Because we finally found them, all three of them together, after years of searching. But believe me, Kegan, believe me, the death of this one really will bring about the cleansing.' She gave a shrug of one bony shoulder. 'At least for me.'

'I had no idea you were going to come over,' said Tana, clinging to her grandfather's arm. 'It's great to see you, but did you not trust me to do the job?'

Brendan Moore patted the hand that had snaked its way under his arm. 'No need to worry yourself on that part, darlin', I just thought you might need a bit of support for the last leg.'

She swung round to face him, forcing a dog walker to break her stride and swerve round them on the path. 'You mean you want in, don't you?' She let her gaze slide from her grandfather's face, towards Kegan – who was leaning angrily against the Land Rover bonnet, staring after them as they walked down towards the estuary.

Moore scratched the side of his nose and gave a small chuckle. 'You have no idea how long I have waited to finish this. How much I … we have lost because of this man.' He allowed himself a quick glance at the wire fence with rolls of barbed wire on its top, and dropped his head. 'Though how the hell we get to him, I don't know.'

Tana laughed. 'No need to hide yourself away. I've walked past here every day for weeks, and the only cameras seem to be on the gates and down the sides. I know how to get him out anyway, and I could use your help – seeing as I've a little problem: two of the followers seem to be in custody, along with the professor.'

'Aye? That's unfortunate. What happened there?'

'They got to us through the professor, I think. Pathetic eejit. Then we made a mistake, a big one.' Unconsciously, she picked at a scar on her arm, rubbing and scratching through the sleeve of her hoody. 'I knew Jay Vine was going to run, and that he would talk. Knew it after the second sacrifice. Kegan and I, we went to his room. We tried to make it look like suicide, but we didn't give him enough, or someone found him too soon. Anyway, he got away. Said on the news the police are holding three people, but none of them have been named yet. Jay texted one of the girls, so he *could* still be on the run, but I'm not hopeful. I'm sorry, granddaddy, I let you down.'

'It's always the same when you bring unknowns into a professional outfit, but it can't be helped now.' Moore stood, looked up at the blank windows of Lympstone Commando training base, and sighed deeply. 'And when will the fire be ready for him?'

'Two days from now, on Saturday night. We'll have to set the fire on Saturday afternoon because of the tides.'

'But worth the effort. Worth the effort to revenge our family, my darlin'.'

Tana nodded seriously. He was the only person who could still make her feel like a child. Comforted by his presence, but slightly scared of his temper, she wanted to please him. It seemed sad that she had only found out he existed after the death of her parents and little brother, but, since then, he had been a constant in her life and that of her adoptive family. And he had helped her to understand that to let the people who had killed her family just walk away, just go back to England, with nothing but a pat on the back, was not acceptable. So, they had waited and planned, and searched and planned some more – for years – until she was ready for the task and they had found a way in. And, watching the first two lieutenants burn had felt good, liberating. She wanted to look this last one in the eye before he died. Wanted to make sure he knew who she was, and that he understood why he had to die, like her family had died, in the cleansing fire.

'Come on,' said Moore, 'walk me back up the path and drop me at the hotel. Let's eat together tonight. Lord, but you're awful thin. I sent you money, what did you spend it on? Not grub, that's for sure. Skinny wee thing. I like the blonde hair though, suits you better than that awful red.'

Tana smiled. He was the only one who could talk to her like this and get away with it. Brendan cared about her, and it was good to know she had one person in the world who cared as much about her mission as she did.

'What about this boy, Kegan, you call him? Do you trust him?'

'I do,' she said, 'he loves me.'

'But you've told him he has to go away on his own? That we can't take him with us?'

'I've told him. Why do you think he's looking daggers at you? He thinks you're some sort of rival.'

Moore snorted. 'Let him think that, if he likes, it'll make the end of all this a little easier for him.'

They arrived back at the Land Rover and Tana seated her grandfather in the passenger seat. Kegan, sulking, threw himself into the driver's seat and swung out into the traffic. This was going to be a bit awkward, she knew, but it was only for two more days. Her pulse quickened. Please let this work, she prayed. We only have the one chance.

Chapter Thirty-Six

Early on Thursday morning, Jay Vine huddled in the lee of a white-painted metal bulkhead. The ferry bucked and thumped in the rough seas, sending spray crashing over him every few minutes. He didn't care; it was better up here than in the seating areas with the smell of puke and chips and screaming kids. He pulled his hood closer around his newly-shaved head. Could he call Scarlett? Make sure she was okay? It wasn't about her, he admitted, he was just desperate to talk to someone he knew. He stared at the screen. This was hard. What if the fuzz were waiting for him in Jersey?

He dropped the phone back into his pocket and wrapped his hand around the wad of notes. Eight hundred pounds should see him right for a while until he got a job. It wasn't as if he was out on the streets, right? At least he was away from Tana, the mad witch. Aching from sitting in the same position for so long, Jay hoisted himself up and turned to let the full force of the wind crash against his face. Other hardy passengers clung on to the rails and ignored the constant blaring of security alarms from the vehicles swaying in the hold. He could just see the outline of Jersey in the distance.

Jay knew he was up against it as soon as he joined the foot passengers in the queue to show passports. The boy staring unsmiling at him from the back page of his passport looked nothing like Jay did now. He had blond hair for a start, and the passport was eight years old. It didn't look a lot like him any more, but *he* didn't look a lot like himself either. What on earth had he been thinking, shaving his hair off in this weather? He pulled the hood further down over his freezing head. Maybe he should make a run for it, but as he'd never been to Jersey he had no idea where that would get him. Or maybe, because he was exhausted and close to collapse, he could just give himself up? He tapped the passport against his teeth and weighed up how long it would take him to get to the gate and the notion of freedom beyond, but he didn't stir as the queue shuffled along. It was beyond him to make a move.

In the end, the decision was made by a sharp-eyed border officer who recognised him from the faxed copy of the photo his mother had given Hellier. The firm grasp on Jay's arm came as a huge relief and he didn't struggle. No more running. No more anything for a long time, he thought, as they marched him into an office nearby.

The call from Jersey police was put straight through to Dan in his office at just after 11am. He held the phone to his chest. Could he justify the expenditure to fly the lad back? It would be a hell of a lot quicker than waiting for a ferry. 'Stuff it,' he said to the sergeant in Jersey's main police station. 'Book two tickets on the next plane into Exeter, one return for an escort, and we'll arrange to pick him up from the airport.' He grimaced when the email to confirm the booking came through, and he hoped this young man would prove to be worth the expense.

Dan surveyed his notes. He felt the need to do something decisive, but, so far, they had several suspects, none of whom had given him a clue about the real identity of Tana. Surely someone had seen her out and about? Knew where she lived? He had the identities of three of the suspects, and could work out their pseudonyms, but who was this unidentified Kegan bloke, and was he hiding Tana somewhere nearby?

He clicked on the Fire Goddess social media links for the third time that morning. Nothing new, thank God. Still full of hyped-up excitable nonsense, but he had the cyber team working to ID anybody they could from the comments that kept coming. He was preparing to do another press briefing, and dreading the point where he would have to admit they had no idea if there would be another murder, or who might have organised the first two.

Sally Ellis tapped on his door. 'Come in, Sal. Nick of time – I was about to slit my wrists.'

'You know, boss,' she said, folding her arms, 'you have to stop watching all those American crime series where they solve murders in an hour. We're less than two weeks into this case, we have suspects coming out of our ears, and the chance of several prosecutions for aiding and abetting. It's only a matter of time before we get the breakthrough.'

Dan regarded her from the desk. 'You're in a better mood,' he said. 'Coming in here and cheering me up.'

'Lost weight,' she said, seating herself opposite him, 'all is good in my world. Well, apart from chickenpox in the Ellis household, but that comes with the parent territory.'

'I haven't had chickenpox,' he said, 'stay back, pestilent one.'

'Too late now. If you're getting it, you're getting it,' she said, with a sly grin.

Dan brushed off an immediate panic about the state of his sperm count if he caught the virus, and updated Sally on the capture of Jay Vine.

'See?' she said. 'Another one bites the dust. Now, if we can identify Jay as Kegan, we'd have the gang.' She paused. 'No, we wouldn't, would we? There's the other unidentified male. We need him, too.'

'One of them must know where Tana is. She can't be invisible, can she? One of them must have a clue.'

'Or be willing to tell us, that's the crucial point. Amber has told us what she knows, I'm sure. Scarlett? She may know more. I'd like to sit in on the Jay Vine interrogation with you.'

Dan nodded. 'Okay. To change the subject, have you met with the awful Lisa Middleton again?'

'I have. I am here to serve. You may find a change in the direction of her articles from now on. Mind you, I did have to sell my soul. It physically hurts to be nice to that woman. In fact, now we're best mates, I'll give her a quick ring and tell her to be at the back door when Vine arrives, that'll go down well in the evening paper.'

'Thanks for taking this on, Sally, I appreciate it.'

Sally raised her eyebrows. 'Do you? How much? Are you willing to put the frighteners on young Adam regarding cakes?'

Dan laughed. 'No, I'm bloody not. Sort it yourself!'

As with the other members of the gang, Jay Vine was brought into the interview room under caution. Dan reckoned on forty minutes questioning before offering a solicitor. Any longer and it could look like avoidance. He didn't mind, Amber had given them enough to hold Vine. Dan leaned against the wall outside the room, watching through the window as Bill Larcombe handed the boy a drink and a sandwich. Apparently, the plane journey, only thirty-five minutes long, hadn't included refreshments. He supposed that would save the department some cash. He waited until Bill and Ben had set up the communications room and were talking into his ear.

Dan checked his watch, it was after 3pm and he wanted a briefing with the team before he held the news conference. He waited for Sally, watching the boy eat, and wondered how long it would take Linda Vine and her husband to arrive from Bodmin. They were so relieved when he'd rung them, he hadn't the heart to remind them their youngest son was wanted for murder.

Jay finished his sandwich and crumpled the wrapper. Then he straightened it out and smoothed it flat, folding and refolding until it became a small parcel. He drained the last of his tea in the paper cup and crumpled the parcel into it. Then he gave a huge sigh and sat quietly with his hands on the table.

Dan caught Sally's eye as she arrived, and pointed at the window. She looked in and grinned. 'Pussycat, this one,' she said, and opened the door.

Dan signalled to Larcombe to start the tapes, and joined Sally who introduced them for the record. 'Jay, nice to meet you at last,' he said. 'You certainly got one over on me, nipping out through the bedroom window while I was talking to your mum. Anyway, let's talk about these murders down at the beach. What would you like to tell us?'

Jay Vine looked from one officer to the other then back at the table. 'I …'

'Best if you just tell it to us straight, Jay,' said Sally. 'We have Scarlett and Amber in custody, as well as your professor, so there's not much point in lying to us, because we can cross-check everything you say, can't we?'

'And,' added Dan, 'you're clearly an intelligent, resourceful young man who got as far as Jersey without being caught. So, use that intelligence now. If you help us, we will do the very best we can to get the court to see that you have been cooperative …'

'You can stop all the crap, now,' muttered Jay. 'I wanted to be caught, okay? I've been almost killed because of all this shit. I ran because of her, not you. She'll kill me properly if she finds out I'm alive, so go on, ask what you like. I'm staying in here where I'm safe.'

'Tana made an attempt on your life? It wasn't a suicide bid?'

Jay snorted. 'She'd obviously never done it before – didn't give me enough stuff, or wait until I was properly unconscious. Then she could have smothered me. Job done.'

Dan shrugged. It was as good a place as any to start. 'Right, Tana came to your room and somehow persuaded you to take paracetamol and whisky?'

'You are going to take this into account when you charge me, aren't you? That I cooperated and told you all I know?'

Sally smiled at him. 'Of course we are, love. We appreciate Tana has treated you badly. You'd like to see her face justice, wouldn't you?'

'Yeah, I would, but, no offence, she's thought all this through. She's untraceable, just like she told us she would be. It was me who realised she would just drop the rest of us in it once she had what she wanted from us. That's why they came after me. She thought I'd tell you. And she was right, I would have.'

'You said "they" came after you. Who else was there, Jay?'

'She had Kegan with her. He's always with her. He's under her spell all right. He hit me and held me down while she poured it all down my throat.'

Sally interrupted. 'So you're not Kegan, Jay?'

'No, I was Idris. I only know Scarlett and Amber's names because they're my friends. Kegan's not at Exeter uni, he's a bodybuilder type. Works at some sort of gym, I think. No idea what he's really called.' He banged a fist half-heartedly on the table. 'She got that right, didn't she? She knew all of us, but we knew nothing about her.' He glanced at the two detectives. 'I told you, she's thought it all through.'

Dan nodded at the one-way glass, hoping that one sergeant would start the checking process for Kegan. It was better than nothing. He stifled a growing wriggle of excitement in his chest. Maybe now they would get somewhere. 'What about an address for him?'

Jay thought. 'Well, we used to meet at Tana's flat. She has a studio flat in Pennsylvania, quite near uni. I don't know the actual street address though.'

Sally leaned towards him. 'Could you point it out on a map?'

'Yeah,' he said, and looked up at her.

'Good lad.' Sally opened her phone and clicked on Google maps.

Dan smiled at Jay. 'You're doing great, Jay. This will look a lot better for you in court.'

'I'm still going down though, aren't I?'

Dan shrugged. 'We don't prosecute the cases, but yes, I think we'll have enough evidence to say that you knew what you were doing, but we need to let the jury decide on the strength of your belief in what Tana was peddling.' He stopped talking. What was he doing, prattling on and giving the kid clues? That's what the lawyers were paid for. He couldn't help but feel a bit sorry for the three of them though. Bravado apart, their lives were ruined.

Sally stood beside Jay, showed him the map, and pointed at the main Pennsylvania Road. 'Go on, Jay, show us.'

Jay followed the line of the road and stopped at a small, square block of flats. 'There,' he said. 'Number 18.'

'Thank you,' said Dan. 'Back soon,' and he took Sally outside. 'A lead, a genuine, honest to God lead, Sal!' He grabbed her by both elbows and swung her in a circle.

'Steady on, boss,' she said. 'Shall we get a team out there?'

He let her go. 'Let's send Lizzie and Adam with a couple of uniforms to check it out first. I'll let Oliver know, just in case we need armed response. I doubt Tana will be sitting there waiting to give herself up.' He dashed off down the corridor.

Sally popped her head round the communications room door to see Bennett sitting alone. 'Where's the other flowerpot?'

'Soon as we got a possible job for Kegan, he was off like a hare, chasing it up. I think we've hit gold here, Sal.'

'Maybe, but we haven't got enough out of him to charge him yet, the girls will need releasing or charging by tonight, and the boss has run off all excited. I'd like to get a bit more before we charge him on one count and then find another three charges we could have made. Just think it's a bit previous to break out the champagne. This Tana has avoided us so far, I don't think we should count our chickens, that's all.'

Bennett made a sad cluck and waggled his elbows, earning him a thump. 'Accessories to murder, I reckon,' he said.

'At least. Or, if the prosecution is so-minded, as murderers under Joint Enterprise.'

'Blimey. That's a tough one.'

'But they knew what they were doing, didn't they? There was intent to kill. They were all, as far as we can tell, present at both murders, no one appears to have been coerced. It's not looking like accessory to me.'

'Bloody shame for those kids: lives wrecked, for what?'

'Kicks, drugs? Who knows? Young, but old enough to know what they were doing.'

Bennett shifted in his chair. 'Boss is on his way back, you'd better get back in there.'

'So, Jay, do you need anything? Drink, snack? Or are you okay to continue for a while longer?'

Jay Vine shrugged. 'Nowhere to be, nothing to do.'

Dan moved closer and leaned across the table. 'Why, Jay? Why did a clever bloke like you end up going along with all this? Could you not see where it might all end up?'

'I … I can't explain it really. Scarlett, she's my girlfriend. Well, she was, and she got involved with Tana first, although we knew her as Kathy Kelly. It was a bit of fun, part of the course. We helped design the website, made up the rituals and the fire make-up that we wore. It was totally secret. Exciting, I guess, to see what we could achieve on social media. You wouldn't believe how many followers we picked up in the first couple of weeks.'

'I would, there were hundreds of thousands following her when we shut the sites down. So, when did you realise that you were going to be setting an actual man on fire? That it wasn't just "a bit of fun"?'

Jay shook his head slowly. 'At the first bonfire. We were sitting around, I was playing a few tunes. I never thought for a minute that Kegan would get an actual sacrifice. Then, along he comes with this old guy, rolling drunk. Kegan bashes him over the head …' He took a gulp of air.

'Go on, you're doing really well,' said Sally.

'I … I helped him put the guy on the fire. I didn't want to, but I did; so did Scarlett and Amber, we all helped,' he said, his eyes full of tears, 'only Tana didn't help. She didn't do anything except take the stupid pictures and video for the website.' Tears spilled over onto his jumper.

'What about the second murder? Same deal?'

'No, it was worse, much worse. He was younger and fitter, and I don't think Kegan hit him hard enough. He woke up in the fire, and the screams … I can't get the screams out of my head.'

'Okay, Jay. I think we should get you a solicitor now, just to make sure we are doing everything by the book. You've been absolutely brilliant. Thank you. We'll leave you here for a short while, then, when the solicitor arrives, you can write out a full statement for us.' He nodded at the PC on duty and took Sally outside.

'I'm off up to see Oliver. Let his parents in as soon as they arrive, and see if the duty solicitor is on the way. Just want to agree the charges for all three of them.' Dan absently patted Sally on the shoulder and shot off down the corridor.

Ben Bennett came out of the communications room with two thumbs up. 'Back in to see the young ladies with all this extra information, I expect?' he asked Sally.

'Absolutely. Looks like the joint enterprise charge was engineered by this Tana woman. Make sure they were all involved, then no one would walk away unscathed, even if they wanted to.'

'It's one way to guarantee loyalty, I suppose.'

'It's bloody clever.'

'Psychopaths often are,' said Bennett, and whistled his way back to the office.

Chapter Thirty-Seven

Dan sat in a chair opposite the two whiteboards, hands wrapped around his fifth coffee of the day. He could see the words and stare at the pictures, but he couldn't read the story. On one hand, he had a naive professor and a bunch of students, charged and awaiting a visit to the magistrates' court, and on the other? Nothing. There was a connection with MI5, and, he assumed, a Northern Irish slash IRA slant to the story. But why burnings? And why this girl, who was apparently working with this guy, Kegan? What would make her want to commit such terrible crimes against men who could hardly fight back? And, if it was about the Troubles, she would have been a young child when all that was happening. How could that be it? 'Bill,' he yelled across the MI room. 'Anything on Kegan?'

'No, boss. Narrowed down the gyms. I've got Jay and Amber doing photofit with Lizzie, hoping that might give us a likeness we can take round with us. Soon as I've got that, we'll get out there.'

Dan grunted, took another slurp of coffee, realised it was cold, and dumped it on the table behind him. He slumped down and rested his head on his hands and his elbows on his knees. Think, man. The room was quiet behind him, everybody engaged in writing up reports from the day. *No, no, no, no.* 'I've forgotten to ask a really important question,' he said, head coming up. 'I forgot to ask if they know if there's going to be a third murder. Idiot! Sack me now, someone.'

He ran from the room and clattered down the stairs to the holding cells. Lizzie sat with Jay Vine as he tried to settle on a likeness of Kegan from the thousands of types on the database. He was nodding at Lizzie as Dan asked to be let in.

'Jay, what do you know about the third murder? Is it still on?'

Jay stared at him. 'Why wouldn't it be?'

'Never mind. When will it be? Where?' He rocked backwards onto his heels, aware that he sounded a bit wild. 'Come on, think, what did she say?'

Jay thought, his eyes wide. 'She brought it forward. It was supposed to be at the end of the month, but it's on Saturday.'

'Saturday? This coming Saturday?'

'Yeah, that's what she said. I'm sorry, I should have said something. I just …'

'Where?'

'I don't know. We never knew until we had to build the fire, but it will be at a beach, somewhere local.'

Dan paced, one step out, one step back. There was no room to do more in the tiny cell. 'Local. One she has already used?'

'Don't know. Probably not, in case of cops hanging about. There are plenty more.'

'Right. Right, thanks,' said Dan, and disappeared as quickly as he had come.

'That was a bit of a whirlwind,' said Lizzie as the door closed on the retreating figure. All her instincts were sending her running up the stairs after her boss, but she had to do this first. She reluctantly turned back to her photofit. 'So, are you sure this is as close as you can get to a likeness?'

Jay nodded. 'Big, muscular bloke, shaven head, bushy beard.'

Lizzie brought up the picture that Amber had settled on, they were similar enough for her to feel happy that it would do as an aide-memoire in a gym-to-gym search. 'Okay, we're getting somewhere,' she said, 'thanks. Right, let's have another look at the photofit for Tana. Happy with this one?'

He was. But Lizzie thought it looked markedly different from Amber's picture, and she hadn't been in to see Scarlett or the professor yet. Tana could change her hair colour and clothes and look remarkably different. Jay saw her as incredible skinny, with pointed features like a witch. Amber, who was plump, saw Tana as slim and beautiful. That's what made facial ID hard, and witnesses unreliable. Everything was filtered through their experiences.

'You know, she has to choose a beach where there is easy access for the Land Rover,' said Jay.

Lizzie stared at him. 'Land Rover?'

'That's how we get the wood and brush to the site, then we unload it and build the fire.'

'Do you know the type of Land Rover? Or the registration number?'

Jay shook his head. 'Not really. Old red type. Like a bus, with seats along the sides, quite big.'

'You're a star, Jay,' she said, 'back soon,' and followed her boss to the MI room as fast as she could.

She burst in as Dan was consulting a map of the area on the whiteboard. 'Boss, he said something else,' she said.

Dan turned, so did Bill Larcombe.

'Kegan drives an old-type, red Land Rover, with seats along the inside.'

'Great, more to work with. I wish we'd caught him a couple of days ago though. Bill, add it to your profile. That has to be a bit unusual in blokes working at gyms, surely. It's not a typical vehicle, is it?'

'And,' continued Lizzie, 'between him and Amber, I think we have a sort of likeness, although he could have changed his appearance by now – shaved his beard off, at least.'

She sent the picture from her tablet to the printer and waited for it to cough out of the tray. With Kegan's picture on the board, under his name, Dan felt a surge of excitement. We can find this guy. Good old Lizzie, she always came up with the goods. 'What about Tana? Any likeness for her?'

'No, they have totally different ideas about what she looks like. I need to get face shape first, and they disagree on that. We know she's thin, and currently has red hair, but that's easy to disguise. I'll need more time.'

'Time, ladies and gentlemen,' said Dan, calling the room to listen, 'is what we don't have. According to Jay Vine, the next murder is planned for this coming Saturday night, at a beach near you. We thought the third victim was Paddy, and he's nice and safe somewhere. But what if we're wrong? What if his involvement was purely to do with IRA activity in the nineties, and nothing to do with our case? What if the third victim is still out there? And going to be killed on Saturday night?

'Come over, all of you. We need to plan. Bill, cadge as many bodies from Team One as you can. I know they've got work on, but I need them. And someone bring me more coffee. You're on overtime from now on, cancel plans for this evening, and no sneaking off until we know what we're doing. Ten minutes, please.'

While the team noisily finished what they were doing, Dan called and asked Oliver to join them. She was good at this sort of stuff, and he was going to need her authority to pull in every spare body they could find if they were going to stop this next murder.

He stared at the map. A beach with access for a vehicle. Somewhere local. Not Exmouth or Dawlish: already used; not Budleigh: too exposed. As far over as Sidmouth? Again, too populated. Where?

Oliver took up her place next to Ben Bennett. 'Are we making progress?' she asked quietly, while the team assembled.

'Of a sort,' said Dan. 'I think I've been complacent. I thought, as Paddy was in custody, there wouldn't be a third victim, but I think we might be wrong. It's on for Saturday.'

She stared at him, shaking her head. 'Really? Two days? Is that all we've got to find this person?'

Dan was relieved when he was interrupted.

'Sir?'

Sam Knowles stood behind Dan, eyes on the floor.

'Yes, Sam?'

'I've been going over every bit of CCTV I can find, from the dates we have, and I think I've found something.' His voice was low, troubled.

What did I do to one of my best DCs? I frightened him when all he was doing was trying his best. Well done me. 'Okay Sam, that's great. Bring it up on the whiteboard so we can all have a look.'

Knowles did so. The typically grainy images from cheap CCTV had been enhanced and hardened up. It was easy, now Dan knew what to look for, to pick out the three students in Exmouth, and on the Dawlish holiday camp, but they were not who he was worried about.

Sam took up a laser pointer and waited until the chatter subsided. 'I noticed this man. Can you see? He's there, in all the videos, but he's always on the edge. It was his clothes that made him stand out. Same homburg hat and overcoat at each location. Doesn't have anything to do with the students, as far as I can tell. Also,' he said quickly, before anyone interrupted, 'now that we know Kegan's vehicle is a Land Rover, here it is, passing along the prom at Exmouth.'

Dan stared wide-eyed at the film. It was clearly the right vehicle, but there was no way to identify it rolling along the unlit prom with its lights off. 'Sam, that's what we pay you for. Brilliant work,' he said. A little over the top, maybe, but he needed to drag the lad back up again.

'Okay, let's focus on suspect Kegan. We have a vehicle. We have a description, and a pretty accurate photofit. Adam, Lizzie and however many of Team One DC level are available, get on to that straight after this meeting. Sergeant Larcombe will oversee the division of labour. Everything routed back through him, please.' He checked the time. 'Most gyms are open in the evenings, I believe. Oh, and no heroics. We're all on phones, call for backup before you do anything brave, okay? We want this guy in one piece.'

Bennett looked thoughtful. 'This bloke who appears in the CCTV footage. Our friends in MI5 have shown huge interest in this case, because of the mysterious Paddy, what if this guy is one of them?'

'Or,' offered Sam, 'could he actually be involved? It's just a thought, sir, but it does seem like a lot of complicated stuff for a very small team of two to organise – one of them a gym instructor and one of them a student. Well, possibly a student.'

'Go on,' said Dan, 'think it through.'

Sam blushed, but straightened his shoulders. 'Well, she's had to build her team, and that started two years ago when she came to Exeter. She had to find her victims, and that would have taken a lot of planning and searching. I mean, how long did it take her to realise they were all in Exmouth? Again, we are going back to when she must have been a teenager. Just doesn't seem likely that she would have had the resources, that's all.'

'And she must have known what she was planning when she stole Kathy Kelly's ID in Ireland, four years ago,' added DCS Oliver, 'and possibly set the fire that killed her. Could she have done that as a teenager, without help? I really don't think so.'

'Yes, that's what I think, ma'am,' said Sam, now in full flow. 'We're looking at a cold, calculating murderer, who had three victims in mind from the start. I don't buy this "find a drunk and chuck him on the fire" business. I reckon she knows them all and chose them specifically. And she's working as part of a bigger team.' He sat back into his chair, having given his longest speech to an audience ever.

Dan nodded encouragement at him. 'Good assessment. I like your thinking on this. Anyone else got anything to add?'

Sally did. 'I think we have to go back to Allport at Lympstone. He was definitely covering something up when we mentioned Paddy. The first two victims were marines, why should the third be any different?'

'MI5's nosiness tells me that the marines were involved in Northern Ireland secret operations, maybe in the eighties or nineties,' said Larcombe. 'And maybe the marines upset some IRA members?'

'That's a bloody long time to wait for revenge,' said Sally. 'It must be twenty years since the peace process.'

'So, going on what we have extrapolated so far, what if the third victim was also part of an operation in Ireland, in what, the nineteen-nineties?'

Lizzie yelped. 'Sir, what if the third man is Allport himself? It would explain how he knows the victims.'

'And all the lying is about protecting himself,' added Sally.

'Or, he could be lying to order, if something happened that isn't in the public domain,' said Bill Larcombe.

'And what if Allport already knows he's the next victim?' Lizzie asked.

Sally snorted. 'Well, as long as he stays on the campus, he's all right, surely? He's got hundreds of marines to protect him!'

Dan scratched his head with his pen. 'You're stretching it a bit, but I like it. It would explain some of what's been going on. Allport definitely knew both men. They could easily have been in a team he was running back then. The involvement of MI5 could point to the fact that they know it's not a closed case.'

'And Paddy's been pretending to be a homeless person to keep an eye on what's happening?' Lizzie punched the air then winced, clutching her injured hand. 'We've got it!'

'Okay, but say it is Allport, and he is somehow forced to leave the barracks?' mused Dan. 'That's what I'd do, if I was Tana. I'd make it so he has to get off the base and be much more vulnerable. Now, what would make him leave the base?' He felt the excitement rise; they were close now. 'We have no idea about his life. Is he married, divorced, single, gay?

'We have to talk to him, Sally. Bill, as you're staying here, can you try to get a better ID photo-fit picture of Tana, and send us the best you can get? She might be recognisable. Also, Sam, the man in the overcoat and homburg hat, whatever you can get, I'll take. Thanks.

'The rest of you, try to ID Kegan, or whatever he's really called, and get an address. Remember, he's dangerous and may be armed.

'Lizzie, you and Adam check out the Tana address.

'Sally, you're with me. Let's go and confront the colonel, see if he's ready to talk at last.

'Ma'am, any chance you could contact the spooks again, let them know what we suspect? We could do with their help. I suppose you should send them a copy of the man in the homburg hat too.'

Larcombe sniffed. 'If they're not already listening, that is.' He put his hand to his ear. 'Is that a helicopter I hear?'

DCS Oliver stood up. 'Go to work, Bill,' she said. She turned to Dan; 'It looks like you're onto something with Allport, but we have little jurisdiction on a marine base without a warrant. I'll contact a magistrate and get one emailed to your phone, just in case Allport is being difficult. I'll have the print version ready if you need it.'

She signalled for Dan to join her on her walk back to her office. 'If I call MI5 now, they'll stop all our activity and throw us off the case, take all the credit, and leave us looking like fools. So, do what you can without them. Get straight on to me as soon as you think we have to inform them. And for God's sake, don't say King of the Sea on any open channels.' She patted Dan on the arm. 'Good luck.'

Chapter Thirty-Eight

Claire answered on the third ring. 'I gather that, as it's six-thirty already and you're not home, you're going to be late?' she asked.

'Sorry, very late, and please tell me we're not supposed to be doing anything tonight that I'll have to grovel about.'

'No, just a night in, in front of the fire, with music and soft lighting and good food. No, you stay at work and play with your friends, you're not missing anything at all.'

He ended the call listening to her laugh. It made him feel better about not being there. He had tried to make it clear to her that jobs could take over, and, so far, so good.

Sally was waiting for him in the MI room, in her coat. 'Spoken to Paul?' he asked her.

'Yes, and to Mum, and to the girls. They're okay, if a bit itchy from all the chickenpox bumps. I just like to be home for bedtime, but it can't be helped.' She picked up her notebook and pen. 'They start school full-time in January, you know. All grown up. It's sad really.' She gathered her bag and stood by the door, checking her notebook.

Dan thought about Sally's kids starting school, on his way to the car. She could step up to DI soon, he thought, if she got cracking on her DI exams and training. How great would that be? He could get Lizzie started on her sergeant's training too, and get in another couple of DCs to stretch out the team again. Bill and Ben wouldn't be here forever either. Ben had dropped enough hints in the last few months, but Sam was also ready to start sergeant training. That could work very well, he thought. He clicked open the car doors and waited until Sally was inside before starting the motor. I just need to broach it when she's not knackered, and minding sick kids, and in the middle of a case. DI exams are no joke.

Colonel Allport wouldn't let them in. The marine doing gate security was apologetic, but Colonel Allport was in a meeting and could not be disturbed.

'Look, I'm not being difficult,' said Dan. 'But he's not in a meeting at seven o'clock on a Thursday night, is he?'

'Sorry, sir,' said the marine, 'but that's what he said.'

Dan shrugged, and brought up the hastily signed warrant on his phone and held it in front of the guard's face. 'I hate to have to do this, but we have a warrant to enter these premises and search Colonel Allport's quarters. So, if you would open the gate, we'll go about our lawful business.'

The marine stared at the warrant. 'I'll need to get someone more senior,' he said, and disappeared into his booth.

Sally smirked. 'Bet they've never had a warrant served on them before.'

'I wish I didn't have to use it. We're on the same side, aren't we? I've no idea why there is so little cooperation between the services.'

'It's because they like to manage this stuff themselves. They have their own disciplinary measures, and prisons.'

'Hmm,' said Dan, 'but they're not above the law.' He watched as a familiar figure came round the corner. 'Aha, we have action.'

Allport was shaking with rage. 'What the hell are you people up to, disturbing me at a very important dinner to be told you have a warrant to search my rooms? How dare you? You can't just walk in here like you have some jurisdiction over this base.'

Dan held up the warrant, close enough for Allport to read it. 'I think you will find you are not above the law of the land, sir. I regret that this was necessary, but it really is a matter of great urgency that we speak to you, and we thought you might say no. So, please let us in.'

Allport's anger beat out a pulse on his temple. He gestured at the guard to open the gate and stalked off at speed, not caring if they could keep up.

Sally glanced at Dan. 'Worked a treat, that did,' she puffed, as she hurried to keep up with Dan's long strides. 'He'll be a pussycat, won't he?'

In his office, Allport whirled on them. 'I have nothing to say to you. Take what you need then get out.' He folded his arms and stood by the window, looking out into the floodlit square.

Sally took the initiative. 'Sir, we don't actually want to search anything. We just need to talk to you. We think your life may be in danger.'

'Well, it wouldn't be the first time, sergeant. Why now?'

Dan shook his head; why was the fool pretending he didn't know what they were talking about? He sat in a chair and beckoned Sally to join him in front of the desk. He waited until she had switched on her recorder and placed it on the desk.

'We want to share the results of our investigation with you. We want to be open, and honest, and for you to be the same way with us. We're on the same side, Colonel. We know that you're well aware of what is going on, but you won't bring us in on it. We all want to stop any more murders.'

'We're pretty sure you brought MI5 down on our backs, for instance,' said Sally. 'You were straight on the phone as soon as we left your office, and we had to give Paddy up to them. I'm assuming he's now on a new mission somewhere. We know this is to do with undercover operations in Northern Ireland in the eighties or nineties. You know, all that stuff will be released into the public domain in a few years, surely you can tell us just what we need to know to solve the case?'

Allport shifted his stance at the window, turned, and sat in his chair. The high colour had subsided and he had his breathing under control. 'I know what you need, Hellier, but I am bound forever by the Official Secrets Act. I can't tell you what we were doing there. And you can turn that recorder off for a start.'

'It's purely for our records, sir. But you *were* on an undercover mission? With Ongar and Hamworthy?'

Allport gave a weary nod, some of the bluster had fizzled out. 'And the man you know as Paddy, was our informer. He worked both sides. Ironically, Paddy is his real name.'

'Has he been spying on you?' asked Sally.

'Don't be ridiculous. He was keeping an eye on Hamworthy and Ongar. They were addicts, could have opened their mouths to anybody when they were half-cut, but it suited the powers that be to keep them in that terrible state – dependent on me for money, unable to do or say anything that would lead back to …' Allport rubbed his hands across his face and glanced at the phone. 'I thought *he* had killed them. Paddy, I mean. That they'd finally become too much of a risk.'

Dan could hardly breathe. *Tell us, just tell us.* He forced himself to sit in silence and wait for Allport to talk. Several minutes ticked by.

On a small outbreath, Allport talked. 'I am aware that I am the intended third victim, Detective Chief Inspector. If whoever it is gets to me, then they will have killed the whole team.'

'Can you tell us what happened, sir, even if you can't tell us what you were doing there?'

Allport suppressed another sigh. 'I suppose it was a long time ago, and, much as I have tried, I've never been able to forget what happened.' He stared out into a well-lit courtyard. 'Maybe it is time for it to come out. At least in private.' He helped himself to water from a carafe on the desk. 'I was not a marine when I joined the armed forces, I was in the army. I led an elite group of men in undercover work. That was my team: Ongar, Hamworthy, and two others – dead now. We worked across the services, including marines.

'We had a tip-off that there was an arms cache in a remote farmhouse. There was, but we encountered a woman and her two sons at the farm, all armed. We should have captured them and taken them off-site, but Ongar, bloodthirsty sod that he was, said he wanted to finish it properly. He set fire to the barn. Only we hadn't found the ammo we were looking for, it was hidden under the floor of the barn. The explosion could be seen for miles, and the family and the men guarding them were too close to the fire to get away.'

'Who did you kill that night?'

Allport looked across at Dan, old wounds naked in his eyes. 'The family of Brendan Moore: a major in the IRA, his two boys and their mother. And the two soldiers guarding them.'

Sally cleared her throat. 'So, has Moore tracked you down after twenty years?'

'For the second time, it looks like he has.'

She caught Dan's eye. Second time. 'Can you tell us about the first time?'

There was a hesitation in Allport's voice. 'I have never talked about this to anyone. It must not come out in court. Do I have your word?'

Dan could hardly answer. He couldn't lie. 'I will try my best to save you from that, sir. I think MI5 may help there.'

Allport nodded. 'I lived on a base in NI at that time, with my family. Moore found us and set fire to my house one night.' He ran a hand over his face once more. 'My wife and son died at the scene. I managed to get out and I rescued my daughter, who was badly burned in the fire. I thought that would be enough. I thought that would be enough, Brendan,' he shouted to the walls.

'What happened then?'

'The authorities thought it best to change my identity. Mike Shepherd disappeared, I became Mike Allport and transferred into the marines over here. I've been here ever since.'

'But what about your daughter, sir? What happened to her?' asked Sally.

'Ah, yes. Maria. She was in hospital for many months having skin grafts. They thought it was safest for her to think I had died as well, to avoid further retribution. They had her adopted into a family somewhere in Ireland. She was eight years old.

They thought that was best for her. As if she would just forget me, or I, her. Took my daughter, took my life.' He shaded his face with one hand. 'So, here I am, and out there is Moore.'

'And somehow, he has found you again, through the woman we know as Tana?' asked Sally.

Allport nodded, all anger spent. 'It has taken him twenty years to track me down, but I believe it is him.'

'And Tana?'

'His daughter, or a granddaughter? I don't know if he married again after his wife was killed, but he may have spent years grooming her to take on this role. Certainly, he would be bitter enough to never let it lie.'

Dan found he was struggling to keep up. 'When did you realise what was actually happening?'

'Oh, only this afternoon. We keep detailed surveillance of the gate and wall CCTV, and any odd behaviour, or change in patterns, is brought to my attention. Mostly it's regular dog walkers and people riding their bikes. The woman, Tana, and her companion, a large young man, have been walking around the perimeter for weeks, obviously checking out security. Security teams just keep an eye on people like that. It's a difficult place to break into, as you can imagine, but we keep them under surveillance.

'I had no idea that they might be the killers until this afternoon, when I saw Brendan Moore, after twenty years, large as life out there with a young woman hanging off his arm, staring up at the fence. It didn't take me long to work out who had killed the other two, and why they were here: they are after me. But it was only when I saw Brendan that I realised the depth of his need for vengeance. He won't stop until he has us all.'

'Or until we stop him ourselves. We can do this with your help, sir.' Dan tried to catch the man's eye, but Allport seemed far away in his thoughts.

'No need, I know how to sort it out so it will be over very soon.'

Dan felt dread. What had the bloke done? 'What do you mean, sir?'

'I shall make myself available. While I have been in here they have been unable to touch me, whereas if I go out on Saturday as usual, as if I suspect nothing, they can pick me up, do their deed, and I can end it.'

'Saturday? Why that day in particular?'

'Let's not kid ourselves, Chief Inspector. They have studied my routine. They didn't try to pick me up yesterday, and my next evening off base is always Saturday nights. I have a ... lady friend who I see on Wednesdays and Saturdays. They will know that, of course.

'I shall set off as usual, and I imagine they will take me. I hope it will be before I meet Sandra, as there's no need for her to be involved in this.' Allport lifted his eyes from the table to meet Dan's. 'It's better this way. Do you both want a drink? I need a whisky.' Allport walked to the cupboard and took out a decanter and three glasses. 'I'll just top up the water. Won't be a moment.' He picked up a glass jug and walked calmly from the office.

Sally leapt to her feet. 'I'll follow him,' she said.

'No need, Sal, he'll come back. He's given up, hasn't he? All the fight's gone; he's made up his mind he wants to die, and you can't blame him, can you?'

She subsided into her chair. 'But we can't just let him do it, can we?'

'No, course not, but maybe we can save him if we play this right.'

They accepted a whisky from Allport. His hand was steady, his eyes clear. 'I think in many ways I've been ready for this moment for the last twenty years. I've certainly known revenge was coming. There was no way Moore would give up. I knew that, sitting safely here in my barracks.' He shook his head sadly, and drank back the whisky.

'Irish whiskey,' said Sally, sipping appreciatively, 'nice.'

Dan watered his well. He didn't like spirits, and especially not when he had to drive and think straight. 'Colonel, I have a proposition for you, if you would hear it?'

Allport looked up from the bottom of his glass. 'I doubt you'll change my mind.'

Dan could see Allport was weighing up the possibility that this might not have to end in his death, but he wasn't convinced he'd bite. His life must have been hell for so many years, that death would be a relief.

Sally placed her glass carefully on the desk. 'Sir, if you had the chance to end this for good, to put Moore away where he belongs, would you at least let us try?'

There was silence, then a slight nod, and that was all that Dan needed. 'Promise me you will not leave the base tomorrow,' he said. 'Give us time to set up proper surveillance and think of ways to protect you. We want to do this right. Can we see the video in which you identified Tana and Moore?'

Allport made a call. 'It will be a few minutes, they're making a copy.'

Dan tore a sheet of paper from his notebook. 'Would you write down Sandra's name and full address for me?'

Allport did so, then poured himself another whiskey. 'I'm not planning on going anywhere on Friday, as it happens. We have a training day on equal opportunities of all things. I shall sit tight and await your visit.'

They finished their drinks in silence.

Dan pocketed the CD as soon as it arrived and stood. 'Thank you, sir, for trusting us. I hope we won't get you into trouble with the spooks.'

Allport shook Dan's hand. 'I shall be writing my resignation letter this evening, Hellier. I really think I've had enough of the military life. Perhaps it's time I found a life of my own, if I can.' He gave a small, tired smile.

Outside, Sally stopped Dan with a hand on his arm. 'Are you thinking what I'm thinking?' she said.

He looked at her. 'Obviously not. My mind is a veritable blank. What you got?'

'Boss, you're letting me down. Tana has got to be Maria Shepherd, the burnt daughter. I'm sure of it.'

'Hmm … You may be right. It makes sense, doesn't it? But why didn't Allport say that? Does he even realise?'

'Would you want to acknowledge that your own daughter wanted you dead? I doubt he's ready to admit that to himself yet, and I'm certainly not going to point it out to him. Poor sod.'

Chapter Thirty-Nine

It seemed that 9.30pm had come all too quickly at the end of that long day. Dan waited until his tired team had assembled round the table. He felt wired in contrast to them. That could have something to do with the sheer quantity of coffee he'd put away in the last fourteen hours, he conceded, slugging down another scalding mouthful.

'We have a chance to sort this,' he said, without any preamble. 'So let's hear it. Do we know where Kegan works?'

Foster cleared his throat. 'We know where he used to work, sir,' he said. 'Core Fitness gym in the city. He stopped turning up two weeks ago – no calls answered.' He flourished a slip of paper. 'This is his last known address, it's a flat in Exmouth.'

'Photo ID?'

Foster shook his head. 'Nothing so advanced. But Kegan is his real name, although he's actually Harold Kegan McAndrew, of Merrell Street, Exmouth.' He wrote the new intel on the whiteboard.

Lizzie interrupted. 'We went for a looksee, sir, but nobody was in. Also, Tana's flat, completely empty. Landlady had no idea where she was.'

'Well, no surprise that Tana has skipped. I presume they'll be back at Kegan's place at some point tonight to sleep, so we'll keep it under surveillance. Currently, I think Kegan and Tana are with an Irish man called Brendan Moore, who was active in the IRA for some years.' Dan took another slurp of coffee. 'He was on the perimeter of Lympstone barracks today, with Tana.

'We need to change her description, by the way,' he said to Bill Larcombe.

'Sam, stick this in the machine,' he said, and threw him the CD from Allport's perimeter watch. 'Tana is now blonde, with much smarter clothes. Kegan is bald with a bushy beard; we can assume he has shaved the beard off, or made some adjustments to his appearance.

'The guy with the overcoat and hat is Moore; well done for spotting him, Sam. He's the brains behind all this. His family was killed by an undercover team from the UK, in, guess what? A fire. And guess who was in that team? No prizes, our two victims and Allport.

'Allport told us about his daughter. Making the connection, I want you to find out everything you can about a girl called Maria Shepherd. Her name may have been changed. She was adopted after believing both her parents and brother were killed in a house fire. Turns out Allport saved Maria, and himself, but was then sent away undercover to save both their lives; she was told her whole family had died in a fire and was adopted.'

Sally coughed. 'What the boss hasn't said, is that Allport is definitely the next victim, and ta dah! His Maria could well be our suspect, Tana.'

Dan jumped in before the team got carried away. 'We need to find out about her adoption before the connection is properly made, but, if she is Maria Shepherd, and Allport, Ongar and Hamworthy killed Moore's wife and children in a fire, she is being used by Moore and she may have no idea what is actually going on.'

'Wow,' said Lizzie. 'That shines a different light on Tana's motives, doesn't it?'

'And possibly on the outcome, if we can take her alive,' said Dan.

'This must have been eating Moore up for years. That poor girl didn't have a chance for a normal childhood,' added Sally. 'Wow, think about the planning he must have done. It's a life's work.'

'A life wasted, you mean. What a mess this truly is,' said Dan. 'Anyway, that's enough for tonight. There's nothing we can do now, we're tired and need a break. Go home, sleep, and be back here at eight tomorrow; I have a little plan that might just save Allport, and capture the others. But I need time to think about it. See you in the morning. Good work out there today.'

He almost rang DCS Oliver, but figured she wouldn't be impressed if he did that at 10pm. He needn't have worried; she came in through the door as the others were leaving, and he had to brief her there and then.

A quick chat with the duty DI got him overnight surveillance on Kegan McAndrew's flat, and a pool car to follow him in the morning if he left it.

It was almost 11pm when Dan got home, and he barely managed to remove his clothes before he crept in beside Claire and fell off the exhaustion cliff.

He was so deeply asleep that Claire had to shove him to wake him up to answer the phone that was vibrating on the bedside table. 'What?' he mumbled, unable to open his eyes properly. It must be the middle of the night. Who was it? Unknown number. He propped himself up on one arm and pressed the button.

'Hello? Is that Daniel Hellier?'

Dan sat up straight, a flash of adrenaline jolting him into wakefulness. 'Mr Tregowen, are you all right? Has something happened at the flats?'

'Well, it's your sister, I can't seem to rouse her and her fire alarm is ringing. I only noticed it when I got up to go to the toilet just now. I'm concerned that she hasn't answered the door …'

Dan's heart hammered. What the …? 'It's okay, I'm going to put the phone down now, Mr Tregowen, and ring the fire brigade.'

'Oh, no need. I have already done that. They are on their way. There's not much smoke that I can see from here.'

Dan attempted to wrestle with his shirt whilst holding the phone to his ear. 'Thank you. Thanks very much, Mr Tregowen. Please, would you wake the other neighbours and get them outside where it's safe?' He rang off.

He turned to Claire, white-faced in the light from his phone. 'It's Alison. She's set fire to the flat.'

Claire threw off the duvet and began pulling on clothes in the dark.

'What are you doing?' he barked.

'I'm coming with you. Anything could have happened.' She switched on the overhead light and they both screwed up their eyes against it. 'Just get a move on.'

Dan didn't argue as he clambered into the rest of his clothes. Anything could have happened? No. Alison happened, that's what this was all about. The sinking dread of being such a fool, yet again, of what this might mean, of all the times he'd wished her dead, of what his parents would think – they all weighed on him, and he drove like a demented man.

Drizzle fell onto the small crowd of people from Dan's block. He could see no sign of smoke, no flames. Had they put it out already? He could hardly look at his neighbours' concerned faces as he found the fire officer in charge and showed his warrant card. 'Can I go up?'

The officer nodded at him then waved at the neighbours. 'You can go back to your beds now, folks,' he said, 'all clear. Nothing major.'

Claire clutched Dan's hand as they all followed the officer up the stairs. The front door of the flat had been broken open. Dan stood outside and waited until he was able to thank old Tregowen for ringing him, and offered apologies to all three neighbours. He was embarrassed that they were sympathetic about his 'poorly' sister.

Alison sat, head bowed on the sofa. He scanned the flat. Living room fine. Someone was in the kitchen, he could hear the kettle boiling. Had to be the bedroom then. He let go of Claire's hand and let her sit next to his sister. He wasn't ready to acknowledge her yet. He could see that she was drunk and only just becoming aware of her surroundings.

A paramedic came in from the kitchen holding a mug, and knelt in front of Alison. 'She's just got a bit of smoke inhalation, shouldn't need A and E. I'm just trying to sober her up a bit before we go. Here you go, sweetheart,' she said. 'Now, Alison, are you on any medication, love?'

They were all being so nice to her. She didn't deserve nice. She deserved the life she'd had, and the prison she was due, and the misery she had brought on herself.

The left side of his bed was a black, wet mess, the rug was burnt and the duvet crisped. A fire officer prevented him from going further. 'We need to look for the cause of the fire first,' she said.

'I can tell you,' he said dully. 'She would have been smoking in bed, fell asleep blind drunk, and set fire to the bed.' He looked down at the woman's face. 'It's not the first time.' And he was taken straight back to when he was ten and Alison had done exactly the same thing at their old house in Exwick. Only that time, the whole bedroom had gone up. The house only survived because the dog had started howling outside his door and woken them all up.

He knew he was tired when he felt tears squeezing themselves out of the corners of his eyes. He turned away abruptly from the fire officer. How many times could she do this before they all called it a day? Before they let her kill herself like she wanted, and just did a bit of mourning and got over it? Didn't they mourn every single time she did something like this?

Dan turned back to the mess. He would have to throw out the mattress and bedding, and the rug, and redecorate. There would be serious trouble with his landlord, but the damage was superficial, he could tell. The smell might take a while to go, and he'd have to pay for a new front door lock. But he could handle all that. It was the rest he couldn't handle. He went back into the sitting room and stood in front of the sofa. 'Come on,' he said to Claire, 'let's go home.'

'We can't just leave her here like this,' protested Claire, rubbing Alison's arm.

'Why not? She got herself into this mess. She can sleep on the sofa. And then she can get out.'

From the sofa, Alison looked up at him, pleading. 'It was just a few drinks. I just couldn't handle it. Not used to it,' she mumbled. 'I'm sorry Dan. I'll pay you back. It was an accident.' She gripped Claire's hand tighter, and that made Dan angrier than ever.

'Accident? Look what you did. Again. Out of your brains on God knows what. And who were you with, getting drunk and setting fire to my flat, eh? How could you break my trust like that? Again?'

Dan pulled Claire up by the arm. 'Come on, she can sleep it off. Don't get caught in her web, Claire. She's bloody poison.'

He glared at the paramedic who was kneeling on the floor clutching the mug. 'And, before you have a go at me, check out her medical record. And her police record.

'I would ask you to close the door on your way out, but I guess you can't, can you?'

He stormed off down the stairs, leaving Claire to offer an apology to the paramedic, who was only doing her job.

Chapter Forty

'I haven't got time,' he said.

'You have. Eat it or I'm going to be really angry. You've barely had four hours sleep, you look awful, and now you tell me you'll be working late again. Eat.'

Defeated, and not wanting the row, Dan sat at the little table in the kitchen and ate scrambled eggs, bacon, and toast, and tried not to check his phone. Claire sat opposite him. She looked tired too, but, as she had pointed out, her day would end at 3.30pm as it was Friday, and his wouldn't.

'Good,' she said, watching him shovel down the food. 'I'm not turning into your mother, Dan, but you need to eat properly if you're going to do a decent day's work; and lay off the coffee today, eh? You were thrashing and fidgeting all bloody night.'

'Sorry. It wasn't the coffee, it was thinking about Alison that kept me awake.'

'I'm not surprised, love. It was awful, wasn't it? Well, we'll talk about that later, when we have more time. Meantime, I've rung your mum and I'm going over there after school so we can come up with a plan. We'll go to the flat and arrange for the mattress to be collected, and take the rest of the ruined stuff to the recycling centre. Meet me at your mum's straight after work. Okay? And don't be late.'

'It's Friday night. We go out on Friday night, just the two of us. I like Friday nights.'

'I think you need to sort a few things out first, Dan. Come on, it'll be better to do this straight away, not sit on it. Oh, and if you give me your credit card, I can buy you a new duvet, and a cover, and a mattress …'

He pursed his lips. It wasn't that he didn't trust Claire with his cash, more that he didn't trust her style. 'No way. It's bad enough I have to see my waste of space sister, there's no way I'm agreeing to flowery sheets in my man cave. I'll need a new rug and stuff as well. We'll go shopping together. Alison's got a lot to answer for.' He sat back and chewed moodily on a crust of toast.

Claire sipped hot tea. 'You do know she could end up back inside, don't you, if you take this any further? We have to make sure this is just a hiccup and not a return to previous modes of behaviour.'

Dan finished his tea, kissed her on the cheek and forced a smile. 'Okay, madam psychiatrist,' he said. 'Most women would be glad to see the back of my sister, she's such bad news.'

'But she's still your sister. I'd have done anything to have a sister, and I'm not abandoning her, whatever you think. And that's that,' she said, with a determined lift of her shoulders as she loaded the dishwasher.

Dan finished getting dressed. It was already after 7am. He wouldn't have time for a walk before work, so he decided to head straight to his office and at least get a little thinking time in before the gang arrived.

The duty DI from the night before was waiting for him in his office. 'Morning, Dan, no sign of anybody returning to the Exmouth flat overnight, sorry. Looks like the suspects know we're onto them.'

'Damn, I suppose that was too much to hope for. Thanks, anyway.' Dan dropped his bag onto the desk. Things weren't getting off to a good start.

'Right, well, I'll hand over to the day DI and get her to speak to you if you want to continue surveillance.' He turned to leave then turned back. 'Err … the fire at your flat? Paperwork is done for that, too.' He placed a sheet on Dan's desk. 'Go get 'em.' He waved as he left the office.

Right, thought Dan, we might not have got them at the flat, but they will have to go to the barracks at Lympstone on Saturday in order to follow Allport. Or, if they could communicate with Allport some other way, his team would have to follow Allport the following night and intercept them whenever possible. Dangerous. So, he needed a team, outside the barracks, to follow Allport on Saturday evening. Dan assumed that Allport would follow a regular path to his girlfriend's house in Topsham. He seemed like a man of habit, so all they had to do was stake out the best route, find the location of the fire, stop Tana burning her own father to death for a crime he didn't commit, and save his completely innocent girlfriend. Easy.

He made the first pot of coffee strong, because he needed the caffeine, but made a promise to himself that he'd ease off as the day went on. Not that there was much chance of that happening.

First, he rang Allport and got through in seconds. He doubted the guy had got much sleep the night before. He asked Allport to email over his routine for when he went out with Sandra, and it arrived in his inbox within minutes. He printed off a copy and forwarded it to the team – including DCS Oliver who wanted in on this case. As she did on all his cases. Good job she was an asset.

Dan liked to get in the office before the others so he could spend a few moments looking over reports from the night before. That didn't happen this morning. They were all in, bright and keen, by 7.45am. Even Sally, who always scraped in last, was making herself a drink.

'Okay, good morning everyone, thanks for getting in early. This is a crucial day. We must not cock it up. Allport will meet his girlfriend, Sandra Eastman, aged forty-eight – poor quality photo on the board – on Saturday evening.' He read the schedule from the sheet of paper. 'So, he leaves Lympstone at seven pm, arrives at Sandra's flat on the Strand in Topsham at seven twelve. Goes in for a few minutes, then they go on to eat at one of two regular places in the village. Tomorrow night, they will go to the French bistro down on the quay.

'Sam, bring up the map of the area, please.' While he did so, Dan checked the high and low tides for the following day. 'Low tide, sixteen forty-five at Topsham; high tide, four in the morning. I guess they will need to be putting up that fire in the afternoon.'

'Or, if they have a dry spot, they could have taken some of it there already,' said Foster.

'Good point, Adam. You and Sam get down there straight after the briefing, and see how far you can walk round the Strand, onto the beach, before you get cut off. Also, what would be the best route to get a vehicle onto the Strand without attracting too much attention? Ask the owners of that pile,' he pointed to a grand house whose garden looked out over the estuary, 'if you can have a snoop over their hedge. Jay Vine told us there was a trailer with the wood in – find that trailer. Could be at the flat in Exmouth, could be already in situ, could be hidden nearby. Find it.'

The map flashed up on the large screen and Sam changed it to satellite view. By chance, the photo had been taken on a low tide. The long red sand beach wrapped itself from the Strand right around to the Bowling Green Marsh bird sanctuary.

Sally got up and traced the line of sight from the big house to the estuary. 'Won't they see the flames? And there are another couple of houses in the sight line, here, and here.' She frowned in concentration. Where could you put a fire that is accessible but not visible? It's not going to be easy.'

'Hmm,' agreed Dan. 'Might not matter though. By the time the flames really catch, our three would expect Allport to be unconscious. He'd be dead soon afterwards, and they can leg it as soon as they are sure. What would you reckon, an hour, hour and a half?' He traced two possible routes with his finger. 'They could drive straight along the Strand and onto the causeway, which is very public, I agree, or take a detour up Monmouth Street and down Bowling Green Road. That way, there are very few houses as you get to the beach end, and there's a boat ramp, down onto the beach, which gives a quick way back off.'

'And then it's a quick drive back, dump the Land Rover in Exeter, and away they go. I can see why they left this murder to last, boss,' said Lizzie. 'It's tight, time wise, but they're close to where they need to be. Clever.'

'So, how do we thwart them in their clever plan?'

DCS Oliver came in at that moment, and Dan suppressed a sigh as the junior ranks shuffled about and made room at the table.

'Sorry to be late,' she said, 'but I've had the MI5 woman on the phone again. They are to be kept informed of our movements at all times. Note they are not offering their considerable resources to capture these murderers. Anyway,' she continued, 'they have let us know that Brendan Moore is still a wanted criminal, with half a dozen murders to his name, and they would like us to pass him over to them. I have agreed that we will do so. As long as we get Tana, or Maria, and Kegan, they can do what they like with the other one. Right, I'm all ears, what do you need?'

'If Allport and Sandra go to the bistro, and leave there around …' Dan checked the printout, 'ten o'clock, then that would be the best time for the suspects to pick them up. They won't want to kidnap them too early, otherwise they would have to subdue two people until the fire is ready and most people have gone to bed. My best guess is, just after 10pm as they are leaving the restaurant.'

Sam zoomed in to a close-up of the area around the bistro. 'There's parking all over this area. They could stash the Land Rover anywhere, cosh the pair of them over the head, throw them in the back, and be away before anyone sees them.'

'There will be other people out on a Saturday night, Sam,' said Sally. 'It needs to be a bit more subtle than that.'

Abashed, Sam sat back down. 'It's what I'd do,' he muttered.

'Also, this Sandra person is a weak link. We actually have no idea whether they will bring her along, dump her outside the restaurant, or what,' said Dan.

'They'll need to tie her up or knock her out though, boss, or else she'd be straight onto the police,' said Bennett.

There was silence for a few minutes as the team attempted to work out what a more subtle approach might look like. Dan watched their faces. I can't think of any other way to do it either, he thought. Unless … 'What if they wait until Allport gets back to Sandra's house, which is a short walk from the bistro to here.' He put his finger on a block of modern flats situated on the Strand. 'It's a much more private car park, just for residents, and closer to the scene. That's what I'd do. I'd grab him, knock Sandra out and leave her there, and take Allport just down the road.'

There was nodding round the table. 'Any other scenarios we haven't thought of?'

Sam looked up. 'Sir, can we call up the drone team for this? Their help would be invaluable. And I hate to think of them sitting there with all that kit doing nothing.'

'Another good point, Sam. I'll get onto them and organise it.'

'Do you think we need armed response?' asked Oliver.

Dan had been worrying about this all night. The problem with guns is that they are there to be fired, and he really wanted all the suspects alive at the end of this. He just didn't know whether Brendan Moore would be armed or not. 'I guess so, ma'am,' he said, 'but I'm reluctant. There's been no mention of firearms in any of the murders, nor have they been mentioned by the suspects in custody. Shall we keep them on standby in the village?'

She nodded. 'I'll bring Sergeant Lake in immediately.'

Chapter Forty-One

Kegan stretched and looked at his phone. It was after 9am and they had work to do today. Tana was out of it, curled into a ball and snoring lightly. He took a shower and shaved the two-day stubble from his chin and cheeks. Having a beard had made him lazy and he didn't like the look of his pale, winter-white skin. Still, once he got away, he could do what he liked, couldn't he? He certainly wasn't going to hang around and take the rap for this, whatever Tana had planned.

When he emerged from the bathroom, Tana was alert and on the phone – to her grandfather, he presumed, in the same hotel somewhere. He dressed and put the kettle on for coffee, slopping boiling water into both mugs and putting hers next to the bed. He turned on the TV and switched to the News channel. He watched until their story appeared, and he grunted. Good. They still didn't have a clue about him and Tana, although it looked like they had caught Jay Vine after all, as they now had four people 'helping them with their enquiries'. It was only a matter of time, of course. He tossed the keys to the Land Rover from one hand to the other and considered going now. Just walking out the door, jumping in, and getting a ferry across to France. He wouldn't have to do any more of this if he dumped her.

But then he thought about what Brendan had told him last night. About how Allport had killed his and Tana's family in a terrible fire. Burnt them to death for no reason except that they were Irish Catholics in Belfast. And Kegan had to agree it was wrong that Allport had been taken away and given a new identity and a great job. Like being rewarded for murder. And that just wasn't right. No, the bastard had it coming to him, and he may as well see it through now.

Bill Larcombe took the call just after 9.30am. 'Boss,' he shouted, 'patrol car has spotted the red Land Rover in the car park at the Premier Inn. What do you want them to do?'

Dan shot to his feet. What indeed? Should he try to take them now, in the hotel? Or wait and catch them later? He didn't really have a choice, they weren't ready. 'Err … tell them to back right off, we'll take over from them.' Who to send? Half the team were out anyway, and he hadn't got armed response yet.

'Sally, Lizzie, the Land Rover has been seen in the car park of the Premier Inn. Take a pool car and get over there. Try for a clear photo, but do not approach under any circumstances. Stay with them, I'll get a surveillance team en route asap to take over from you. Move it then.'

Just after 10am, Sally Ellis and Lizzie Singh pulled into the hotel car park. The Land Rover was backed into the furthest corner, but there wasn't much cover in the grounds of the newly-built hotel and it was easily spotted. 'It's there,' said Sally, pulling into a bay that faced the exit.

'I'll go and have a look round, Sarge,' said Lizzie. 'They might be having breakfast.'

'Okay, I'll talk to the receptionist.'

They took separate routes, once through the sliding door, and Lizzie was back before Sally had even asked the receptionist a question. 'I think they're in the restaurant,' she said. 'Come and look through the window.' She led the way back outside. 'What do you think? Is it them?'

Sally remembered the grainy film that Allport had provided the day before. 'I think it is. Right, what to do?'

'I'll ring the boss, let him make the decision. I'm not kidding myself that we could arrest them without backup.'

Dan took the call as soon as it was sent through. 'What are they doing, Lizzie?' he asked.

'Sir, eating breakfast with an older man, as far as I can see through the steamy window. Moore, I reckon.'

'Can you get close enough to get a photo of them?' asked Dan.

'I'll try; I'll get back to you, sir.' She pocketed her phone. 'Sarge, the boss wants a photo.'

'Right, we could wait in the car for them to come out. Or, do you fancy a bit of breakfast?'

Lizzie shook her head. 'We've been told not to approach them, just to follow them. They're murderers, Sarge, they could be armed.'

'Oh, come on, Lizzie, we're just going in for breakfast, why on earth should they suspect two women having a natter? Get a grip.'

Lizzie followed her reluctantly, and chose a table set against the wall that had a clear view of the older man – Moore – and the back view of who she assumed were Tana and Kegan. She was struggling not to stare at them, and kept her eyes on her phone until Sally returned with the tray of food.

'Eat this, and let's play best friends,' said Sally, adding a sweetener to her tea from a small box in her handbag. 'Take my photo eating a sausage, go on.'

Brendan Moore had spotted them as soon as they entered the restaurant. They were just a little too loud and chatty to be believable. He sipped coffee and let Tana rattle on about something with her fella, while Moore kept the women at the very edge of his vision. After a careful ten minutes, they were not making any suspicious moves and he began to doubt himself. How could they possibly know where to look for him? The pair were chatting away, tucking into a full English, when he at last began to relax. They had shown no sign of noticing him or the others, and had made no attempt to ring for backup. Maybe he was getting paranoid. Then again, maybe not. 'Let's get moving, you two,' he said, breaking into their conversation.

Tana finished her tea. 'What's the hurry? Not much we can do until this afternoon, you know. Then it'll be all hands to the deck.' As she spoke, one of the women in the corner spilt her tea over the table and into her companion's lap. The subsequent screech caused all three of them to turn towards the table, at which point Moore understood that they had been photographed, face-on. 'Get outside, now,' he barked. 'We've been rumbled.'

The three bustled off through the door at speed and headed for the Land Rover. On their way out, Moore stared at them and pulled aside the edge of his coat to display a holstered gun.

There was a moment's silence. Lizzie said, 'So are we just going to sit here, then?'

'Are we buggery. Come on, Liz,' said Sally, shoving back her chair and heading straight for the car. 'They know we're onto them, we'll call it in and get someone to take over the surveillance. Meanwhile, we'll just be brazen about following them and try not to lose them.'

The Land Rover had bullied its way into the traffic, leaving Sally's pool car a whole set of traffic lights behind. Sally hoped the distance would make them more difficult to spot, as she brought the car slowly into the same lane. They were in real danger of losing the Land Rover in the press of traffic. 'Keep your eyes peeled,' she said, 'don't want to lose them.'

'Equally, don't want a bullet in my head,' Lizzie muttered, straining to see beyond the busy morning traffic.

Sally saw the problem as they drove past the Met office. At the next major roundabout, the gang could turn left up towards Pinhoe, take the left lane ahead and hit the motorway, go straight down the A30, take a right towards Sowton and Exmouth, or even go back into town. Nightmare. She slowed down and hovered between lanes as they approached the roundabout.

Lizzie rang Dan on Sally's phone. 'We got a picture on both phones, but Moore's onto to us, sir. Sorry. We're tracking them, just keeping our distance. Approaching the start of the A30 roundabout. Yes, sir, the photo has been emailed straight to your phone. Err … there's something else. He had a gun, in a holster, and he made sure we saw it. Yes, sir, terrified to be honest, but we're on them now.'

She listened, then rang off. 'The boss is sending a two-car team out to relieve us. We just have to keep them in sight. Then he wants us back in the station. He's not impressed.'

'There's a surprise,' muttered Sally. 'Look, they're taking the Sowton turn. Might be heading back to Kegan's flat in Exmouth after all. Let's just slow down a bit here,' she said, as she chose a lane and followed the Land Rover. She cursed as a bus pulled out in front of her and there was nowhere to overtake. 'Can you see them?'

Lizzie, hanging out of the passenger-side window, watched the Land Rover approach the next roundabout, then she lost it. 'No,' she yelled, 'I can't see them. Get round that bus if you can.'

Sally indicated, pushed her way into the traffic, ignoring the honks of indignation from the rear, and approached the roundabout too quickly. Slamming on the brakes, she scanned the exits. Services left, motorway or Exmouth straight ahead, city centre right. There was no sign of the Land Rover.

'Dammit!' Sally banged the steering wheel. 'I don't believe this. Where are they?' She jumped as a big SUV swerved around her and onto the roundabout, gesturing imaginatively. Then she followed its line, going around the island so quickly that her tyres squealed on the tarmac.

Lizzie held on and kept looking. 'No, we've lost them, Sarge. Slow down a bit.'

'I know,' Sally growled, thumping the steering wheel. 'I'm such an idiot. Best lead we've had and we lost them. Amateur.' Glowering, she took the city road and headed for the station.

Lizzie tried to turn up the heating in the car – she was cold and damp from the tea. 'That was a bit of excitement,' she said, flopping back into her seat and lifting her wet trousers away from her legs. 'Yuk. I nearly wet myself when he showed us his gun.'

'It was too much excitement for me. I thought we'd had it when he spotted us.'

'Me too. But it's not about us, is it, Sarge? He's after Allport, and he won't want to attract any more attention. Mind you, I don't want to bump into him again without backup.' She shivered. 'I feel really bad, you know. We could have stopped this whole thing there and then if we'd handled it better. Should have gone straight in there and arrested them, no messing about.'

'I know, love, I know. But we could both be in the hospital if we'd tried to do that on our own. They're not rational, these people. No, we need to stick to the plan, and go when we're all ready for what this lot can throw at us. I guess we'll need armed response tonight after all. I might need it for my own protection,' she added, under her breath.

Chapter Forty-Two

Dan sent the images – Lizzie had managed to get two – to the colour printer and waited for them to print. He watched their faces emerge a few lines at a time, face-on, startled at whatever Sally had done to get their attention, Tana: blonde, thin-faced, intense, close-set eyes; Kegan: rounder, muscled, closely-shaven head and face – resembling a tortoise more than anything; Moore: a mass of tangled grey hair and a beard to match. He pinned them to the whiteboard and invited Bill and Ben to have a look. 'We need a quick meeting, get everybody back here. If Moore is armed it changes our approach. I need Lake's team here, we'll start when they arrive.'

He stared at the latest intel, which included the first photos he had ever requested from the force's drone squad. They gave him a good aerial view of potential sites for the fire in Topsham, but there was no sign of a trailer or fire-building in the area.

'Boss,' said Bill Larcombe. 'Do we put this image out to the press? It's the first positive ID we've had on any of the main suspects.'

Dan stared at his sergeant. He wasn't firing on all cylinders today and he knew it; he was knackered. Make a decision. 'No, we only have a day and a bit left until the deadline. After that, we will either have them, or they'll be dead. We can release it on Sunday morning, let Lisa Middleton have a heads-up first, like we promised.' He chewed on the skin around his thumb. He'd have to hammer the budget to keep up surveillance for the next twenty-four hours, but it had to be done, and as for the overtime bill, it didn't bear contemplation. Shrugging, he washed his mug and made some tea, in deference to Claire's commands at breakfast.

At his desk, where he was going over a hastily rearranged plan for the following day, he took a call from Neil Pargeter. Usually he was pleased to hear Neil's voice.

'Mate,' Neil began, 'I'm glad you've got time to talk. Wasn't sure you would have, with, you know, everything going on and that.'

'What can I do for you, Neil?'

Dan heard the blowing out of a huge breath through Pargeter's teeth. 'I don't know how to say this but, Dan, I'm sorry. Really sorry.'

'Sorry? What for? Can you get to the point, I'm trying to catch a murderer or three here, you know?'

'You don't know? Sorry. It was last night. Alison. She was out with me.'

'What? She was with you? And you let her get in a state like that? What were you thinking of? I warned you, I told you what she was like, Neil, I thought you had more sense.' Fury made his voice tight and hard.

'No, it wasn't like that. Just listen, all right? She's on antibiotics. Shouldn't have been drinking at all, but she didn't realise it. Mate, I didn't just dump her, I made sure she got home and into bed before I left. She was okay when I left her, honest.'

'First I've heard of antibiotics,' Dan said, the sick feeling in his stomach had come back. 'I think she's having you on, Neil.'

'No, I've been round to your mum's this morning and it's true. That's why she asked me to ring you and explain.'

What the ...? Neil had been at his mum's? 'You seem to be getting very close to my family, Neil. Anything else you want to tell me about my own sister? Shoe size, bra size?' There was silence on the other end of the phone. 'Well?'

'Well? You're making this too hard. You're not her dad, you know.'

'Well?'

'Why do I feel like I'm being interrogated? Okay, okay, let's do it. Since that night the other week, Alison and I have seen each other a few times. Just a few times, we haven't, you know, or anything.' He seemed to gather strength from somewhere. 'Anyway, we like each other and we're going to carry on seeing each other. I thought you'd be pleased. You did introduce us, after all.'

Dan rubbed his tired eyes. Yeah, it was his own stupid fault; of course it was. He'd got suckered in yet again. *When are you going to understand that she's not your responsibility? Let her see whoever she likes.* He wriggled his stiff shoulders and tried for emotional detachment. It didn't work. Instead, his head threw up for his consideration: *but what about my flat? Who coughs up for that? Not Alison, that's for sure.*

'Well, thanks for letting me know, have to go now.'

'No! No, wait, Dan, please. Don't be angry about this. She knows she messed up. I'm just trying to show you that she hasn't gone back to her old ways. That's all. Okay? Dan, are we okay?'

'I haven't got time,' Dan mumbled. 'Got to go,' he said, and cancelled the call. He really didn't have a clue how he felt about all this. He hadn't had time to process what had happened at the flat, and had certainly not had time to work out how he felt about his only friend seeing his sister. Voluntarily. Or that Claire was in on it with them. His mum, too.

Dan gathered the paperwork from his desk and headed back into the MI room. He was glad to see most of the team had assembled, and he could focus on that for a few hours instead of thinking about his family. He glared at Sally and Lizzie, and mouthed, '*Lost* them?'

Shaking his head, he threw his paperwork on the table and perched on the corner, waiting for the shuffling to stop.

He welcomed Duncan Lake of the tactical team. 'Nice to have you with us.'

'Always glad to be of help.' Lake nodded to the team, most of whom he had come to know when they had raided the animal rescue centre a few months earlier.

Dan filled them in on the morning's encounter with the gang. 'They know that we have the details of the vehicle, and of Kegan. They don't know that we also have the identities of the other two, thanks to Allport. They might not think we have a photo of them, but they're wrong. So, we have something, at least.

'Lizzie, get back onto the Irish Garda and find out what they can tell us about Moore. Also, can they trawl the newspapers, say between 1995 and 1997, looking for people killed in fires, IRA caches set on fire, anything like that? Can they shed any light on Tana?'

'Boss,' said Bill Larcombe, 'I know this is a bit off the wall, but if Tana *is* Allport's daughter ...'

'Go on.'

'Well, Allport told us she was adopted into an Irish family, and I assumed it would be in Northern Ireland, but what if it wasn't? What if Moore *did* adopt Tana, or at least nosed his way into her adoptive family, and has been grooming her all these years?'

'She's his instrument of revenge,' said Lizzie.

'The ultimate killing machine,' added Foster, earning him a dig in the ribs from Sam Knowles.

Dan chewed the end right off another nail and ignored the buzz of excitement. What if they were right? Revenge. It would explain who this guy Moore was, and how the plan had come together over many years. How long would you wait to avenge your dead family? 'You know, that may be on the money. Vengeance is right at the black heart of this.

'Right, Sally and Lizzie, find out where that daughter was fostered. As you've been seen by the gang, we can't have you out and about in Topsham, in daylight, can we? May as well get some use out of the pair of you.'

Lizzie's cheeks burned, and even Sally didn't have a smart comeback. Dan took a breath and sifted his notes. It wasn't fair to take out his temper on his officers, in front of the team, but he was angry. They could have taken the three suspects down today, this very morning, and avoided all the worry and expense of a major take-down tomorrow. If they hadn't lost the bloody Land Rover.

Bill Larcombe interrupted his brooding. 'Got four teams out looking for the vehicle, boss. Just sent the photo ID for the suspects. All foot patrols are looking, as are area cars on their rounds. They can't go too far away if they're picking up Allport tomorrow.'

'Right, thanks, Bill,' Dan said. He indicated the drone images of the area around the Strand in Topsham. 'Clearly, we are basing our plans on this area of the town, mainly because everywhere else along the river estuary is either too populated, or too dangerous to get a vehicle onto the sand. If Tana follows her usual pattern, she will choose an area close to where her victim lives, and set the fire in a dip, or a quiet place away from houses.' He held up a hand. 'Before I hear objections, I know it's speculation, but what else do we have to go on? We have to start with a reasonable assumption.

'Sam, Adam, what did you see this morning?'

Sam cleared his throat. 'The tide wasn't out far enough for us to walk round earlier, but we talked our way into the garden of the big house that overlooks the estuary, and there are two places on the south side of their sea wall that are dry already, even this early in the day. The gang could start building a fire as soon as the tide has gone out a bit further. Tomorrow afternoon would be the best time.'

'We checked the best routes in and out, sir,' added Foster, 'and agree that it would be logical to bring the colonel along Monmouth then down Bowling Green Lane beside the bird hide and onto the sand. There are not many houses on that route.'

'Good work. Okay, everyone, I'd like to think we could track them down this afternoon, so we keep looking. They know we spotted the Land Rover, and I doubt they will go back to either Kegan's or Tana's flat. Where would they hide out?' He slapped the incident board with the flat of his hand. 'Could be anywhere. Needle in a haystack.'

He turned back to the room. 'As I said, we can only assume that Tana will follow her usual pattern. Logically, she will do what we hope she will do. But, Brendan Moore is a wild card, probably IRA trained, which means he might be getting on a bit but he'll be tough and wary.'

'And clever, if he's avoided capture all this time,' said Sam Knowles. 'He knew how to put the frighteners on Lizzie, anyway.'

'Thanks, Sam,' she mouthed at him.

'Yes, and he'll be putting all his efforts into getting hold of Allport before we do. So, we need a plan that allows us to move quickly and react to changes.' He nodded to Sam.

Sam clicked his keyboard and brought up the map of the barracks and main road into Topsham.

'Allport must be followed from the moment he leaves the barracks. One of Lake's officers will be in the back of his car. And PC Lynch from family liaison will stay with Sandra Eastman from tonight, just in case. They may make their first attempt on the road, so the rest of us will be situated along the route into Topsham.' He pointed at three positions on the A376.

'If all goes well, and Allport gets to Sandra's flat, we will then take up positions,' he indicated to Sam to bring up the street map of Topsham, 'inside and outside the restaurant, and here and here along the road to her flat. One team on the Bowling Green Road, and a team in the garden of the house, here.'

He faced the team. 'I know it's risky, but I still think they will go for Allport as he and Sandra return from the restaurant. They'll be more relaxed after a few drinks.'

He scratched his head. *Got to make a decision; so make a decision.* 'We make the locus that car park in front of the flats. It's big and we can hide several vehicles among the parked cars. Duncan, I'd like your team near the entrance, in your vehicle, ready to go.'

'That's fine,' said Lake. 'I'll go along tomorrow afternoon and have a proper look. I need to brief Sandra Eastman anyway.'

'Sir, we'll need to alert the public to stay indoors – if you think there will be arms fire,' said Sally.

Dan pursed his lips. Could be a disaster if he did, and a disaster if he didn't. Make a decision. A sick feeling swirled in a stomach already acidic from too much coffee. And knowing that they were working entirely on assumption, threatened to make him throw up. *Make a decision, Daniel. Keep putting one foot in front of the other.* 'No, we can't. Moore is on to us. This morning will have made him edgy. Any sign of them being watched and they'll abort. We could lose them altogether.'

'Not even the people in the flats?'

'No. The last thing we need is people hanging out of their bedroom windows. The plan is to take the gang down before they get Allport anywhere near the fire. If the residents call the police at a disturbance in their car park, well, we'll deal with that. Okay, Sergeant?'

Sally sniffed. 'Suppose it'll have to be, sir,' she said.

'I'll come with you for a walk round Topsham, sir,' said Duncan Lake, 'I like to see the locations for myself if I can. It's a bit of a rarity in my job.'

'Great. Okay, worst case scenario: they get Allport as far as the fire and prepare to chuck him on it. Allport is a fit bloke, so he will have to be unconscious. Their pattern is to use a rock to bash the victim's head in. We can only assume they will do the same for Allport. In that case, we'll have the tactical team move along and set up in the garden of this house, behind the sea wall,' he stabbed a finger into the map. 'Sergeant Lake's team to lead from this point on.'

Sally raised a hand.

'Yes, Sergeant Ellis, I will make sure we have permission from the absent owners to use their property.'

Sally dropped her hand. 'Thank you, sir,' she murmured, 'just checking.'

'We could park behind their gates as well,' he added, 'that would help hide our numbers.'

He surveyed his notes. What else? 'Sam and Adam, get back to Topsham and check out all the possible parking places for us.

I want pool cars used, not your own vehicles, and I need you in casual gear. Look like people out for a walk, or going to the pub.

'I'm sure Allport is safe as long as he stays on the base, but we'll have an armed officer with him all day too.' *Sure?* He buried the doubts.

'Right, you lot. We had a late night last night. Go home early tonight, have a rest, but be on call. If a patrol spots the gang today, we're going in, whatever the time. If not, I'll brief you again at eight tomorrow morning.'

Chapter Forty-Three

As arranged, Dan drove straight to his parents' house after work. He was knackered, frantic, but totally stuck unless they got word of the gang's whereabouts. So he left the station as he'd promised, even though every part of his brain was screaming at him to stay on, just in case. Now, he sat in his car outside the comfortable home of his parents, and wondered what on earth he was going to do about Alison. Compared to this problem, catching a multiple murderer was easy.

He took a bottle of red wine and some flowers he'd bought hastily from Waitrose to the door. Dinner somewhere else was what he needed. With Claire. Food, bit of alcohol, Friday night sex – always the best – and a few hours of oblivion. Not this.

Inside, they were lined up on the sofa: Mum, Alison, Claire. They were holding hands. He felt a bit sick. Off to the side, his father sat in an armchair, head determinedly buried in the newspaper. Dan took the wine and flowers into the kitchen, came back and took the other armchair. At least Neil wasn't sitting there. The worry on his mother's face hurt him. It had been her default expression for so long that her face fell into those lines and furrows whenever Alison was around. 'Okay, I'm here as summoned. Any chance of a drink, Dad?'

Geoff Hellier virtually danced off the chair. 'G and Ts all round? It is Friday night, after all,' he said, rubbing his hands and disappearing into the kitchen before anyone could respond. Or stop him.

'Dan,' said Claire. 'We've been talking this afternoon. Sorting a few things out.' She let go of Alison's hand – it was impossible for Claire to talk without using both her arms.

Dan suppressed a surge of love for her. 'You have?'

'Yes, and I think we have a solution.' She nudged Alison.

'I know I'm a mess …' his sister began.

Dan bit his tongue to stop himself from agreeing with her. He had to listen, had to at least hear what they had cooked up between them. He wasn't enjoying feeling like the outsider in his own family, though. Short memories, some people.

'… but my teeth are in a terrible state, and the dentist put me on antibiotics for an abscess, and I just forgot you shouldn't drink with them. I'm really sorry.'

Claire chipped in. 'Anyway, the bed base isn't damaged, your mum has replaced the rug, and we can pick new bedding and a mattress tomorrow and get it all back to normal in the flat.'

Dan sank back into the chair, arms gripping the armrests. 'You know, I'm not worried about that stuff, Claire, it's replaceable.'

He looked at his sister for the first time. 'Alison, what are *you* going to do? As usual, everyone is running around, looking after you like you're a bloody invalid, but when do you take control of your own life?'

'That's why we wanted you to come here,' said Alison. 'I had another job interview this morning, and it went really well.' She gave a nervous laugh. 'Not like at the charity shop. Anyway, she's offered me a job. Part-time at first, but it might lead to more.' She turned pleading eyes to him. 'I'm straightening out.'

Claire interrupted again, 'You know my friend, the one with the online baby clothes business?'

Dan vaguely remembered her going on about someone. 'Yeah.'

'Well, it's really taken off, and she needed someone to help, so …'

'So, what's the actual job?'

'Well,' said Alison, 'I'll be steaming and cleaning the second-hand baby clothes, and packaging them up to send out. I'll be based in her house, and she's paying me eight pounds fifty an hour, for twenty hours a week.' She sighed. 'I can live on that, maybe look at getting a room in a shared house. The social will top up my rent for a bit, until I'm out of probation.' She took Claire's hand again. 'I can't thank Claire enough for helping me. It's like a miracle.'

Dan watched his mother's eyes fill up with tears. She squeezed her daughter's hand. It was hard to watch. He was relieved when his dad bustled back in with drinks, and nibbles in bowls.

'Dan,' Claire said. 'We know how upset you were about the flat, and how angry you feel, but it was a genuine accident, and you can see things are getting better, can't you? It's time to move on.'

Dan took a swig of a ridiculously strong gin and tonic. He didn't know if he could let his anger go, just like that. Claire didn't know what they'd been through. Time to move on? As far as Claire was concerned, she was helping a woman who had fallen on hard times, not giving in to someone who would let her down, again and again. But he guessed she would learn the hard way, as he had.

He looked at his father, who shrugged back. What did they want from him? Approval? 'Okay,' he said, 'well done on landing a job, Ali. Hope it all works out for you this time. Can't stop. If you finish your drink, love,' he said to Claire, 'we could get to the Indian before it starts to fill up with Friday nighters.'

'Oh, but Daniel, I've cooked,' wailed his mother. 'There's a leg of lamb resting and loads of roast potatoes. Please don't go.'

Dan stood and placed his empty glass on the coffee table. 'You ready?'

Claire shared a look with his mother and sister that cut him deeply, gathered her coat and followed him to the door. 'I'll leave my car on your drive, if that's okay?' she said. 'I'll come for it tomorrow morning. Bye, then.'

There was silence in the car for the first few minutes as Dan negotiated the traffic and got on the Pinhoe road. He let it lie. He was evaluating exactly where it left him and Claire if she wanted to side with his family against him. Of course, Claire didn't know the background, hadn't been there. It was hard for her to see Alison for what she was. He risked a glance in her direction and found her staring at him.

'Your mother cooked specially for you tonight. She spent three hours at your flat cleaning up the mess, replacing the rug out of her own money, making you a lovely meal because she knows how upset you are, and you repay her by storming out? How old are you?' She turned to stare out of the window at houses closed up for the long winter evening ahead.

Dan drove in silence, trying to fight back the urge to shout at her, to make her understand. 'I know what you're saying. I feel bad for my mum. I wouldn't hurt her for anything. But you've got to understand, Claire …'

'No, Dan, you have to understand. No one can hope to come up to your standards in your family, can they? Why? Because they can't bear to cut their daughter off completely, even though you've written her off as a waste of space. I get it, I know what's happened in the past, I just don't like it. I don't want to be a part of a family that is fractured like this, it's too painful.' She scrubbed at her eyes.

Dan parked outside the Indian restaurant, the dim interior light of the car catching the tears that were forming in the corners of Claire's eyes. 'Love, I really don't want to hurt you,' he said, taking her hand in his, 'it's just the way she makes me feel.'

'I'm not saying you're doing it on purpose,' she said. 'It's that you're so bloody ramrod straight about everything that you can't move on. She isn't *making* you feel anything, you're doing that to yourself.' She blew her nose on a tissue dragged from her pocket. 'Look, can you give Alison a bit more time to make her mistakes and find her feet? At least she's clean, and she has got a chance to make it with us helping her. Don't expect so much at first. Not everyone is as brilliant as you.'

Dan winced. She was right. Not about the brilliance; he knew she was being sarcastic. He'd made enough mistakes in his time. Was he being totally unreasonable about Alison? Yes, course he was. Was it related to his childhood? Yes. Could he move on? No, not at the moment. But he could make things a bit better for

Claire and his mum, couldn't he? 'I'll try. I'll support you in this mad idea to get Alison working for your friend. It may work. I actually want her to stay clean. But don't ask me to forget all the crap from the past twenty years, because I can't, and don't ask me to let her back in the flat, because I can't do that, either.'

She took hold of his face and pulled it round to look into his eyes. 'Okay, that will do for now. Thank you. Shall I ring your mum and see if there's any of that lamb left?'

Chapter Forty-Four

Dan was amazed at how well he had slept, considering all the stuff that was crashing round his head as soon as he woke up. He stepped under the shower and scrubbed at his hair, glad that he had gone back home and made it all right with his parents. He didn't want to risk losing Claire over his sister. He was just going to have to learn how to detach himself from her while she was in his life. The thought that she and Neil might end up together, permanently, didn't bear thinking about though. Who could he whinge to if they became a pair?

His phone buzzed in the bedroom and it wasn't even 7am yet. Claire was downstairs making him breakfast again, even though it was Saturday and she must be knackered. It occurred to him that she might be worried about him. She could tell that he was approaching crunch point in the inquiry, even though he'd told her very little. It was what broke police marriages apart: the inevitable distancing that came when a case got critical, the closeness between the team that left out spouses. They had to leave family out of the loop for their own safety, and because it was the rules. And, as she'd pointed out, he liked to stick by the rules, didn't he? He dried himself off and got dressed into warm, casual clothes, ready for a day on stake out.

The briefing was, for a change, brief. His and Lake's teams knew what they had to do. Bill Larcombe had dispatched PC Lynch to stay with Sandra Eastwood. The team tracking Allport were in place and had radio contact set up.

Foster's suggestion of using the drone team had been a good one. They set up their monitoring equipment in the MI room and did a sweep of the Topsham beach area at 9am. The plan was to act like it was a new toy, and take it to different parts of the coast to play with it. That way they could get a thorough view of any suspicious activity. Dan was impressed. True, their range was limited to a few kilometres at the moment, but he reckoned the force would rely on them more and more as they improved. Those little machines would save so much leg work in the future. And, of course, help to reduce his staffing levels even more.

Dan sent the team off to work and briefed DCS Oliver over the phone. Later, he and Duncan Lake would take a walk and check out the area for themselves. He did trust his officers to have done it properly, it was just a matter of seeing it in the flesh and getting a feel for the place. For the next couple of hours, however, Dan needed to go over the plan and look for any weaknesses.

Brendan Moore sat at the wheel of the small white van he had stolen late on Friday night. He'd taken it from a garage in Exwick, and was hoping it had been put away for the whole weekend. The side of the van said: Hopson and Son, Painters and Decorators.

He then found a barber's shop in Exeter, and got the guy to shave off his wild beard and crop his hair close to his head. Under a baseball cap, and wearing white coveralls, Brendan thought he looked sufficiently different to confuse any cop looking for him.

He'd parked the van behind the garages of the flats on the Strand, to allow him to watch the girlfriend's flat from one window, and the sun twinkling off the water from the other. Beside him, Tana kept an eye on the passing walkers and traffic, checking for anyone who looked like police. She resembled a boy, with her hair bundled up in a cap and her slim frame buried under the coveralls, he thought. Brendan drank from a takeaway coffee and finished the last of his sandwich.

Tana rang Kegan to check on the fire-building status at the site. It was all going ahead as planned. Brendan listened in and was relieved. It had been a good idea to change the plan. This fire was so important to him, and he didn't want police interfering.

He thought about his long-dead wife and his two beautiful boys, and felt his anger like a stone where his heart once was. Anger had been a hard, tight fist in his chest for such a long time, he thought he would miss it when it went. It would be a wonderful thing to finally send the whole of that damned undercover cell to hell. He was already prepared to join them there. And the English police, well, they weren't going to ruin it for him now, that was for sure.

An hour passed, then another. He checked his watch, it was almost 1pm. Two women carrying gym bags strolled down the road, towards the car park, chatting away. 'You say she comes back from the gym around now, darlin'? Is that her? With the other woman, in the gym kit?' He watched them walk straight past the front of the van, immersed in conversation.

'It is, granddaddy,' Tana murmured, 'but I have no idea who the other woman is.'

'Hmm. Well, let's pay Sandra a call.' Moore got out of the van and stretched his legs. He expected the next bit to go smoothly. The Topsham estuary was blue and calm. It was a lovely place, indeed, he thought as he checked on the gun in its holster.

Dan paused at the entrance to Sandra Eastman's block of flats. He and Lake had scoped out the beach area, which was still viable as a site for the fire, but for every passing hour the fire wasn't built, he got more worried that they'd made an error. Where were they setting the fire? Why hadn't they started it yet?

He checked his plan again. Lake knew where to position his team. They were ready to respond quickly. The car park at the flats was overlooked, a point that worried Lake, but Dan still preferred it as the best place to bring down the gang. There were street lights and fences, which meant it would be harder to slip away than if they were on the dark beach.

Dan thought back to the fire his sister had started all those years ago. The fear was still in him, a strong fear of fire of any sort, and he was desperate to bring this whole thing to a close before they got anywhere near one. Even in training, going into the smoke-filled room had terrified him. He admitted to himself, standing on a beautiful November afternoon, face up to the sun, that his anger with Alison was all to do with the fire she had started in her bedroom when he was a child. She'd burnt not just her own stuff, but all his toys, all his special things. Nothing had been saved. The fact that she had done the same thing in his flat, his private sanctuary, was more than he could cope with, even though it had been a tiny thing, really.

He zipped up his jacket against a cool wind coming off the water. A break from it all was what he needed. Getting away for Christmas with Claire, that would be good. They could afford two weeks somewhere warm, surely? Of course, everyone had already booked their time off over the holidays, but, no point in being a DCI if you couldn't manipulate a bit of holiday time for yourself, was there?

Feeling cheered he made his way up to Sandra Eastman's flat. It was after 2.30pm, as arranged. Time to brief the lady without terrifying her.

There was no answer when he buzzed the intercom. Odd. His heart did a funny little skip. No, please no. He buzzed all the other flats on Sandra Eastman's floor, and finally got hold of her next-door neighbour who let him into the corridor and up the stairs. He banged hard on Sandra's door then checked the lock. There was no sign of forced entry, the door was firmly locked, and there was no noise coming from inside.

'She always goes to the gym on a Friday morning,' said the neighbour, a purple-rinsed elderly woman. 'Then we play whist, if she's not doing anything else. Has something happened?'

'Did she come home this afternoon?'

'Oh, I think she did. But possibly I didn't hear her. My hearing's not good these days. She had a friend with her this morning, a nice girl. They went out together to the gym. They could be having lunch, couldn't they?'

'No, I don't think they could. Do you have a key to Sandra's flat, by any chance?' he asked.

The old lady was flustered. 'I really don't think I should be talking to you. Who are you again?'

As calmly as he could, Dan showed her his warrant card, and waited while she studied it over her glasses.

'I really need to check that she's not ill,' he said. 'You can come in with me if you like.'

Slowly, she checked through her keyring and fitted the key to the lock.

As soon as the door was open, Dan almost shoved the woman back into her own flat. 'Thanks very much,' he said, 'I'll deal with this. Just go inside and lock your door, you'll be perfectly safe.'

The body lying on the floor of the lounge was PC Janice Lynch, red hair haloed in a pool of dark blood. Dan sank to his knees, put his ear close to her mouth and listened; she was barely breathing. It looked like she had been hit on the back of her head. He called for an ambulance, but didn't dare move her. Scanning the impeccably tidy flat, he saw two gym bags and a bottle of water flung into a corner. There was no sign of damage, and there was no Sandra Eastman. They'd taken her already. He was too late. Keeping one hand on Lynch's arm, he radioed Lake to come back to the apartment.

Stuck there on his own, and able to think, his horror grew. Panic-stricken, he rang the barracks to speak to Allport. The colonel wasn't on site. His secretary said he had left an hour ago to start his weekend early. No, that wasn't normal; no, she had no idea where he was going. Dan asked to speak to the armed officer who should have been accompanying Allport. He came straight to the phone. He'd been told to grab some lunch while the colonel went to the gym. The colonel's car was still in its parking space; he'd had no idea that Allport had left.

'Shit.' Dan looked down at the blank face of Janice Lynch, and saw his whole plan disintegrate before him.

Chapter Forty-Five

Back at the station, Dan called in as many of the team as he could. He also called in DCS Oliver; she needed to know what was going on, much as he dreaded telling her. All of it, all that careful planning, gone to hell.

It was uncharacteristically quiet as the team gathered, bringing their drinks and notebooks. They stared up at him, perched on his usual corner of the table, and waited for him to salvage the disaster. He always found it hard to look at Lizzie's huge, dark brown eyes when it was bad like this. They showed total faith in him and he didn't know how to live up to her expectations this time.

'Sam, can you run a check on Allport and Eastman's mobile phones, please? We may be able to trace them.' He didn't hold out much hope, but there was no point in beating himself up even more.

'So, they've taken Sandra, and it looks like Allport has sneaked out of the barracks. Presumably they are using her as bait to get to him. The guard on duty confirmed that Allport left, in jogging gear, by the rear gate onto the estuary path and headed back east, towards Exmouth town. He could be anywhere by now. Caught a train, a bus, who knows?' He shrugged. 'I shouldn't be too hard on him, they could have done anything to Sandra to make him give himself up. I just wish people would leave it to the professionals. Why didn't he tell us?'

'With all due respect, sir,' said Lizzie, 'Colonel Allport *is* a professional, has been for his whole life. Maybe he's not as undefended as we think.'

Dan shook his head as if to clear it. 'You're right, I'm not thinking straight. Allport was a soldier, then he trained marines.

He's fit, and undercover combat trained. We need to bear that in mind when we catch up with them. Try not to mow him down in the rush. You never know, he could have them all trussed up and ready for nick by the time we get there.' He felt better when that raised a titter.

'We know that the murder has to take place soon, because the gang are aware that we are onto them. For them, the sooner the better. Adam, what did your drone team tell you?'

'Nothing at all on the beach around Topsham, sir. No sign of wood, or of fire building.' He hesitated. 'I think we're looking in the wrong place, sir. Sorry.'

'No need to be sorry – I think you're right. I think the gang changed their plans as soon as they knew we were onto them, and decided to go early, even though that would put them in more danger.'

'Not if they disguised themselves properly,' said Bill Larcombe. 'The front desk took a call from a resident at the Topsham flats to say there was a white van, belonging to a Hopson and Son, that had been sitting in the same place for three hours. She was concerned that they weren't doing any work. Appeared to be an older man and a young boy in the van.'

Dan smacked his head with the heel of his hand. 'They were already in place while we were sorting ourselves out, weren't they? They'd checked out her address, and just went in and took her, while I was pratting about having a walk and looking in the wrong place at the wrong time. Bloody hell's teeth.'

'Hang on a minute,' said Larcombe, 'the woman said there was an old man and a young man in the van. What if the "young man" was Tana, and Kegan went off to set up the bonfire this afternoon? They could be burning Allport now, for all we know. We should be out there, boss.'

Dan shouted the noise level back down. 'I know it feels like we're wasting time, but we need to have a plan. We can't go running about the seaside like headless chickens.' They subsided, the atmosphere worsening.

Sally interrupted the negative mutterings. 'How's PC Lynch doing, sir?'

'She has severe concussion and a possible bleed on the brain.'

Sally looked down at her notebook. 'She's a mum of three.'

'I know. I know that, Sal.' He didn't know what else to say. 'Look, I seriously underestimated this gang. If we'd had armed response with Sandra, as well as with Allport, we may have held on to her. But we didn't. Fat lot of good that would have done us with the colonel, anyway. Allport just took off when he wanted to and made amateurs of us.'

'I can't believe he did that, boss,' burst in Foster. 'I mean, we could have worked with him to capture them.'

'I know, that was the plan. And now we don't have a clue where they are.'

DCS Oliver allowed the silence to hang for a short while. 'When you get a setback like this, DCI Hellier, the best thing you can do is go back to the beginning. Where have they already set fires? Exmouth and Dawlish. Where else could they set fires? I don't know, say Budleigh, Sidmouth, Seaton? Or round the other way, towards Teignmouth? So, Team Two, if you were the perpetrators, and you wanted to kill someone in a fire today, where would you do it?'

'Ma'am,' said Foster, 'I could get the drone team to survey the different beaches for us …'

Dan waved his hand to stop his junior officer mid-sentence, an idea forming as he spoke. 'Good thinking, Adam, but it would be too slow.' He turned to his boss. 'Ma'am, we need the helicopter. It could do a sweep of all the local beaches, high up enough not to be spotted, and give us a heads-up on any likely sites. Can we do it?'

She pursed her lips. 'How far over the budget are we? Sod it, I'll call them up. Let's do it before it gets too dark for them to go out.' She took herself off to a corner of the room and got out her phone.

Invigorated, Dan stood up. 'Right, that should get us a head start. We're not giving in at this stage, even if our intended victim has given himself up. Any news on the phone tracking, Sam?'

Sam came back from his desk. 'Sandra Eastman's mobile was used about an hour and a half ago, in the Topsham area. Probably at home. And Allport must have his switched off. We've got nothing since last night. The gang may have destroyed it already, if they have him. Otherwise, we have to wait until he switches it on to track him. Sorry I haven't got more, sir.'

'No, that's okay. The last call from Sandra's phone could have been to Allport to tell him where to meet them. We need that location, fast. Find it, Sam.

'Right, as Bill says, we need to be out there. So, let's split into teams. Duncan, your lot will go in your usual vehicle, please. Sally, Lizzie and Adam together. Sam, Bill and me in the other vehicle, with your portable rig, Sam. Bring what you need, you can have the back seat to yourself. Ben, I need you in a van with as many PCs as you can bring in. I want paramedics on standby, too. Bring up a map of the coastline, Sam.'

He studied it. 'The main thing is for us to get out of the station before we get stuck in the teatime rush hour, or we won't be going anywhere fast. We need to be able to respond immediately to any sighting. I know, let's rendezvous at Exeter Services at seventeen-thirty, we'll be on the motorway and close to the main roads. It's sixteen-twelve now, synchronise with me, please.' He waited for DCS Oliver to finish her call, feeling the faint tingle of anticipation in the room. They weren't total idiots. They could do this.

Oliver gave him a thumbs-up from the far side of the room. 'Twenty minutes and they'll be in the air,' she said. 'First sweep will go across Lyme Bay in a fast circuit, then slowly back up the coast from Lyme Regis round to Torquay. I'll key them in to your radio frequency. Oh, and I'll be up there too, keeping an eye on you. Good luck.' She ran from the room.

Foster whooped. 'Way to go, ma'am! Action at last,' he said. 'Sitting here doing nothing is killing me.'

Dan wanted to whoop as well, but he held steady. They could still be completely wrong about this. 'Get ready; I want all of you in full protective gear. Sally, we'll need night vision goggles for at least two people in each team. Everyone to have a radio – on the EX1 frequency. Okay, have a pee, grab a snack while you have a chance, and cancel your Saturday night plans. Let's see if we can catch some murderers. I'll see you in the car park at the services at seventeen-thirty.'

Chapter Forty-Six

The air inside the pool car was steamy with takeaway coffee and the waft of warm Cornish pasties. Dan wiped his fingers on a paper napkin and sighed. That was good. He passed the remnants to Sam, sitting in the back, who took the rubbish to the nearest bin. Bill Larcombe tapped out a tune on the steering wheel and waved at Sally in the car next to him.

Dan's phone buzzed. It was an unknown number. His heart gave a lurch. 'Hellier?' He let his shoulders drop as he listened, and said little except 'understood' and 'yes', and ended the call by stabbing at the screen and growling.

'Bad news, boss?'

'MI5 again.'

'I knew they were tapping our office,' shouted Larcombe. 'I knew it. How could they know what we're doing? How?'

'Well, keep your hair on. It's worse than that. They want us to detain Moore, but not arrest him, as they want to take him away for interrogation *before* we arrest him, and don't want him, and I quote: "languishing in the prison system". They are on their way, in a van this time, and want in on the take-down.'

'It's gonna be like bloody Piccadilly Circus, boss,' Larcombe grumbled. 'They'll steal all our glory.'

'That's not all. They asked us to keep an eye out for Patrick O'Leary, known to us as Paddy, who disappeared from his accommodation early this morning. They didn't see fit to tell us that he was also part of Allport's team all those years ago. Or that he was also part of Moore's team. I knew he was a snitch, but that's all.'

'Whoa, double agent! That could get very messy indeed,' said Sam.

'And exactly whose side is he on now, boss?' asked Larcombe.

DCS Julie Oliver swallowed her fear. She'd never been up in a helicopter, and, although there was no way she would have turned down the opportunity, she hadn't expected it to be so stomach-churning. This was a small, light, agile craft, meant for pursuit and detection, not a big, solid people carrier. The pilot skimmed across Lyme Bay as the day faded into a pink and grey streaked sunset. 'Gorgeous,' she shouted. The pilot grinned at her, and pointed towards the shoreline below them. Oliver stared hard at the beaches as they sped past. It had to be accessible, sheltered ... and there it was. She pointed for the pilot. 'Sandy Bay, look.'

The pilot nodded but didn't change his direction. 'Back to base, ma'am?'

'No. Make a big circuit around the bay, far enough away that they can't hear us, but close enough to get back if they need us.' He nodded, and set off out across the water.

Oliver radioed the cars. 'Got it! Back at Exmouth, Dan. Go to Sandy Bay for access to the far end of the beach. It's further along from where the last fire was, sheltered by a bit of the cliff that sticks out towards the water, near Orcombe Point. Go through the caravan site and down onto the beach, but be careful, they will be able to see you coming in a vehicle. Have a patrol car block off the entrance in case they make a run for it. Keep me informed.'

She looked with dismay at the call waiting icon on her phone. MI5 again. Now what did they want?

Allport jogged towards Exmouth town centre. He was wearing earphones, a cap pulled down low over his face, and jogging clothes. His priority was Sandra. First, though, he needed to get the location sorted in his head. He swung in to the town, up onto The Beacon, past the houses of the rich and famous from the town's history. He felt safer up away from the beaches and main roads. He had no idea where Moore was hiding out.

Moore had used Sandra's phone to contact him, the bastard. It made him sick to think that the police had been so incompetent as to let her be captured. Did they have no idea at all who they were dealing with? That Detective Chief Inspector, he was young. What did Hellier know of the IRA? Of how far they would go to punish a man? Nothing. The poor girl would be terrified, if she was even alive.

He'd been told to be at the end of the promenade, seated on the metal bench overlooking the sea, by 5pm. There, Moore would exchange Sandra for him. She would be unhurt if Allport came alone and gave himself up willingly. That gave him an hour and a half to recce the position and work out a plan to rescue Sandra and himself. Of course, he could call the police, but he thought they'd just take him out of the action, and he wanted to watch Moore die out there, not waste away in prison.

He paused to let traffic pass, and then cut across onto Trefusis Terrace. He could follow the pedestrian pathway for a while yet. The main task was to take out the young man and woman. Once they were disabled, he could tackle Moore. But he had to get Sandra out first, and that was where his planning fell short. What if Moore had left her somewhere, and he killed Moore before he found out where? He coughed up phlegm and spat it into the bushes. No point thinking like that.

The path led down, past the back of The Maer – a wide expanse of sandy grassland that separated the houses from the sea. He was most vulnerable here, out in the open, so he spurred himself on across the field and up to the South-West coastal path. There, he stopped to drink some water and get his breath. They wouldn't be expecting him to be up here, behind them, would they?

Slowly, now, Allport walked the path until there was a break in the greenery, and he could edge along treacherous, soft red sand to lie full-length and peer over the edge of the cliff. Below him, a hundred feet or more, the sea was retreating over hard-packed sand. Nothing down there. He shuffled backwards and checked his position. Orcombe Point was a few hundred yards ahead. If the gang's vehicle used the Sandy Bay ramp onto the beach, rather than the Exmouth end, they could be further round the bay and not where they had set the first fire. He jogged again, rounding the point and heading towards the campsite in the distance. Again, he found a place to crawl to the edge and look over the cliff. This time he did it right. There was a figure building a fire, tucked into a natural alcove in the cliff, a few hundred feet away. Invisible from the Exmouth side, because of the cliff walls, it was only really visible from the caravan site or at sea. Allport wormed his way closer to the crumbling edge and used his binoculars to get a better view.

The young guy was completing the building of a fire, with brush and thin saplings surrounding what looked like small-cut logs. It was a good fire. A good pyre, he thought, with a little space at one side to fit a body. Neat.

Taking stock, Allport realised he felt better now than he had in some time. At last there was a chance to end the horror of what had happened all those years ago; to make some reparation for the idiocy of Ongar, always full of himself, setting fire to the Irishman's house. To silence the screams of the dying. And then to put to rest his own beloved little family, killed, of course, in the same way. An eye for an eye.

A quiet cough made him swing round, body tense and ready to fight, but it was Paddy, as expected. 'Glad you could make it,' he whispered.

'Took me a bit of effort to get away, but I'm here. Want to see the bastard dead too. Hate loose ends. I thought I'd never find you, it's a long path.' He flopped down on the damp grass. 'It's not that long since I was up it, either.'

'I didn't know where they'd be, but peep over there and you'll see the lad, Kegan, finishing off the fire.'

Paddy grinned, his newly cleaned teeth gleaming out of the darkness. 'Yes, sir.'

Allport pointed Paddy towards the caravan site. 'Right. Slip down the path into the caravan park, wait, and you sort Kegan out as soon as I get there. Then take the girl. I want Moore to myself.'

'I didn't know Moore had a granddaughter, sir.'

'Neither did I, Paddy, but she takes after him - a cold murderer. So, keep walking that way, watch out for dog walkers. The caravan park is closed for the winter, but there's a guard in the main building and you'll see the light on. Straight down the path and onto the beach. The only place to hide is close up under the cliff, so try not to be seen.'

Paddy muttered, 'Grandmother suck eggs,' at him, and slipped away into the gloom.

Allport made his way back to the rendezvous point. With every step along the darkening path, he became more convinced that Moore was the devil himself. The girl worried him, too. Moore only had sons, he was sure of that.

He ran along the last few hundred metres of the cliff top walk, to overshoot the rendezvous point, then made his way back along the prom. There were several vehicles parked at the end. Some motorhomes had clearly come for the weekend and were parked up. Others were dog walkers, taking a last stroll before night set in.

He walked warily, not wanting to be grabbed before he could negotiate Sandra's release. As he approached the final parked-up vehicle, a white van with writing on the side, the driver's door opened and a large man got out. He was holding a gun.

Allport stopped on the pavement and watched the man and the gun. 'Brendan,' he said, 'I'm unarmed. Let Sandra go and you can have me. I'm ready.' He held out his hands to the side and stopped breathing when Tana edged up alongside him, checking out his clothing, staring all the while into his eyes like hers were lasers she could kill him with. The eyes. He knew those eyes. It couldn't be, could it? Allport found himself shaking, and it wasn't with fear.

'He's clean,' Tana said, and gave Allport a little push. 'Over here, now.' She led him towards the rear of the van, where the back double-doors stood open, and he could see a drugged Sandra slumped on top of paint pots and a ladder.

Moore took a step to the rear and held the gun on him. 'Pick her up.'

Allport reached in, picked up Sandra in his arms and waited, unable to take his eyes from the girl.

'Over there,' said Moore, indicating a metal bench. 'Leave her on there, she'll come round in a while and can go home. No harm done. See, we keep our word, you murderous bastard.'

Allport held Sandra close to him, breathed in her flowery scent, and felt sorry that she had become embroiled in all this because of him. He had to finish it tonight. He would. A surge of adrenaline shot through his body, making him stumble as he laid the comatose woman on the bench. He removed his lightweight jacket and placed it over her. *Stay in control. Don't do anything stupid here with all these civilians around. Don't look at the girl, you can't think about her yet. Paddy and I will do it as a team, in the quiet, like we used to.* He stood back. 'Where do you want me?'

Tana walked out onto the causeway, Allport followed her, with Moore bringing up the rear.

'Walk round the beach,' said Moore. 'Keep going until I tell you to stop.' Moore pushed Allport's shoulder and they set off in a tight line. For Allport, the walk was short. He studied the girl's walk, the shape of the back of her head. *It couldn't be.* Even Moore would not do that. Not that. Not to a child.

They heard a helicopter approach from the east, flying low. Allport peered up but could only see its outline. He had a feeling they would have company soon, and picked up his pace behind the girl. It was time for Moore to die.

Chapter Forty-Seven

Dan rang ahead to the caravan site and arranged to have the gates opened. He deployed Ben Bennett and his team at the promenade end of the beach and told them to secure it. The cars rolled into the deserted caravan site and down, almost to the causeway, onto the beach. He gathered the teams together for a quick briefing, and none of them saw the slight figure, dressed all in black, slip down the causeway and onto the beach before them.

Team Two followed Duncan Lake and his team, keeping low and close to the cliff. Ahead of Dan, the fire was burning well and he had to keep a hold on the fear that they were already too late. His night vision goggles showed no movement, other than the flames, so he signalled the team forward once more. They came to a halt fifty metres from the fire. Dan waved them down. He crawled across to Lake. 'The fire's just burning on its own. Where are they? Wait, I can see Kegan.'

Lake shrugged. 'They're coming from the other side?'

His guess proved accurate. Dan flattened himself to the sand as Tana came round the promontory, leading Allport, with Moore at the rear, gun pointing at Allport's head.

'Kegan,' hissed Tana. 'Where are you?'

Kegan shot round from the other side of the fire. 'I didn't hear you over the crackling,' he said. 'So, you got him.' Kegan picked up the rock he had chosen for the purpose and advanced on Allport.

'Forget that,' said Moore, shoving Kegan out of the way. 'I'll shoot the bastard and have done with it. He'll still burn.' He raised his gun as Allport viciously drove his elbow back and up into the older man's throat. Moore doubled over, gasping, windpipe crushed. The gun slipped from his fingers onto the sand.

Tana screamed, and threw herself down, scrabbling for the gun and pointing it at Allport. 'You bastard!' she cried through her tears, and pulled the trigger. She missed by a mile.

Allport dropped to the ground, rolled, and came up next to her. He knocked the gun from Tana's hand, forced her head down into the sand, and kicked her feet from under her. 'Not going to happen,' he muttered. He flipped her over, knelt on her back and tied her hands with a cable tie. 'Stay there.'

Paddy came running out of the rock debris, twisted Moore's arms behind him, secured them with a plastic tie, and laid him on his side to get a little air.

Kegan stared around him, dropped the rock, and ran.

'Let him go,' shouted Allport. Help me with Moore.' They dragged Moore towards the cliff face, away from the fire.

Kegan headed along the beach towards the caravan site, straight into the arms of Lake's men. He offered no resistance when one of them tripped him up and knocked him to the ground.

Dan signalled his team to follow, as Lake's armed men ran in and surrounded the remaining four.

'Stop! Lie face down on the ground,' yelled Lake.

Tana struggled to her feet, arms pinned behind her. She edged towards the flames, bent double and ran for Allport. She headbutted him in the stomach, knocking him into the edge of the fire, yelling cries of triumph and pain as Allport's screams of shock tore the air. 'At last! I have him, Mammy. Burn, burn.' She kicked at Allport's feet.

Paddy didn't hesitate: just as he had done all those years ago, he dragged his commander out of the fire, rolled him on the damp sand until the flames were out, and collapsed next to him, holding his burnt hands close to his body. 'Jesus, but that hurts,' he yelped.

Lake moved in quickly, removed the fallen gun and checked on Moore who was barely alive. He called for paramedics and asked Bennett's team to come along from the promenade end. As soon as he gave the signal, Team Two moved in.

The sound of Tana's uncontrolled keening when she saw that Allport was hardly burnt at all was hard to hear. Left alone for just a moment, she took her chance and threw herself backwards into the fire. Dan reacted without thinking. He ran and dragged her from the terrible heat, feeling the hairs on his arms frizzle and smelling her long hair burning. He did what Paddy had done for Allport and rolled her on the wet sand until the flames were out. Her head was a mess. He shivered. The gloves and Kevlar had protected most of him, but he still hated fire – more than ever.

'Let me go. I'll burn. I'll burn,' Tana sobbed, writhing and kicking as Lake's officers cut the plastic ties and strapped her onto a portable stretcher. 'Granddaddy,' she cried through her blackened, blistered mouth, writhing and bucking under the restraints.

Dan lost patience. 'Tana,' he yelled in her face. 'Listen! Shut up and listen.' He held her shoulders until her eyes stopped rolling and she could focus on his face. 'This man,' he indicated to Allport, who was kneeling close by. 'He's not the man who murdered your family.'

Tana only moved her eyes to flick over Allport's face. 'He is. I've watched him all this time.'

'No,' said Dan, quieter now. 'No. Allport is your father, Tana, and you are Maria Shepherd. He saved you in the fire that killed your mother and brother.'

Allport let out a choked cry. 'Is it true?'

'No!' yelled Tana.

'Why would I lie?'

'No.'

'My Maria?' Allport crept closer to the stretcher, peering down at the terribly injured woman. 'You really are Maria?'

'And Moore,' continued Dan, determined to get it all out, 'he's not your grandfather. He's the one who groomed you to kill your own father, because your father and his men killed *his* wife and children.' He shook her shoulders again, gently. 'It's the truth. Can you see it?'

'Granddaddy?'

Moore lay on the sand on his side, struggling to breathe. He didn't look at her.

Paddy O'Leary, sitting on the ground nursing his hands, laughed a long and pained cackle. 'Ironic, isn't it, sweetheart? What he's done to you?'

Allport forced himself to stand in front of his daughter. 'It's a long story, Maria. Will you let me tell it?'

Her eyes flickered past him to the body on the floor. 'Granddaddy?'

Dan realised that Tana had no way to process the information he'd given her. She lay quietly on the stretcher and her eyes were lost. 'Do that later, Allport. Let's get out of here.'

Above their heads came the whine and roar of the helicopter returning. This time it put on its spotlight and hovered above them, illuminating the scene. It also illuminated another group of armed soldiers who were approaching from both sides of the beach. 'Dan,' said DCS Oliver, 'you've got company. Guess who?'

Lake backed away out of the light to regain some night vision, but Dan just waited. He knew who this would be.

Commander Alice McCarthy strode into the bright arena. 'Right,' she yelled over the down draft and roar of the helicopter engines. 'We will take Moore, if you haven't permanently damaged him, Colonel. Patrick O'Leary, you are on a charge of treason, so you're coming with us, too.' She held up a hand to prevent Dan's objection. 'You have the murderers. This is nothing to do with you.' She gestured at her commando troops. 'Seize them.'

Paddy used the time it took McCarthy to give her order to scramble out of the light on all fours and start clambering up the cliff. Dan watched him climb like a spider up a drain. He wasn't about to alert the commander, who had come in and stolen their thunder, just as he'd predicted.

Paddy wasn't quite fast enough, however. On a nod from the commander, a soldier aimed his rifle at the retreating figure and shot him in the back. The wiry Irishman fell back to the beach with a crunch of bones as he hit the rocks.

Dan and his team stood, shocked, as the commandos bundled both men onto stretchers and ran them away along the beach as quickly as they had come. In his ear, he could hear DCS Oliver swearing profusely.

'Come on,' Dan shouted to his team, 'secure this scene.'

Larcombe bustled in, arrested Kegan and charged him before he was taken away. Knowles and Foster accompanied Allport and the injured Tana to hospital.

Ben Bennett's team came in from the west. 'Found Sandra Eastman,' Bennett said. 'She was fast asleep on a bench. We've got her in the van.'

'Good,' said Dan. 'Why don't you take her back with you, get her statement, and then get her home?'

It was a relief when the helicopter rolled away and gave them some peace and quiet. Dan stood down Lake's team; only the remnants of his own team were there, standing beside him in the golden firelight. He tried to let the rage of impotence die down before he said anything. The arrogance was hard to stomach. Walking in and taking over. Shooting someone in the back without a second thought. And he'd bet there wouldn't be the kind of investigation the police would put him through if he'd done something rash like that. Oh, no.

Into this seething contemplation came the awareness that the rest of his team were standing listless, staring into the flames and not even grumbling at each other. *Adrenaline with nowhere to go does this to you*, he thought. *That and feeling cheated.*

'Hey,' he said, 'we caught the Fire Goddess and she hasn't got a leg to stand on in terms of defence. We got Kegan, and the rest of the gang. And we stopped another murder. Result! And it's only just after seven pm. We could be in the pub for nine if we get a move on.'

Sally managed a weak smile. 'True. But that poor, poor girl.'

Dan ignored her. 'Bill, you'll have to stay to set up the crime scene. Can you send for forensics?'

'Sure, boss,' said Larcombe, on the phone already. 'Forensics is going to be a bit odd though, seeing as we can't mention the spooks, and there's blood on the cliff face, and at least two bullets but no body.'

'I know,' he shrugged. 'You know, I've got no idea how we're going to deal with that, and frankly, I don't care. Let the guys do their thing and we'll work it out in the morning. I'll get someone from late shift to come and take over as soon as we're back at the station.'

'Least I'll be warm,' said Larcombe. 'Should have brought burgers and beers.'

Dan turned to Lizzie and Sally. 'You two all right? You're very quiet.'

'That poor, poor girl. How do you come back from that? Moore really is evil, isn't he? I hope he bloody well dies,' said Sally.

'I've never seen anybody shot before,' said Lizzie. 'Only on the telly. Poor old Paddy.'

'Yeah, well, it looks like poor old Paddy was not just Allport's informer. McCarthy said he was wanted for treason; I think we can work out how Moore found the men he was looking for, can't we?'

'You think he was working for Allport and Moore at the same time, boss?' asked Larcombe.

'I do. It was the thing that puzzled me all along. However hard you looked, how the hell would you know that two losers like Ongar and Hamworthy would end up hanging round the back door of the place they had been ejected from? They were nobodies. Not on anyone's register. Unless someone who knew about Allport taking care of his men at Exmouth ...'

'… told Brendan Moore where to look,' said Sally. 'Wow, bad news indeed.'

'No wonder MI5 were hacked off when he disappeared again today.'

'But they just shot him.' blurted Lizzie. 'In the back. How can they do that and just get away with it? How can it be legal?'

'Okay, ladies,' Dan said, 'I know I'm brilliant, and know practically everything about everything, but I have not got a clue. And frankly, I don't really care. Because nothing we say or do will make any difference to what just happened. So, if you can just put it to the back of your minds for a minute, can we get off this beach, write our reports and go for a drink? Because I don't know about you, but I really need one.'

Sally put her arm around Lizzie's shoulders and walked her back to the car. 'The boss is right, let's move on, love.'

Chapter Forty-Eight

The team parked up at the back of Exeter Road station, checked in their protective clothing and took themselves off to their respective desks to write up reports. Dan told the duty sergeant to oversee the booking in of Kegan.

He and Sally then concocted the best story they could, without giving out much actual information, and Sally took the ever-present Lisa Middleton into an interview room to give her the story first, as promised.

He and press liaison would need to prepare a much better story for the nationals. He knew the security of his country was paramount, but, as a copper with over twelve years in the job, he also knew that the law of the land is supposed to be for everybody. It rankled when he understood how little power the police actually had when the big boys brought out their guns and trampled all over them. It bloody hurt.

He had seen people killed before, of course. In his first case as a detective sergeant in the Met, a boy was shot in the head as Dan was arresting him for drug dealing. He had been splattered with gore, which no amount of washing could shift. It had taken him a long time to come to terms with how shallowly some members of society held life. That most precious thing, casually blasted aside. And then there was Ian Gould, shot a few short months ago, and he still wasn't able to go there.

Dan avoided hiding in his office and took himself and his laptop into the MI room, where he sat typing, and waited for the team to come to him. First in were Sam Knowles and Lizzie. 'All right, you two?' he asked, eyes on the screen.

Lizzie slumped in a chair beside him. 'Feel crap, actually, boss.'

'I know you do, Lizzie. It'll pass. You might find it useful to speak to someone about it though; I did.' He slid a phone number across the table to her. 'Don't let it build up. You'll see more death the longer you spend as a detective. Find a way to deal with it, okay?'

'Why, sir? Why did Moore do that to Maria? She's the same age as me, you know. She really has been groomed, hasn't she? All those years, fed lies by Moore.'

Dan shrugged. 'What better punishment than for Moore to tell Maria that it was her own father burning on the pyre when it was too late to save him? For her to understand how foully she had been betrayed. Revenge, indeed.'

'But how can someone be so twisted? What possible pleasure could Moore get from forcing a child to do that terrible work? The years he must have put into turning her, and all for this one act of vengeance. Sick.' She shook her head and slid down until the back of her head was resting on the hard back of the chair. 'A large G and T might help,' she murmured.

'Might, probably won't.' Dan said. 'Don't see why that should stop us researching it thoroughly, though.'

He walked across to Sam Knowles, who was rearranging his computer equipment, and put the same phone number down on the desk next to him. 'If you need a professional to talk to, she's very good.'

'I'm all right, sir, thanks,' said Sam, but he had two pink spots in the middle of his cheeks, and Dan didn't think he was all right at all.

'Just in case,' he said, then cast around to change the subject. 'I know, help me get the rest of the detail on the board, Sam, then we can do a proper sign off tomorrow.' He picked up the felt-tipped pens and dropped two on Sam's desk. 'Now, how do we tell the story, make a proper report, and completely miss out the main event of the evening?'

Sally Ellis bowled in with Bill Larcombe at her side. They were arguing loudly.

'Hold it,' shouted Dan.

The sudden silence was a relief. 'Know how you feel, but we have to let it go. This must not leak out to the press, and currently you two can be heard all over the building. There is no time limit on murder investigations, as you well know, so we had to let the spooks take Moore and O'Leary. So, stop it, and come and help us sort out the events as if they happened without the interference of MI5.'

Larcombe threw up his hands. 'Just makes me sick, boss, that's all.'

'Get on with it, man. Where's Foster?'

'He's gone to Waitrose for a snack,' muttered Sally. 'He and I will be having a little word if the snack is a tray of cream cakes.'

Dan's phone buzzed, it was Claire. 'Just taking this, then we'll get started.' He went into the corridor. 'Hi, gorgeous.'

'Dan, how's it going?'

'Actually, brilliantly. We've caught the Fire Goddess gang.'

'Wow! That's fantastic. Oh, I suppose that means you'll be late home, then?'

'Well, we should have a little drink to celebrate.'

'Of course you should. Oh, I've invited your family and Neil over for lunch tomorrow.'

'Whoa, need a bit more notice for that kind of bombshell. Why?'

'Why? You're not on rota tomorrow, are you? It's Sunday. Thought we should clear the air – and we've not had them over yet.'

'No, but, love, I've just solved a major case, and I'm up to my ears in paperwork …'

'There's always paperwork to do, Daniel. It will wait. You can have until one pm, but then I want you home. Understood?'

Since when did she start calling him Daniel like his bloody mother? And ordering him about?

'Are you still there?' she said.

'Just about. Any more instructions, ma'am?'

'Don't wake me up when you get in, and I'll get you up nice and early tomorrow with aspirin and eggs so you can get back into work. Love you, bye!'

He stared at the phone for a few minutes. Did you always sign up for a life of servitude when you entered a relationship? You did if you knew what was good for you, his dad would have said. Claire was angling to get his family back together. Got to love her for trying.

Mike Allport, or Shepherd as he now preferred to be known, stood quietly outside the maximum security psychiatric wing, and watched his daughter through the glass.

Next to him, the psychiatrist assigned to Maria Shepherd read through her notes and made a few pen marks.

He wanted to cry when he looked at the top of his daughter's head: dark tufts of baby hair had begun to grow through the burnt scalp. Maria's eyes were open and she was looking at him, but there was no recognition. No sign of life at all.

'She's in what we call a dissociative fugue state, Mr Shepherd,' said the psychiatrist. 'It's very rare, but in it, the person detaches themselves from their identity. They have total amnesia about their life, because who they are and what they have done is too painful for them to contemplate.'

'Will she get better?'

'Usually time heals, but sometimes we never get them back. I don't know how anyone could come back from what has been done to Maria, but there is always hope.'

She placed a cool hand on his arm. 'You don't have to come every day, you know. We will ring you when we see any change.'

Shepherd rolled his shoulders and waited until her hand had dropped. 'She's my family. Where else would I want to be?'

The End

Acknowledgements

A small tribe of people make a book happen, and I couldn't have done it without the following stars; early readers Liz Pinfield and Jill Turner, who gave constructive feedback on the draft; stalwart Andrew Vernon, who checked the police procedure; Joanne Craven, editor extraordinaire, who picked up on my most ridiculous errors, and to Betsy and Fred at Bloodhound Books, who devised the re-launch of the West Country Crime Mysteries, giving me the opportunity to revise and polish the earlier manuscripts and round off the series with a bang! Thanks all.

Digatartis